THE JOINING

BOOK I OF
THE CARROWKEEL SERIES

NINA ORAM

Text Copyright © 2019 Nina Oram
Cover Art © 2019 Bede Rogerson

First published by Luna Press Publishing, Edinburgh, 2019

www.lunapresspublishing.com

ISBN-13: 978-1-911143-84-0

For Joe, as Albert Hammond wrote and The Hollies sang.

Thanks to everyone for their love and support, but especial thanks to Francesca and Luna, Coirle, Helen, Bill, Roy and Mum.

Contents

The Beginning

She stood on the edge of the mountain, feeling her heart pound, her head floating with the height of it, and for a moment she thought the world was going to tip and her body slide inexorably down and over into space. Behind her the shouts were coming closer, the sounds reverberating in the cold crisp air and the stone around and beneath her. She turned; running towards her with their legs stretching over thick clumps of grass, taking them with ease, were men half-dressed in animal skin and leather, their long hair flying in the wind.

They were shouting her name, not calling for her, but coming for her, their voices rhythmic, chanting. She looked wildly about her. It was dusk, the landscape around her beginning to fade into night, and all she could see were the sides of the mountain below her, the green and brown of grass, the yellow and purple of gorse and heather, the steely grey of granite. There was nowhere left to go. The men were much closer now, the first of them only a few paces away, his knife raised high above his shoulder. She did the only thing she could. She jumped.

She fell, the wind pummelling the breath from her body, the speed of her descent knocking all but one thought from her head, that she could hear her own voice screaming. A second passed and the ground was already coming closer. Incredibly, impossibly, as if he were only a few feet away, she saw a boy she didn't recognise, his hair dark, his eyes blue, standing, watching from far below. Heard him shouting her name. He calmed her, this strange boy she didn't know, and quickly she focussed, trying to stop her descent. Her body began to slow, but still the ground was coming. With a sickening lurch of her stomach, she realised she'd left it too late. She pushed harder, feeling the pressure squeeze her body, her limbs as she continued to slow, but it wasn't enough. The ground was a heartbeat away and she shut her eyes, anticipating the crunch her body would make as it hit the earth.

Chapter One

The ferry rolled to the right as it turned, taking Jasmine's stomach with it. The sensation jolted her from her sleep and, lifting her head, she looked about her. Her mum and John had come back and were sat, eyes closed, in their seats opposite her. They snuggled into one another, her mum's head nestled into the curve of John's neck, her arm draped lazily across his body. Jasmine's lip curled and she looked quickly away. Her book had slipped off her lap and into the gap between the seats. She picked it out, tried half-heartedly to flatten the bent pages before giving up and dropping it, closed, on the seat next to her.

"You're not enjoying that, are you?" John's voice asked suddenly.

He was watching her again, his pale blue eyes unreadable. She couldn't shake the feeling that he was studying her, like a scientist trying to figure out a new species or come to a decision about them. It was beginning to grate, to annoy her, like his fussing, the overprotective clucking of a male mother hen. And a surrogate one at that.

"What?"

He frowned at her tone, pushed his black hair out of his eyes. Curling around his ears, the collar of his shirt, it needed a cut. He was too old for the style, though she guessed in his head he was going for the hip oldie look with the greying temples, the lines around his eyes.

"Oh, the book? No, not really," she replied quickly, flushing.

She didn't know if she would enjoy it or not; she couldn't get past the first page to tell.

She leant in towards the window and looking out, pretending to be engrossed, studying the sea. It worked; his eyes moved away and she sighed with relief, keeping her own carefully where they were.

The sea, far below, was grey, dull, and flat, the mirror image of a sky without sun or colour, filled with nothing but thick, heavy cloud. Jasmine pressed her nose to the glass, trying to see further out, to see past the grey, but it was too dense. After a moment, she sat back. This fog did strange things to her head. Made her imagine that there was nothing beyond it, that the world beyond had gone, disappeared, faded away altogether while she'd been sleeping. As if she, her mum and John and the ferry carrying them, silent but for the odd white-haired, hard of hearing pensioner talking too loudly and the insistent, metallic chugging of the engines, were the only things left in the universe.

It was an unsettling thought. More disturbed by it than she cared to admit, she pushed it away. A better one was to imagine that somehow, miraculously, they'd passed Ireland by, missed it completely and were now heading out across the Atlantic. A tin boat, stuffed full of oldies chugging manfully across the ocean to Canada. She imagined her father, waiting for her on a Canadian beach, blue sky framing the jagged rock and cliffs behind him. No one would have to tell him she was coming; he'd know, feel it instinctively, just as he'd know exactly where she would land. A stray hair tickled the side of her nose and she rubbed at it irritably, feeling anger hot in the pit of her stomach. *Ireland! Why not Spain or Greece or even Southern France? Or anywhere warm, for that matter.* Somewhere with hot, hot days and balmy nights, with crystal blue seas and golden beaches, and men darkly handsome and smouldering to make Sarah insanely jealous and give her some sort of consolation. But she knew why, even if it didn't help. She frowned and, in the glass, two foreheads wrinkled simultaneously. Outside, the cloud brightened suddenly, as if the sun was trying desperately to break through, hoping to be seen at least once before the end of the day. Jasmine watched it for a moment then returned her gaze to the waves created by the side of the ship, her eyes drawn to the white surf and spray as water and metal collided.

A woman's voice sounded suddenly, high, tinny and crackling across the tannoy. Jasmine missed most of it, just caught the end: disembark. They were almost there. Curious despite herself, and wanting to catch a first look at land, she stood up, climbing out between the chairs and the low table. Her mum opened her eyes and lifted her head. Long light brown hair slipped from John, revealing an open button in his shirt. Her mum's hair was silky straight, giving it the shiny, luscious look of melted caramel, whereas Jasmine's was a boring shade of mouse, thick and wayward. Which was why she'd persuaded her mum's hairdresser to add red highlights and fried it with straighteners; the only way to stop it from floating around her head in mad professor waves.

"You OK, Jas?"

She nodded. "Yeah, just going to the deck to have a look."

Her mum sat up, and her hand, with her Portobello market

wedding ring flashing, moved across John's body, finishing on his stomach. Jasmine watched as her fingers slipped into the gap and began absently to stroke the skin underneath. Her stomach tightened. "Don't forget we have to be back in the car before the ferry docks. If you hear the siren, get back to the car and we'll meet you there."

"Yeah, OK."

Clear of the table and all their stuff, Jasmine struggled into her coat.

"You do remember which deck the car is on?" John asked, lifting his head up so that it joined her mum's.

"Of course!" she said witheringly, moving away before anyone could say anything more.

Three D, she said to herself as she followed the signs for the stairs, *or was it Three G?*

The deck was almost deserted; only a few people seemed determined enough to brave the chill of the wind as it whipped along the side of the ferry. Jasmine found a spot along one side, the side she thought she'd see land from, and looked out across the sea hopefully. Still nothing, still the same endless grey. She folded her arms over the top of the rail then rested her chin on them, scanning the water, prepared to wait.

Her mind drifted, as if caught by the waves, the endlessly restless tide. She was in Canada, living with her dad in a white wooden house with the beds covered in knitted patchwork blankets, an orchard at the bottom of the garden. They'd have a dog, a big Canadian one that would follow her around. And they'd be happy and her dad wouldn't be broken, not knowing how to fix himself, like pieces of fruit in a bowl slowly rotting one another, souring bit by bit.

Someone was watching her. Jasmine knew it, suddenly, instinctively, and lifted her head to look. At the far end of the boat, standing all alone and leaning on the back rail, was a man dressed in a worn black suit covered by a long dark grey coat that was way too big for him. Even from this distance, she could see how white his skin was, his face, his hands stark against the cloth, and the blackness where his eyes should be. The blackness bored into her, making her shiver. She pulled the sides of her coat together and wrapped her arms around it, keeping it there, as she looked away and back. He was still staring. *Don't be silly*, she told herself, *he's looking ahead, past you, the way we're going.* As if to prove it to herself, she looked left, towards the front. But she couldn't help herself; she had to look back.

He was still looking, still staring, and this time she found herself staring back. *Don't,* a voice inside her urged, but it was too late. She couldn't stop. Couldn't seem to blink. And then her head began to spin and the ferry shrank suddenly, the sides slipping away as the back moved towards her. The man came with it, his face growing as it drew closer and closer, blocking almost everything else out. His white skin gleamed, looked as if it had been bleached not once, but over and over and then stretched, pulled tight over the bones that lay underneath. His eyes were deep set, sat in shadow and the irises, Jasmine realised with a shudder, were completely black, almost as if his pupils had leaked outwards, obliterating any trace of colour.

Something touched her shoulder. She jumped, turned to look, her breath coming out in a rush.

"There you are; we've been looking for you. Thought we'd join you."

It was her mum. Jasmine's head span again and the ferry returned to normal. She looked back. The deck was full of people stood along the rails, eager for their first glimpse of land. It was hard to see past them, but she thought she saw the edge of the man's coat, his arm.

"I don't know where John's got to. He went one way and I went another—" her mum murmured, looking all around, "—oh, there he is now."

Coming from the front of the ferry, he was walking towards them. Jasmine looked away, back towards the man, but he'd gone, the space he'd left taken by a family of four.

John joined them, standing the other side of Jasmine's mum and snaking his arm around her waist, pulling her close. He gave Jasmine a nod over her but, still thinking of the man, she ignored him.

"There," her mum cried out suddenly, leaning forward in her excitement and pointing. "Do you see it?"

They all leant forward, but to Jasmine it was nothing more than another, darker patch of grey. The ferry moved towards it, the patch growing in front of her, becoming bigger and bigger. And then suddenly, without warning, the grey, the mist slipped away altogether and she was staring at the dark green of grass. Land, she thought eagerly, in her excitement forgetting all about the man. The tip of a peninsula, low lying, with craggy little inlets. The ferry turned slightly and, hugging the coastline, began to steer towards the harbour. The land slid smoothly by. Stone walls began to appear, dividing the grass into fields, signs of human habitation that strangely made the land seem bleaker, more remote. Something clicked in her head, like recognition, but not quite. She dismissed it, thinking it reminded her of Devon, the northern coastline, near when her Nan lived.

"What do you think?" John asked after a few minutes, breaking the silence.

It took Jasmine a moment to realise he was talking to her. She sneaked a look at him, at his face still turned towards land, expecting to see something there, some clue to how he was feeling, returning home after so long, but it was smooth, empty.

"It looks nice."

Even as she said it Jasmine mentally kicked herself. Her reply seemed so stupid, inadequate, reflecting nothing of what she saw before her. John didn't even seem to notice.

"It looks quiet enough, but Ireland's a strange place. It has a funny way of getting under your skin, in your blood. When it does, it doesn't let go easily."

He'd lifted his eyes as he'd talked, gazing at her over the top of her mum's head. There was something new in his gaze, something different, as if he had something important to tell her. The siren sounded suddenly and John turned quickly away. Then her mum was leading them back, towards the stairs and the moment passed as if it had never been there.

Chapter Two

"Jasmine. Jasmine! Breakfast's ready."

Half-asleep, Jasmine stumbled towards the bathroom.

"You only just got up?!" Her mum gazed up at her from the bottom of the stairs, her brown eyes narrowing. "We're leaving in half an hour. I told you, I want to be gone by nine thirty — so we can make a day of it."

"I won't be long," Jasmine dragged a hand through her hair, catching sight of herself in the hall mirror.

The mad professor waves were back, somehow managing to point in every direction simultaneously. She stopped and puffed out her cheeks. Looked, with her hair, her round face and small features, like a chipmunk, with his paw in a socket. It needed a cut. She breathed out, deflating her cheeks.

"You'll be half an hour on that hair of yours."

"Oh, very funny," she replied acidly, going into the bathroom and closing the door firmly behind her.

*

Autumn sun shone through the car window. Magnified by the glass, its heat warmed Jasmine's face as she watched the countryside fly by. Soft greens were interspersed with flashes of brown, gold and russet as leaf and grass slowly began to turn. And yet it was so mild it was hard to believe it was October. It was hard to believe it was October full stop. Her first month here had flown by, whirling her along with its busyness, the minutes, hours, days of the new squeezing out the old. *Malachy*. Just thinking of him made her smile. Out of all the things she'd been surprised to find here, Malachy was definitely the most surprising. From the first day she'd met him, she'd felt there was something different about him, something interesting. She'd been walking home from the bus stop after her first day at school, had been walking past his house, deep in thought, replaying the day over and over in her head and fretting.

"How's it going?" he'd said, poking his head around a gap in the hedgerow, the unexpectedness of his appearance making her jump.

She'd stared at him, noticed the garden gate he was leaning over, his dark hair, his wide cheeks and strong nose, his eyes a deep vibrant blue, not pale, like John's...

"What? Oh — hi."

He seemed strangely familiar. An image flittered through her mind, like a butterfly seen out of the corner of her eye, moving too fast for her to follow.

His grin was wide, unexpected, "Hi. Do you always look like that?"

"What? Oh, er, right," Ten seconds too late, she got it. "Like what?!"

"Annoyed. You were frowning."

"Oh, I was just thinking."

"First day at school." He nodded sympathetically. "Did Pat the Baker introduce you to your year? He always does that. I think he likes to see us cringe."

"Pat the Baker?"

There was that grin again, making his eyes bright with mischief.

"Pat the Baker. Mr Corcoran, the head teacher. His first name's Pat and his dad used to own a bakery in Ballaghaderren, and with the bread you get... y'know the brand... in the supermarket, Pat the Baker?"

He saw her blank face and waved the joke away. "Forget it."

A thought occurred to her. "How did you know it was my first day?"

He flashed her a look, a look that said how stupid she must be.

"You're the new girl in the area and you're wearing the school uniform."

She flushed. "Oh, yeah. I moved in up the road."

He gave her that look again then nodded. "In Kelly's house. You're from London."

"And how do you know that?"

He laughed. "With that hair, you had to be from London or Dublin."

Her hand went to her head. She had to admit it did make her stand out. But that was why she liked it; it felt punky, with attitude, even if she wasn't.

"I'm only messing. You really are new here! Word gets around pretty quick. There's nothing we don't know."

"Is that because you're all so nosy?" Jasmine asked tartly, getting annoyed now.

To her surprise he just laughed again. "Yeah of course. What do you expect when there's nothing else to do but look at the fields? You wait; after a winter here you'll do anything to stop the boredom."

His mischief was infectious. Leaning forward, she lowered her voice conspiratorially. "I won't. They have this amazing thing now called the internet, I don't suppose you've heard of it?"

For a moment, he didn't say anything and then he put out his hand.

"I'm Malachy, Malachy Costello," he said, pronouncing it cost-de-low.

"And I'm Jasmine. Jas." Grinning, she took his hand.

"Hello Jasmine," he said seriously.

They shook hands. From the field opposite came the deep, low throb of an engine and then the roof of a tractor appeared over the top of the hedge.

"That's me dad." He dropped her hand and straightened. "I've got to go, can't stand around talking to the new girl. I've got to help me dad with the cattle."

"I'd better go anyway," Jasmine said, moving off. "Wouldn't want to part a man from his cows. See you around."

"They're not cows, they're cattle."

The tractor, so small it looked to be in miniature, chugged loudly as it shot out of the field and crossing the road just in front of her. Malachy's dad turned to look at her as it flew into the open gates of the farm and headed off down the driveway.

"If you're good I might give you a ride on it," Malachy called after her.

She turned back. "Your Dad's tractor? It's a bit on the small side."

"For a city girl, you sure know how to wound a farmer!"

They'd grinned again at one another, and then with a vague wave Malachy had gone, running down the drive after the tractor. She'd watched him go, marvelling at how fast he could move in wellies.

The car jerked as John accelerated out of the corner, pulling Jasmine forward and then back. Sighing to herself, she grabbed hold of the door handle, braced herself as he headed towards a corner. What a time for John to find his inner Lewis Hamilton. Normally cringe-makingly slow, today he was managing to find every dip and pothole in these madly twisting country roads. They hit a line of dips, three in a row, that sent the car and Jasmine's bottom bouncing and the front wheels lifting. For a moment the car flew, suspended in midair, then came thudding to the ground, Jasmine's bottom crunching with it.

The soft green hills and fields gave way to baby mountains, their tops jagged, misshapen with exposed rock. John slowed to negotiate a roundabout then accelerated again, through it and out the other side. The road, a dual carriageway, opened up before them, the countryside around them doing the same. Jasmine shifted, wanting to see past her mum's shoulder, to see the view ahead. And then she saw it.

It was a hill, but not like any she'd ever seen before. It was stood so completely on its own that it towered over everything around it, dominating the low fields surrounding it and the sea beyond. And it had the strangest shape: it looked almost as if someone had cut it into two and discarded the top half, leaving the stone in the centre open, exposed, the summit flat. Very flat. And there, on the very top, was something… she couldn't tell what, couldn't quite make it out. It was sat slightly back, away from her and towards the sea. Jasmine squinted, shifted again then moved to her side window as the hill came closer. It looked stone, like someone had carried boulders, pebbles up there and made a mound. And then something clicked. *A cairn!* She thought to herself excitedly and leaning forward.

"John, what's that hill?" she asked, pointing.

He glanced to the left then returned his gaze to the road. "It's Knocknarea."

"That cairn on top, can you get inside it?"

"The tomb? No, I don't think so. The legend says it belongs to Queen Mebh, but I don't think anyone really knows."

"Who was she?"

"An Irish Queen. She was the Queen of Connaught, I think, and some sort of pirate. Met Queen Elizabeth. Apparently they got on really well. Or am I thinking of someone else?" He shrugged. "I can't remember. We did it in school years ago. I'm sure you'll be able to find her on the internet."

Jasmine sat back, frustrated: it was so typical of him not to know.

"You'll do it as soon as we get home, won't you, Jas?" Her mum threw her an affectionate look over one shoulder. "Do you remember when me and your dad took you to Stonehenge? We had to drag you away, even though you were so tired." She turned to John, "She's always been the same. Fascinated with old things. Like when you sent her a keyring shaped like Chichen Itza from Mexico. She took it everywhere. What happened to it in the end?"

"It broke."

John was saying something, but Jasmine ignored him. She looked out of the back window instead and wondered what the cairn would be like. If only she could get inside it. Out of nowhere an image flashed through her head, and for a moment it was so clear it was as if she was really seeing it. She was in the tomb, standing with the stone ceiling high above her head, the walls lit by a faint, amber light. Ahead of her a stone crypt lay tucked into one corner, covered by symbols that twisted and turned into one another as if the stonemason's work had gone beyond rushed and into frenzied. The image faded and Jasmine blinked, shaking her head slightly as if to clear it.

"This is it. Sligo, where I went to college," John was saying loudly to her mum.

Behind her, Knocknarea had disappeared into the distance and, reluctantly, she turned around to look.

At first there wasn't too much to see, just the usual tops of buildings with one lone grey spire of a church towering high above them, reaching into the clouds. Looked almost like a pin on a map, marking the spot. And then the road curved slightly and she saw the mountain. It was huge, sat just behind the town, and filled the vista. Stretched inland as far as the eye could see. It reminded her of something out of the Grand Canyon, with its top heavily lined and eroded, the exposed rock cut deep by the water flowing downwards. But there was no sandy yellow here, just the same deep green, brown and granite grey tinged with purple. It was stunning, made doubly so by the sea sweeping into the bay beneath it. Her first views of County Sligo and already she was falling in love with it.

"Look at that," her mum breathed, seeming to say it all.

"That's Benbulbin." John smiled, with a sideways glance at Jasmine's mum. "I knew you'd like it."

A few minutes later and they were in the town, John parking next to a cathedral, the spire Jasmine had seen. Getting out, he led them across the empty spaces towards a set of worn stone steps, the exit to the street below. Jasmine tried to put her coat on as she walked, but a wind, coming seemingly out of nowhere, whipped at them and streamed her coat away from her.

"God, it's windy!" she exclaimed, managing to get one arm in.

"It always is; we're next to the Atlantic don't forget," John explained, stopping at the top step and holding out his arm to Jasmine's mum.

She took it, laughing girlishly, and allowed him to lead her down the steps.

"*Next to the Atlantic don't forget!*" Jasmine muttered, straightening her coat.

At the bottom, her mum and John waited for her to catch up. They kissed, long, passionately, their mouths working furiously. A pair of teenage girls passing by stared at them, at the grey at John's temples, then nudged one another and snickered. Flushing, wishing desperately for the ground to lift up and swallow her, Jasmine flew down the steps and straight past them.

"Jas, wait," her mum called, but she ignored her. "You don't know where you're going."

That stopped her. Reluctantly she turned around and waited. Still walking arm in arm, she had to admit they looked good together. Both tall, closer to slender than to plump and dressed casually in jeans, they looked younger than their ages (especially her mum, with only the faintest of lines around her eyes), but not self-consciously so.

"You want to go left at the end of the road," John explained as they drew close.

"Hold on." Jasmine's mum stopped. "Maybe we need to decide where we're going first. I mean, is that the way to the shops?"

"It is." John nodded. "But there's something I'd like you to see first."

"What? What is it?"

"I'm not telling you," he teased her, his eyes bright. "Wait and see."

"Here we are," he announced, stopping in the middle of the pavement.

He spread his arm wide, enjoyed the effect as Jasmine and her mum stared at it in surprise. It was a shop, or rather a shop that was more of an old one-roomed workshop. A huge, rough wooden bench lay along one half of it, covered with carving tools strewn any old how. Behind that, an enormous pile of wooden logs, all different sizes, reached almost to the ceiling. There was sawdust everywhere. Even the silver-haired man, the owner, the carpenter, was covered with it. Standing behind the bench, he tightened a block of wood in an enormous vice with one hand while talking vigorously to a couple stood across from him. Jasmine moved around her mum and spotted his window display. Her mouth fell open. She took a step closer and, pressing her nose to the glass, peered at the wooden statutes he'd positioned into three rough rows. They were very intricate, and for a moment all she could see was lines, and then slowly symbols; figures, animals, began to emerge and she saw a mish mash of eyes, noses and tails. The carpenter had placed a small piece of card below the statues, giving each one a name, written in English and Irish.

"Oh John, they're beautiful," Jasmine's mum breathed. "But I wouldn't know which one to choose."

"You don't have to." He grinned, his eyes shining as he looked into hers. "He makes commissions. Is well known for it. With his help, you can have exactly what you want."

"Oh, John — really?"

They kissed long and deep. The man in the shop picked up a hammer and chisel and chose that moment to glance out of his window. He watched them for a moment, his face expressionless, then set to work.

Jasmine tutted, straightened up. "So are we going in or what?"

Her mum and John broke apart.

"After you then, if you're so keen," her mum retorted with a wave of her hand.

The sawdust seemed to have permeated the very air of the shop, for as soon as they stepped inside Jasmine's nose began to tingle then itch. She rubbed at it furiously. The old man, still chattering away, paused in mid-flow to welcome them and then with barely a breath continued on. He worked as fast as he talked, his movements smooth and effortless, his hands working to their own, long-used rhythm. His accent was unfamiliar and very broad and for a few minutes she had no idea what he was talking about. Then suddenly, as if someone had flipped a switch in her brain, she got it. He was telling them about the stories, the Irish legends, his work illustrated. How he'd drawn out the different threads running through them and united them in his carvings so that each statue was an eclectic mix but also a distinct whole. He punctuated his words with a point of his chisel at each statute, his work a labour of love, his passion for his art verging on the obsessional.

The couple, with wide smiles and many thanks, made a swift exit, making Jasmine wonder how long they'd been trapped there, too polite to walk away from him in mid-sentence. She watched them go with a barely suppressed smile; her mum was far too impatient to get caught like that. She'd cut through his patter. She waited, but to her amazement her mum didn't say anything, just stood there with John, listening, her eyes intent, as if she had all the time in the world.

Jasmine shifted. The man was still talking, seeming to have an almost endless repertoire of stories. She glanced around the room, looked up at the ceiling, the white discoloured and flaking, then back to the carvings in the window. Her mum said something and John laughed. Ignoring them, she moved towards the window. Made of wood the colour of honey, the carvings were thick and deep, making her think of an old stone hearth warmed by a winter fire. The old man's voice softened and slowed, lingering enticingly on the Irish words, giving them an almost magical quality. They floated through her head, evoking sights, tastes and smells, as if he were bringing his carvings to life. Lost within them, her mind drifted, imagining people, places she'd never heard of.

"—and this one represents the three women in folklore; the young beautiful girl, the strong knowing woman, the mother of men and the hag, ugly but wise, Brid or Brigid. This one is the warrior Queen Medb, and you can see her tomb is on top of Knocknarea—"

The voice stopped. The images faded and Jasmine was back in the shop, conscious suddenly of the silence in the room. She turned around. The old man was examining her with a look on his face she couldn't place, her mum and John following his gaze. She blinked. She felt very strange, lightheaded, woozy, as if she'd been too long in the sun.

"Jas, are you OK?" her mum asked anxiously, starting to move towards her, but she stopped her with one hand.

"Yeah, I think so."

Without a word, the old man spun the handle on his vice and removed the statue he was working on, replacing it with a small square piece of wood from his bench. He began to talk again, except now he was telling them his prices and about the pieces he'd commissioned for different customers, the poet giving way to the salesman. He paused, picked up his hammer and chisel and gave Jasmine another piercing look.

"What's yer favourite animal?"

"Madra Rua," John said from beside her mum, answering for her.

Jasmine stared at him, caught between curiosity and outrage at his presumption.

"What's that?" her mother asked for her.

"A fox. Or more accurately the "Red Dog", Rua being Irish for Red and Madra, Dog. Of course," the carpenter answered, nodding.

He looked down and began to carve. Taking only a few, sharp, definite strokes, he finished almost as soon as he'd started. He loosened the vice slightly and flipped the wood over.

"Yer name, what is it again? Yer mother said it."

"Jasmine. I'm Jasmine."

"Like the flower."

A few strokes more and he lay down his tools and loosened the vice completely.

"Here." Moving down his side of the bench, he held it out to her. "It's for ye. Madra Rua on one side and Knocknarea, the final resting place of Queen Mebh and the fabled entrance to the world of the Tuatha de Danann, and yer name on the other."

Jasmine took it from him without a word. She traced the outline of the fox with her finger and then turned the wood over, seeing the crude but unmistakable outline of Knocknarea etched above her name. She heard her mum and John protesting, saying that it was too much, but the carpenter dismissed them impatiently.

"It's nothing. Call it a sample if you like. But it's for the girl. Just for her."

She sensed rather than saw him move forward and lean over the bench towards her. She lifted her eyes. He was staring straight at her, his lips close to her ear. And then he was talking, his voice so soft that afterwards she wondered if she'd heard right.

"For you, Jasmine. To keep you safe."

"John, I don't think I need a commission. I like all these," her mum said loudly. A few feet away she was oblivious. "But I can't quite decide which one."

The carpenter straightened and, still looking at Jasmine, answered her mum, "There's no rush to decide, I'm always here. Come back when you're ready."

"What about this one—"

"I'm closing now," he interrupted, his voice abrupt, rude almost. "Come back another day."

"But…" her mum began again, but John took her arm and gently propelled her towards the door.

"Come on Kate, let the man close. It'll give us time to think about it."

Feeling slightly dazed, Jasmine followed them, the old man coming after so he could lock the door behind them. She hesitated then turned back towards him.

"Thanks for the carving," she said awkwardly.

He smiled for the first time, "Yer welcome." His face turned sombre. "Take care, young Jasmine."

And then she was out on the pavement with the carving in her hand, her mum and John next to her and the door shut behind her. She looked at the carpenter through the door, saw him nod to John then flip the lock and turn the sign to closed.

"Let's have a look at it, then," her mum said.

"What?" Jasmine turned.

"The carving," her mum explained slowly, rolling her eyes at John.

"Oh." Nonplussed, she passed it over.

"It's lovely." Her mum examined it for a moment then passed it back.

Jasmine quickly put it in her pocket. Her mum and John moved off and she followed, glancing at the shop as she passed. The carpenter was stood at the window watching, his hand poised on the edge of a blind as if he'd been stopped, frozen, in mid-action. Seeing her look, he began to move again and pulled at the blind, drawing it down, obscuring him from her view.

It was getting late when they'd finished shopping and made their way back to an almost empty car park, the sky already beginning to darken. The roads out of Sligo were still busy, but the traffic dispersed quickly and it was quiet by the time they'd reached Knocknarea. The hill, lying half in shadow, half in the golden light of the setting autumn sun, looked eerily magical. Jasmine sat back, settled her head on the rest behind her and watched it glide by, her hand moving to the carving in her pocket. She traced the lines with her fingers. The surface of the wood was strangely smooth, as if it had been prepared earlier and was not just a piece of scrap the carpenter had grabbed impulsively. The whole thing was strange if you thought about it; the way the carpenter seemed to single her out, the way John had spoken for her. *And why did he say the fox was her favourite animal?* She liked foxes; he was her favourite animal in the book her Dad had bought her once, "The Animals of Farthing Wood". But apart from that she didn't think she had a favourite. She glanced over at him, catching the reflection of his eyes in the rear-view mirror. He was watching her again. Hiding her annoyance, she gave him a deliberate smile, bright and false. Behind her, framed in the back window of the car and with the sunlight faded from every part of it but the tomb, Knocknarea disappeared into the distance.

Chapter Three

Jasmine woke early the next morning, disturbed by the sun shining in around the edges of her curtains and a dream about the carpenter she'd met yesterday. The house was quiet; her mum and John were still asleep and she snuggled back down, determined to get her lie-in. But it was too late; she couldn't sleep. The carpenter's eyes were still with her, looked almost black as they stared out at her bizarrely from Malachy's dad's tractor. And besides, the sun was calling her, her bike too, telling her that it was a perfect day for a cycle. Getting up, passing the wooden sculpture left on her bedside cabinet, she dressed quickly, throwing on layers against the cold and stuffing her feet into trainers.

Her bike was in the corner of the shed, the front wheel at right angles and a garden hose twisted somehow around the mudguard and the bottom of the handlebar. Cursing John, Jasmine tugged impatiently at the hose. Her bike lurched, looked for a moment as it was going topple over, and she quickly let go. She tried again, going slower this time and taking more care. The hose fell away finally and then she was dragging, heaving her bike out through the shed door and wheeling it around the house and into the road. Slipping onto the saddle she tilted the bike then span the pedals and kicked off. It was her first ride since the move and it took her a moment to find the rhythm. Then she had it and was pedalling hard, enjoying the sensation of legs pumping smoothly beneath her. She hit the apex of the hill and let the pedals go, letting the bike plummet down the hill, bouncing manically over the uneven surface. Wind whipped her hair and her hood straight back, caught in her throat and chilled her nose and cheeks red, but her heart sang with exhilaration. She passed Malachy's house, glimpsed his dad crossing the yard and then she was gone, down to the main road and onwards.

She followed the main road down to the village, turning arbitrarily left and left again. The road was quiet, the houses too as she passed. She saw a lake to her right, boats left on the shore, the bottom of people's gardens, then she was moving under trees and into a dim half-light. Branches arched over her head and the lake disappeared behind a thick, overgrown wood. She was cycling through an avenue, a tall, high roof straight ahead of her. She pedalled closer. Three tall chimneys appeared, then upper windows, long and narrow and built in the Georgian style. An old stately home; it had to be by the size of it. She passed an old brick wall, saw gateposts ahead, the original rusty iron gate covered in thick metal barriers. Red and black warning signs told her there was danger and to keep out. It was empty then, derelict. The upper windows stared out at her. She stared back and for a moment she had the strangest sensation, as if there was someone behind them, standing deliberately to one side so that she wouldn't be able to see their face as they watched her ride by. As if she'd know them. Unnerved by the thought, she continued on, pedalling as fast as she could to get through the trees and out of the shadow and shade. And then finally she was out and back in the sunlight, seeing the lake again and the village behind it.

With legs tired and protesting, Jasmine headed for home. Halfway up the hill to the house her legs gave out, forcing her to a stop. She slipped off her bike, feeling the stiffness in her thighs. The hedgerow to her left rustled, the wind picking up or maybe a bird. She ignored it and began walking. The top of Malachy's house came into view just as she heard the sound of a car. She looked back; it was coming along the main road and as she watched it began to slow. Thinking it would turn, she stopped, moved to one side, but it continued on, speeding up as it passed the junction. Next to her, the hedgerow rustled again, louder this time. She shivered. Felt again as if someone was there, just the other side, watching her. She imagined them crouched, their face pressed close to the branches, their eyes peering at her through the twigs. A tiny bird appeared suddenly, hopping from branch to branch.

Jasmine, you silly… she laughed to herself, realising that it was the second time today she'd let her imagination run away with her. She continued on, walking fast, her head lowered with the effort.

"You been for a ride?"

She jumped, looked up. It was Malachy. In his usual place, hanging over the garden gate.

"Do you have to keep doing that?" she complained crossly, her heart beating furiously.

"What?" he asked innocently, but his grin gave him away. "So you've been for a ride."

"Na, I don't actually ride it. I just wheel it around."

His grin widened. "So how far did you wheel it?"

She laughed at that. Couldn't help it, not with him.

"Not far. Around the lake, past the old house."

"That's not an old house, that's a convent."

"A convent?" she repeated in surprise.

"Yeah, y'know, where nuns live. Didn't you see the church?"

"No." She shook her head.

"With the big gold cross on top?"

"No." Another shake.

"You're weird."

"I kind of like that." It was her turn to grin.

"Which makes you even weirder."

"Not like you, hanging over a garden gate without a coat on a freezing cold Sunday morning."

"I'm helping my dad! Besides, it's not cold."

"Not cold?!" She rolled her eyes.

They laughed, heads bent towards one another.

"So, you got out early, away from the parents' Sunday morning love fest?"

"He's not my dad!" It was out before she could stop it.

"Sorry, I keep forgetting." His eyes slid away. "I don't know what you've got against John; he seems OK to me."

"He's not my dad."

"I know that," he began impatiently, "but—"

"I mean it. He's not my dad, but he acts like he is, always telling me what and what not to do." She sighed.

They'd never really talked about it before. Malachy was a boy and generally she thought he wouldn't be interested, but now it seemed important to explain and have him understand.

"It was only supposed to be a trial separation, but John came back. Usually he goes again, but this time he didn't. And then him and mum got together and that was it for Dad. He and me dad were best friends at University; they were still supposed to be close and then he goes and does that to him. And then they couldn't even wait for my dad to get used to it. They had to go and get married, rubbing his nose in it. No wonder he went to Canada—"

She stopped, realised that her first instinct had been right. Malachy was looking even more embarrassed and very uncomfortable.

"Sorry," she apologised quickly, but she wasn't, not really.

"It must've been hard." He gave her a sympathetic look, she guessed trying his best.

"It was. And weird. I knew John before, when I was little I mean. From what me mum said he worked all over the place, y'know, all round the world. But he used to stay with us sometimes, in between trips. And he always brought me back something, a present, something from the country he'd been in, something that sort of represented it, if you know what I mean. But he was like an uncle or something. I never had one; me dad's an only child and me mum just has one sister and it was nice, and he was… exciting, exotic… had all these stories."

She stopped again. Malachy was looking at her and she could guess what he was thinking, wondering. *Why was he so bad?* But she couldn't say, couldn't explain why she couldn't accept John, how disloyal she'd feel.

"So, have you heard from him yet? Your dad, I mean?" Malachy asked, interrupting her thoughts.

"No." Realising she didn't want to talk about it anyone, she pulled herself together. "I'd better go," She gave him a weak smile. "So you're helping your dad all day?"

"No." He shook his head, making a face. "We've got visitors later. My dad's oldest friend and family."

"Oh, have fun."

"Yeah, thanks," he said sourly, straightening up. "See you Monday."

"See you Monday."

She left him then, continued on, still thinking of her dad. Wondered for the hundredth time, the thousandth, where he was, what he was doing and why he didn't even try to call.

*

Arriving home, coming in through the kitchen door, the first thing that hit her was the aroma of bacon frying. Her stomach growled furiously, hungry suddenly. "Where have you been?" her mum asked, looking up from the bacon just beginning to curl in the pan.

"Just out for a ride." She closed the door behind her.

"I bet you didn't have any breakfast. I'll do you a fry-up."

"Just—" She stopped as John appeared, yawning.

"Morning, Jasmine," he said cheerfully, pulling out a chair from under the table and flopping heavily into it.

She didn't answer.

With a slight, almost imperceptible shrug, John reached for teapot and one of the mugs her mum had left in the middle of the table, "Kate, that smells great. I'm starving."

"I'm not surprised." Her mum's answering laugh was deep, throaty and full of meaning.

John eyed Jasmine over the top of his mug. "Want a cup?" He took a loud, greedy slurp.

"No, I'm going for a shower," she replied, pressing toe to heel and levering off the first of her trainers. "I'll—"

"Have some breakfast first," her mum interrupted, putting three rashers of bacon onto an already groaning plate and handing it to John.

"Thanks, love." Immediately John began sawing awkwardly through a half-charred sausage. "Jas, you were out early."

"Yeah, just for a cycle." Bending, she picked up her trainers, "Just round the convent and back. Mum, I'll get toast later."

"But there's plenty here!" Her mum protested, looking up from the pan.

"The convent?" John was asking, his fork lowered.

"Yeah, that's what Malachy said it was. It was hard to tell." Jasmine started across the room, heading for the hall, "OK, Mum, maybe some bacon, for a butty. But I'm having me shower first."

"But it'll be ruined. You can shower after. Besides, it's nice to eat all together." Her voice hardened. "Sit down, Jasmine."

"I don't… I won't be long." Her mum's neck swivelled. "OK, then." She sat into the chair opposite John and, resisting the urge to let her trainers drop, placed them on the floor next to her.

"You didn't go in?" John's voice was suddenly sharp.

"What?" She straightened. "No, why would I?"

"Good. You shouldn't; it's not safe."

"I know. I saw the signs."

"The roof's dodgy," he continued as if he hadn't heard her, taking a half slice of toast and dunking one corner into his egg. "They were talking about it at work."

"Here you go," her mum interjected brightly, handing Jasmine her plate.

"It didn't look that ba—" Jasmine found herself arguing.

"It might look OK, but it's not," John interrupted, still chewing. "That's why they have the signs."

"I know, I saw them!"

"Jasmine, there's no need to be rude. John's just concerned about you."

Her mum joined them, sitting in the chair between them.

"But I didn't—?" She fell back, speechless at the level of the unfairness.

"John, how is it?" her mum asked, ignoring her.

"Kate, it's great, as usual."

Smiling, they leant in towards one another and kissed. Jasmine watched as her mum sat back, wiped a fleck of egg yolk from her lip, and looked down at her plate. Jasmine saw a trail of fat oozing along one side and was no longer hungry.

"Mum, I'll just be two minutes—" Already, she was moving, her bottom sliding sideways off the seat.

"Jasmine, your mum cooked breakfast for you, the least you can do is sit and eat it!" John snapped suddenly, his face like thunder.

Jasmine's bottom froze and she pushed her plate away, her anger easily matching his. She was on her feet, the chair scraping, before she realised.

"But I didn't even want it… not everyone's a pi—"

"Jasmine!" It was her mum's turn to snap. "Don't you dare talk to John like that. This is his home too."

"As if I could forget," Jasmine shouted, turning on her.

"And don't talk to your mum—" John began, but she was too angry to stop, to listen.

"Just shut up," she shouted. "Leave me alone, you, you, bastard!"

She flew out of the kitchen, ran along the hall and up the stairs. Her heart thudding, she opened her bedroom door and, stomping inside, slammed it behind her.

Too angry to cry, Jasmine lay on her bed and watched a thick, white cloud move slowly closer, leaving a thin streak of blue behind it. Five minutes passed, turned to ten, eleven, and twelve and then, in the silence, she heard footsteps on the stairs. Guessing that it was her mum, and knowing immediately what would follow, she sighed and pulled herself upwards until she was sat with the pillows bolstered behind her.

Knock, knock.

"Jasmine." Her mum's voice was muffled, as if she were leaning into the wood of the door. "I want a word."

"OK" Her voice sounded sullen, so she tried again. "OK." That was better.

The door opened and her mum's face appeared, stiff and cold.

"I won't be long." She stepped into the room, keeping one hand on the door handle. "Me and John are going for a walk."–

"OK." They locked eyes, Jasmine the first to look away. She studied the legs of her jeans, the faded crisscross of the denim.

"I just wanted you to know how disappointed I am in you. I expect better. And I'm telling you now that we had planned a surprise for you. You know those megalithic tombs John told you about? Well, we were going to go today. It was John's idea; he knows how much you love things like that. But after this morning we won't be going."

Her mum paused. Jasmine frowned, noticing the small indent on the right leg, just above the knee; the start of a hole.

"It'll give you chance to think about your behaviour. If you want to behave like a child then we'll treat you like one."

The door creaked. Jasmine looked up in time to see her mum leaving the room. She turned for one final, parting shot. "So, we'll see you later." The door closed. Hearing her mum going downstairs, Jasmine threw her body over, laying with her back facing the door. *A megalithic tomb*. Suddenly, she didn't know who to hate more, John, her mum or herself. She thought of her dad, wished it was him here instead of John, having lie-ins with her mum, eating her cooked breakfast, smearing his fried egg across her lips.

*

The afternoon sun lengthened. Jasmine woke, her lips and around her mouth wet with saliva. Someone was knocking at the back door, the sound loud, insistent. Sighing to herself, she dragged herself off the bed and went downstairs, her feet flopping as they took the stairs one reluctant step at a time. With the kitchen door open, she could see the back door from the hallway, see the outline of a man through the frosted glass, pacing impatiently. He knocked again, even more furiously. Thinking it must be something urgent, she flew into the kitchen and, grabbing the door handle, opened the door. A man aged anywhere between fifty and sixty-five stared at her. His face, brownish-red and heavily lined, had been tanned by the bog, then flushed red and creased by the elements. His hair, what she could see of it poking out from under his hat, was grey and wiry. Behind him was sat a collie, his head cocked quizzically to one side, his brown eyes fixed on his master.

"How's it going? I'm Seamus. Your neighbour."

It took a moment.

"Oh, hello."

They stared at one another for another moment and then Seamus smiled.

"And you're Jasmine. John told me about you."

"Yes—" Her voice faltered. "He's not, er, Mum and him have gone out — they've gone for a walk."

"A good day for it." His smile widened. "And so Jasmine, yer welcome home."

"But I'm not home. I'm from London and I don't know when they'll be back."

He looked at her in silence, still smiling, his eyes bright.

"Er, would, would you like to come in and wait?" she heard herself say. *What on earth made her say that?*

"I would, yes, thank you Jasmine." He glanced back, towards the dog. "Bran, stay."

"Oh, you can bring him if you want."

He shook his head. "He's grand outside."

He stepped inside.

"Would you like a drink? Tea, er, or coffee?" she asked, waving vaguely at a chair.

"Coffee would be grand." Picking the seat John used, the one facing the kitchen door, he sat down heavily.

"So how are ye settling in?" He slipped off his hat and smoothed his hair; she saw patches of auburn in amongst the grey. "How do you like us here?"

"I like it here." Filling the kettle, she returned it to its base and flipped the switch. "Much more than I thought I would."

Surprised by her own unexpected admission, she grabbed the cups, coffee for him and a teabag for her, then bent down to the fridge to get the milk, keeping her face carefully averted. For a moment neither of them spoke. "It must be hard leaving your home and coming here to live among strangers," Seamus said quietly.

Soft, like the whisper of the wind through the trees, she almost missed it. Still hanging onto the fridge door, she looked over at him.

"But we're not as strange or as different as we might at first seem." His eyes, fixed on hers, seemed to glow. "And now I've met you I have this feeling that you're going to fit in with us just fine."

His eyes, his words, warmed her, like sun on bare skin. Embarrassed, she looked away again and finished making the drinks.

Seamus talked as they drank. Afterwards, she couldn't remember what he'd said, or what they'd talked about. All she knew was that he was someone who would understand, no matter what you said. Someone to be trusted.

"Well now, I'd best be going," Seamus said abruptly, draining the last of his coffee.

"But… didn't you want to talk to me mum, John?"

"It'll keep." He smiled, put his hat back on and stood up, favouring his left knee slightly. "I've cattle to feed."

Moving to the door, he opened it and Bran leapt forward to greet him.

"It was grand meeting you, Jasmine." He waved a hand at Bran, dismissing him. "You're exactly how John described you. A lovely young woman."

"What?" she spluttered, couldn't believe what she was hearing.

Seamus flashed her a look that was impossible to fathom.

"Thank you for the drink, Jasmine."

He stepped outside, one hand on the door handle.

"That's OK," she murmured, still taken aback.

But it was too late; he'd gone, closing the door behind him.

Jasmine put the cups in the sink and went back upstairs, thinking of what Seamus had said. Wondered if John had told him how it was between them and decided not. He was far too sensible to confide in someone he hardly knew. And yet she was surprised to hear him talk about her like that. Surprised, and a little bit pleased. *Don't even think about it*, she told herself quickly, sternly. It doesn't change anything. She stepped into her bedroom, heard voices coming from outside and went to the window to look. Seamus was leaning on his bike, talking to her mum and John as Bran scampered restlessly around them. As she watched, Bran raced away and began darting in and out of the fields, first one side of the road then the other. Seamus said something and she heard her mum laugh and then he was climbing awkwardly onto his bike. Another word and a wave and the three of them parted, Seamus moving off, pedalling so slowly that the bike meandered beneath him. Jasmine noticed the back of his saddle, the masking tape crisscrossing it, keeping the innards carefully in place. Then he was gone, disappearing under the trees. Her mum and John continued on, up the garden path and out of view as they followed it around the house to the back door. Jasmine turned away, but her eyes caught something moving in the field opposite and automatically she looked back.

A figure, dressed in a black suit and heavy overcoat, slipped out from behind a tree. Turned upwards, its white face stared at her through the bedroom window. Jasmine jumped, her heart thudding as she recognised the figure, remembering him instantly as the man from the boat. She opened her mouth to shout, to call her mum or John, her eyes sliding to her bedroom door and back. She stopped. There was nothing there; the field was empty. She glanced swiftly to her right and left, but the road too was empty.

"What is it with me?!" she muttered. It wasn't like her to be so jumpy.

Her mum and John were in the hallway; she heard them talking as they put their coats and shoes away. Maybe it was the carpenter yesterday, his oddness unsettling her? Or falling asleep during the day. That was it. Her mum laughed, the sound echoing upstairs. It called to her, and suddenly, she didn't care if it was John here and not her dad, she just wanted to be with people, to feel and see them close.

Later, Jasmine helped her mum clear up after dinner as John chopped wood in the barn outside. From the field opposite the house, a figure stepped silently out into the road. The night was clear, the cloudless sky a myriad of stars and the air chilly. It was almost time. He was so close. She was almost ready, almost... he could sense it in her, smell it. *Almost*, he rebuked himself sternly, feeling the excitement build. He'd come so far; now was not the time to lose patience, to become careless, over-confident. With the one known as Madra Rua near, if anything he was going to have to be even more careful, even more cunning.

Chapter Four

Sunday, three weeks later, Jasmine, her mum and John were again on their way north, heading, finally, for the elusive megalithic tombs. Sat in the back, she clutched the tourist leaflet John had brought home for her. She should've known the words off by heart, she'd read them so many times, but she couldn't help reading it again.

"The remains of Carrowkeel tombs and Neolithic village is one of the most important megalithic sites in Ireland, although possibly one of the least known. Lying on top of the Bricklieve Mountains, just north of the town of Boyle in County Roscommon, they overlook the plain to the north and the waters of Lough Allen and the Arigna Mountains to the East. On a clear day, you can see all the way to the coast, to Sligo's iconic Benbulben and Knocknarea with its own Neolithic cairn known as Queen Medb's tomb."

The photo above the script looked amazing; she hoped the tombs looked as good in real life.

"There they are, the Bricklieve Mountains." John pointed.

The road ahead sloped downwards in a wide, gentle arc, the 'mountains' rising behind it, low and jagged. They were hills really. Jasmine squinted. It was hard to make out at this distance, but she thought she could see a tomb, a grey dot, like a pimple on a face of brown and green. She leant forward.

"This was a good idea of yours," her mum was saying, her voice low.

"I hope she likes it. She's had a tough time, what with everything."

"You're a good a man," Smiling, her mum gave him an affectionate look.

Briefly, they held hands. Squeezed each other's fingers then let go. Jasmine sat back. They looked so happy. She couldn't remember the last time she'd seen her mum and dad look like that. Maybe Malachy was right and John wasn't so bad after all. Maybe she should give him a chance and try, at least, to see him as something more than man who married her mum and sent her dad spinning to the other side of the world. The hills drew closer. John laughed suddenly at something her mum said. Almost two years of living with him, and only now was she beginning to realise how little she really knew him.

Slowing, the car turned left, off the main road. Following the smallest of signs, they turned again, down a road just about wide enough for a car or a tractor. The ground ahead of them began to climb, the front of the car lifting, and then the top of the hills came into view. John took two more turns, the car crawled past a parked tractor and then Jasmine's mum spotted a second sign, wooden, rotting and crudely painted.

"This is it," John said as he turned into a track off to their right.

They parked on the verge, next to the only other car parked there, and getting out looked about them.

"This way, I guess," Jasmine's mum pointed towards the gate, to where a wooden turnstile had been built alongside it.

Taking John's hand, she walked towards it, Jasmine following. The ground was sodden, saturated with water, and they had to step carefully, minding the puddles.

At the stile John went first, covering the biggest puddle yet with one long stride. He grabbed the wooden post, heaving himself up and over. The post wobbled furiously at the movement, at his weight, but it held. Her mum went next, the post wobbling again as she clambered over. She placed her second foot down, but it slipped, slid off the step, off the mud left by the feet of tourists and other walkers. For a moment she teetered but then John darted forward, caught her arm and steadied her. He helped her down then turned back for Jasmine but she shook her head at him, hopped over by herself, taking the stile with ease. Jumped down the other side, landing expertly between two puddles and giving her mum a grin.

"A bit more surefooted than your old mum," her mum said ruefully.

"Just fitter!"

Her mum aimed a swipe at her, but she danced out of her way, laughing, before starting up the hill, following the road. It was tarmacked but heavily worn and full of potholes, the surface dotted with grass and thick mud. Going fast, her foot slipped out from under her, her arms flailing as she fought to keep her balance. She righted herself, turned back, flashed them both a look.

They were both grinning.

"Or maybe not," her mum said drily.

Jasmine tossed her head, pretended to ignore her as she continued, heading upwards.

They walked up the road, following its path as it skirted the side of the hill, traced out the shape of a wide horseshoe. To their left the ground sloped away into a grassy narrow valley, and to the right huge slabs of granite loomed high above them, leaving them half in shadow. The sky was grey and overcast, although the sun had managed to break through in two places. Its rays streaked through the cloud tipped the edge with gold and illuminated a light, barely discernible rain that wetted the landscape, the stones, into glossy definition. There was almost no grass; the patches of ground that had managed to keep some soil were covered in clumps of gorse and heather. Green and brown, the colours of autumn, interspersed with the odd flash of purple and white. In the distance, a bird, black in silhouette, streaked across the sky, but there were no other signs of life. All was quiet. Jasmine glanced behind her. Her mum and John had linked arms, but were walking in silence. She understood why, felt if she were to speak herself it would be in the hushed tones of reverence, for this place felt special, ancient, as if the long-forgotten ages were seeping out from the rock, the earth.

They reached a fork. The right fork, a grassy track, disappeared over the brow of the hill. The left, still the road, meandered downwards then rose again into the second half of the horseshoe. Next to it stood a sign, saying "To the tombs". Jasmine used it to lean against while she waited for her mum and John to catch her up.

"I think we go that way," John said after a few quick breaths, pointing at the left track.

"Really? D'you think?" Jasmine's mum nodded towards the sign.

"Didn't see that," he replied, looking sheepish.

"That's because you're getting old," she grinned, giving his cheek an affectionate peck.

They carried on, Jasmine leading once more. The track was much rougher than the road and littered with loose stones and even bigger puddles, forcing Jasmine to keep her head down and to look where she stepped. Halfway up the ridge now and she noticed a wind for the first time, chilling her despite the warmth of her exertion. She zipped up her coat as she walked, her pace slowing as she struggled to align the two strands, giving her mum and John chance to catch up with her. Reaching the top together, a gust of wind caught them, sending them tottering backwards.

"Jesus," John exclaimed.

They stopped to catch their breath. Continuing, the path disappeared around a corner, and to their left was a grass promontory.

"Let's have a look at the view," Jasmine's mum suggested with a wave of her hand.

They did as she said and stepped onto the grass, moving along the promontory. Gentle at first, it began to slope upwards, making it hard to see the end. The sides narrowed, the ground on both sides falling away steeply. Jasmine paled and, pausing to let her mum and John go ahead, continued more slowly. The ground beneath her seemed to want to roll, to pull away and pitch her out over the edge, but eventually they reached the apex and the vista came suddenly and stunningly into view.

"My God, that's beautiful," her mum breathed, and despite her sweating palms, she had to agree.

Off to the right, past the main road, lay the still silver waters of Lough Allen, and to the left the knobbed brown summits of the Ox mountains. But it was the view ahead that really made Jasmine's breath catch. The view Seamus had promised: Sligo town sat in the distance, nestling between Knocknarea to the front and Benbulben behind. The sea, bathed in the autumn sunlight, twinkled. Jasmine thought of the tombs, the view megalithic man had given his ancestors and wanted nothing more than to see them.

"Come on you two, time for a photo." Unzipping her coat pocket, her mum pulled out her digital camera and waggled a finger at a vague point in front of them.

They did as they were told, posing first for one photo and then another, just in case. John's arm hovered awkwardly across Jasmine's shoulders as if uncertain of its welcome. They broke apart.

"Right Mum, is that it?" Jasmine asked impatiently. "Can we go now?"

"All done," her mum replied serenely, "After you."

Returning to the path, Jasmine followed it around the bend. In a second horseshoe, the path descended into another steep valley and then upwards again, to what must surely be the final ridge. She traced the line of the ridge upwards. Stone cairns, five in all, sat one behind the other, following the slope in perfect formation. The tombs. Her stomach swirling with excitement, she darted forward. Started down the hill, walking fast. The descent sharpened suddenly, the loose stone on the path beneath her feet rolling away. She slipped and skidded, but didn't slow.

She hit the bottom, her impetus carrying her up the other side, into the second and last ascent, even before her mum and John were halfway down. The hill rose high above her, rock and gorse overhanging. She was beginning to tire, her breath becoming ragged, the backs of her legs protesting, but she didn't stop. She couldn't describe it, couldn't say what it was, but something was pushing, urging her on. She had to get to there. And had to get there, be there, all on her own. She glanced back. Her mum and John had gained ground slightly, but the climb would slow them down again. She pushed on, the top now in sight. A few more steps and she was there. She stopped, breathing heavily as she looked about. The wind whipped her hair across her eyes and, dragging it back, she held it there with one hand. Ahead of her, the path stopped, petering out into grass. Left was a sheer drop; to the right, the side of the ridge went up. Up. She took a step back and tilted her head. Just pass the curve of the land, she thought she saw something, something grey, like stone. The tombs. Quickly she examined the ground, seeing small tracks in the gorse leading upwards where sheep and walkers had worn and flattened the vegetation into rudimentary pathways. The tracks looked easy enough to follow and she started upwards, moving quickly, confidently.

A few steps and Jasmine realised just how wrong she'd been. The ground was boggy, spongy and her feet sank and slipped. She continued, taking care to watch exactly where she put each foot. Her right foot sank and she pulled it back quickly, stared at the imprint it left. The ground looked solid. Shaking her head, she continued for a second time. This time, she made sure the ground was firm before she put her full weight on it. In the boggiest, wettest place she gave up entirely, scampering over the boulders instead, using her hands to stop her slipping on the thick, wet moss. Tired, breathing heavily, she reached the first tomb and stepped out onto flat, iron grey slabs of rock, all that was left of a megalithic pathway.

Alone now, with her mum and John completely out of sight, Jasmine walked towards the front of the tomb. She couldn't take her eyes off it, couldn't believe that no one else was here. In the UK this would've been packed, thronging with tourists. This first tomb was smaller than she'd imagined and perfectly circular. The wall was made from large, heavy rocks layered one on top of the other, and the roof from smaller stones heaped into a dome. Once, maybe, they'd been a myriad of shapes and colours, but over the centuries had been eroded and moulded by the elements into smooth, round pebbles and bleached a startling white. Jasmine tilted her head. The entrance was a wide doorway, created and framed by three flat stone slabs, their edges whittled into flaking by the wind. A fourth, slightly thicker, stone lay in front of them, reaching halfway up the doorway, half obscuring it. She moved closer, hoping to get a look inside, then stopped in surprise. Behind the fourth stone was a gap just large enough to squeeze through, with two stone steps leading down. A passageway. A passageway that could only be seen as a person got near, as if whoever had built it had wanted it hidden until the very last moment. She smiled to herself; she could get inside. Reaching out, she touched the top of the fourth stone and felt its hard, cold surface and the rough, texture of lichen. Her stomach fluttered. Ignoring it, she leant over and looked inside, but couldn't see much, just a yellow, sandy floor. She took a breath, feeling her heart beginning to thud and then using the stone as leverage, slipped down the steps and inside in one easy motion.

She landed on all fours in a narrow, low tunnel. It was dark; her body acted as a stopper and prevented most of the daylight, but she could still see. She raised herself onto her haunches, feeling her head scrape the stone ceiling above her, then inched forward, moving awkwardly as she kept her head bent. A few moments later and the tunnel opened up into a wide circular space, high enough to stand in and big enough for five or six people to stand shoulder to shoulder. Jasmine stood up. Now she was out of the tunnel it was surprisingly light inside and she could see everything: the ceiling, the walls, the small alcoves at the back where she guessed the graves used to be. The tunnel, she realised, had been built, angled, to allow light in, but to keep the wind out. *So much for primitive, unsophisticated man.* She moved about the tomb, touching the walls as she went, following her instinct to feel, to connect with this place, this history. It looked, felt, amazing, so old, and yet here it was still intact, the roof above her head, the walls seemingly as solid as the day it was built. The wind outside sounded stronger; she could hear it howling past the stones above and around her, the stone magnifying the sound, but in here, even with the smell of cold, dank earth and stone, it felt warm, cosy almost.

Jasmine thought of her mum and John. Guessed that they would've arrived by now and would be wondering where she was. It was time to go. She took one long last look around her, trying to fix it in her memory before returning to the edge of the tunnel. It was lower than she remembered. Half crouching, she propelled herself forward. Too fast, she caught the side of her temple on the rough stone. The thud jarred her skull, reverberated through her jaw and into her teeth, making the world spin. She fell back, her legs folding beneath her. Her bottom found the soft floor of the tomb and for a moment thought she was going to pass out with the dizziness, the nausea rising from the pit of her stomach. She closed her eyes, waiting for the moment to pass. The tomb, apart from the howling of the wind outside, was silent.

She opened her eyes. The pain had finally eased; the nausea too. Lifting a hand to her forehead she felt a lump, a split in her skin and her fingers came away with a streak of blood.

"Ow," she hissed.

Behind her came a noise. Faint, low, it sounded almost like a hum. She looked around, turning her head slowly for fear of making the bleeding worse. The hum was getting louder, but she couldn't place it; it seemed to be coming from everywhere at once. Her mouth was so dry. She swallowed, tasted the smell of rotten eggs and swallowed again, wishing she'd brought a bottle of water. The hum increased, becoming almost too loud for comfort and, like too much bass in a speaker, making her ear drums throb. Her head swam, felt suddenly heavy, as if it was going to topple off her shoulders, and instinctively she closed her eyes and raised her hands to it. But it didn't help, just made her feel worse, made her head and her stomach spin, the two of them churning together in perfect unity. She opened them again. The chamber was turning. She blinked. It was still turning. Not spinning, but turning, as if she were sat in the centre, the fixed heart of the tomb, and the walls were moving around her. They began to speed up, to turn faster and faster, making her body sway beneath her. She pressed both hands to the ground, afraid she was going to fall over. The humming was so loud now it was almost as if it were inside her, inside her head, as if it had burrowed into her through her ears and into her brain. The tomb whirled so fast the walls were beginning to blur. The power of it forced her head back and her eyes to the ceiling and she hung suspended, powerless to do anything more than hold on as the world span crazily around her. It was too much, the pressure too immense; it forced her hands and arms away from her body, pushed them upwards and out. Pain shot through her; she felt as if her arms were going to be ripped from her body. She screamed, the sound echoing all around her, and then she was tumbling away, twisting through the air to the back of the tomb.

Chapter Five

Jasmine stood on the edge of the megalithic path and looked about her. Couldn't understand how she'd got there. Couldn't remember leaving the tomb. It was getting late, dusk rapidly approaching, the cold stillness of evening already beginning to settle over the land. There was no sign of her mum or John. No sense that anyone else was near. The hillside around her was deserted, empty.

"Mum. John?" she called down the slope.

She listened intently, but heard nothing.

"Mum! John! I'm over here. Mum, where are you?" she shouted louder this time, her voice shaking.

She ran to the end of the path and looked back the way they'd come. She could see the place where John had parked the car, but there was nothing there, not even the gate or the stile. Nothing but grass and bush. They'd left her. They'd gone home and left her.

"Shit," she swore, partly in disbelief, partly to hear the sound her own voice.

And partly to ward off the panic that was rising within her.

Strangely, the swearing helped, made everything real and allowed her to realise what she needed to do: get off the hill before it got dark. She took a deep breath, steeling herself for the journey down and prepared to step. The track stretched out far below her, snaking, undulating across the hillside. She froze. Illuminating the trail, a column of lights spread all the way from the first ridge to the second and moved steadily upwards towards her. A rescue party, it had to be, Jasmine thought, almost crying with relief. She took one, eager step down then stopped again. Something was wrong. Something about the lights her rescuers were carrying. She had it. They were yellow not white, their glow flickering, like flames in the wind. Her mind whirled, moving too quickly, the thoughts jumbling in on themselves. Now she was looking, the torchbearers were walking strangely too, one perfectly behind the other, as if part of a procession, or some sort of ceremony. And there were way too many of them, far too many for a search party. A bird cried, its voice caught on the wind. Jasmine's stomach dropped. It wasn't a bird, it was human voices, singing, chanting. A second column appeared, coming across the ridge from the opposite direction. Much closer than the first, she knew instinctively where they were going. Up, towards the tomb, towards her. She took a step back. Couldn't even begin to wonder who might be climbing up a hillside towards ancient tombs, carrying flame torches, or why her mum and John had left her. All she could think of was to go, get away. But which way? She couldn't go down; even with the fading light, they'd see her. Couldn't go sideways either; in the dark the boggy ground beneath her would be too treacherous. She looked up, back towards the tombs. The stones of the path gleamed white, showing her the way. It was too much to resist. She went upwards, retracing her steps, her feet flying, as she bounded from stone to stone. She reached the first tomb, the front of her foot catching the edge of one of the stones, and she fell, the world tipping. She dropped her hand, feeling the palms scrape and sting as she hit stone and skidded. One kneecap thudded. Behind her, the chanting was so loud now she could make out distinct words, although they were in no language she recognised, and it spurred her on. Scrambling to her feet she half ran, half hobbled past the first tomb, then the second. Four more steps, halfway to the third and she stopped, the path in front of her ending, disappearing into mud and bog. She looked back and saw a flame appear, rising over the undergrowth, the first of the torchbearers climbing the slope towards her. She froze, not quite sure what to do, and then her feet were taking her back, back to the first tomb, deciding for her.

She paused at the entrance, her heart beating wildly, then threw herself down, slipping in between the stone slabs and into the tunnel. Light flooded the entrance behind her as the first of the torches arrived. And then, ignoring the pain in her knee, she was crawling as fast as she could through the tunnel and into the central chamber. It was pitch-black, she couldn't see, had only a brief remembrance to guide her. She put out a hand, spread her arm out wide, stretching and reaching and feeling the rough stone. Felt the curve of the archway that led to the back chamber and crawled quickly inside. Came to rest by the back wall, gasping as quietly as she could to get air back into her lungs. They were outside; she could hear their voices, muffled by the stone and then, to her horror, she heard a body shuffling, the grunts of someone straining, exerting himself, and knew someone was coming through the tunnel after her.

Pressing into the stone behind her, she pulled her body in on itself, making herself as small as possible. The grunts were getting louder; he was through and she heard him moving around the central chamber, feet away from her. More shuffling, another grunt, and a second man was coming through. This one carried a torch, illuminating the tunnel before him, and slowly, with each shuffle, he scattered the darkness around her. The torch appeared, held out for the first man to take, the second man's head following, his eyes staring into and across the chamber, straight to where Jasmine was crouched. She ducked

*her head and closed her eyes just as the man shouted and the torch span,
illuminating every corner of the chamber.*

Someone was calling her name. Automatically she turned her head to
look, lifting it from the cold stone that was chilling one side of her
face. The chamber span for a moment, then settled. She realised that
she was still in the tomb. Still sat in the darkness of the back chamber,
her legs tucked under her, her shoulder leant against the back wall.
The central chamber lay in front of her, illuminated by the light from
the tunnel. The voice called again and she tried to answer, but her
voice just croaked back at her. She tried again and this time managed
a shaky, "I'm here!"

She was cold, colder than she had ever been in her life.

"I'm coming in. Wait there," a voice called back, echoing around
the walls.

She ignored its advice and, lifting her body from the wall, got down
on all fours. Her head felt light, distant, as if it didn't quite belong to
her, as if she was teetering on the brink of a bad sickness, but she
forced herself to move, to crawl towards the tunnel, to the voice and
the person coming through. She reached the central chamber and
stopped to catch her breath just as the room darkened. John's head
appeared suddenly and then his shoulders. And then he was levering
himself out through the mouth of the tunnel, his body twisting to get
through a gap almost too narrow for him.

"What the hell are you doing here? We've been calling you for
ages."

She stared at him, shivering, trying to smile. She'd never been so
happy to see him. Kneeling down in front of her, he pulled her to him
and held her tight, half crushing her arms.

"Are you OK?" Letting her go, he peered into her face. "Oh my
God, Jas, your head! What happened?"

"I hit it."

"You gave it a good whack." He frowned, pushing her hair carefully
out of the way. "How do you feel?"

"Cold."

"Did you lose consciousness at all?"

"No, I don't think so."

He touched her cheek, the other side of her forehead lightly. "You
feel a bit hot."

He dropped his hand. "Let's get you out of here, back in the fresh air."

"John, John! Is she OK?" Jasmine heard her mum calling.

He answered, stooping to shout back through the tunnel. "I've got her. We're coming out. She's OK." He looked back at Jasmine. "More or less. Now, do you think you're alright to crawl out?"

She nodded.

"OK, if you're having problems just shout; I'll be right behind you. Now, are you ready to try?"

She nodded again and he patted her arm, smiling. "Grand."

She could feel him watching her, checking, as she got back onto all fours and began to crawl slowly through the tunnel. It was hard going, harder even than crawling across the chamber. Her body, still working away beneath her, seemed to have separated from her head completely. Her mum was waiting out the other side, and jumped forward, helping her up as she came through then up the steps. They came to a stop next to the fourth stone. Jasmine leant against it. The air cooled her face, and her stomach contracted.

"What happened?" Clutching her face between both hands, her mum peered intently at her forehead in the same way John had done. "What did you do to your head?"

"She hit it." It was John who replied.

He was coming up the steps, his body again twisting sideways to get through the gap.

"Mum, I'm going to be sick." Jasmine pulled away.

Bending over, she turned her head away just in time. She was sick, bringing up nothing but a vile tasting, greenish bile.

"Sorry," she coughed, wiping her mouth with shaking hands.

Her mum put her arms around her, wiped her hair from her forehead.

"John, what is it… concussion?"

"I don't know. She said she wasn't knocked out but I think we should go to casualty just in case. It's freezing in there, maybe she's caught a chill. These old places—" He paused, frowning. "Jas, are you OK to walk? Because I can carry you if you need me to."

"No, I can walk," she mumbled, determined to avoid that at all cost. "I feel a bit better after that."

As if to prove it, she pushed herself off the stone and straightened up. Her mum reluctantly let her go.

"You don't look it," John replied with a slight shake of his head.

"But let's see how we go."

Somehow, she made it to the car.

"Here." Her mum opened the car door and helped her inside.

"Sligo's closest," John was saying as her mum bent over her and clicked her seatbelt.

They climbed inside. Jasmine closed her eyes.

"No, Jas, open your eyes!" John's voice snapped. Reluctantly she did as he said.

"That's better. You have to stay awake. Talk to us."

"About what?"

"Anything." He started the car.

"Talk about school," her mum said quickly. "You've hardly told us anything. Or about your new friends. Fiona, Lisa and… who's the other one again?"

"Rachel. It's Rachel."

Backing the car carefully off the grass, John pulled away.

Jasmine lay still. Light, golden, flickered in the room around and across the stone ceiling high above. She was in a crypt, could feel the stone beneath her body, see the sides rising around her and knew, somehow, that the lid was lying across the floor, that it had been lifted from her, carefully, reverently. Across the room a man was speaking, his voice echoing as he moved towards her. He was saying just one word, repeating it over and over. A word she'd never heard before. It was a name, she knew, knew it deep inside her, just as she knew it was hers and that he was calling her, wanting her to wake. He came into view. Dressed in a long cloak, with the hood pulled down, over his face, he lifted his hand and the sleeve of his cloak fell back. A knife glittered. His arm swung, and the blade flashed, catching the light as he held it, suspended, over her. She watched, unmoved, as his fingers tightened, his body tensed, and then the knife plunged down. In one quick, seamless movement he thrust it deep into her stomach. A spasm ran through her, but for a moment, there was no pain, and then, as she stared at the hilt sticking out of her, at the outline of the symbol engraved across it, three spirals sat together, combined into one yet still distinct, still separate, the pain started. It consumed her, her body, her every thought, as if it had always been there and always would, and it was all she could do to hold on. And then, as quickly as it came, the pain was gone and so was the knife and the man too. Jasmine, now upright, looked all about her. At the mountaintop, she looked all around her and at the sea beyond and felt the wind rippling through her long hair. Men, shouting, their faces twisted, were running towards her. One

She woke, feeling her heart thud, not quite sure where she was. Then she saw the illuminated digits on her alarm clock, showing three fourteen, and she realised then that she was back home, in her own bed and room. Her head felt heavy, her mouth dry and she swallowed, trying to moisten it. It didn't help; her tongue stuck. She needed water. She thought briefly of going to the bathroom and sticking her head under the tap and drinking and drinking, but then she remembered the glass her mum had left for her on the bedside cabinet. In the dark, she reached for it; her hand caught the edge, grabbed it, and she raised herself up, took a long drink, breathed, then took another. Feeling better, she put it back and, lying back down, closed her eyes.

Something moved. She heard it, the sound faint, like tiny claws scratching. She opened her eyes and listened. Nothing. She snuggled down again, pulling the duvet up around her ears. There it was again. She pulled the duvet down, listening intently. It was still there, coming from her bedroom door, as if someone was on the other side, their fingers scrambling at the woodwork, trying to find the handle in the dark. Her heart pounding, she sat up, pulling her weakened body half out of the duvet. The door clicked, and she felt more than saw it slowly open. A figure stood in the doorway. Framed by the light from the landing, a hooded cloak shrouded its tall frame and obscured its face. Horrified, she watched it step into her room and move quickly, noiselessly, to the foot of her bed. It paused, the hood turning towards her as if unseen eyes were examining her, then stretched a long, bony white hand and darted forward. Fingers touched her duvet, sliding upwards as the figure skirted around her bed. Caressed the creases in the cloth, the folds, inches from her body. Jasmine shuddered, pressing her body backwards into her pillows as if trying to find a way through them, but there was nowhere to go.

It crept closer. The fingers slipped sideways, moving across the bed. They touched her, tracing the curve of her body through the duvet. Her head span. A voice inside her was screaming, screaming at her to do something, to move, to fight, anything, but she couldn't.

It reached her stomach. Flexed its fingers and then slowly began to press, the tips curling as if their owner were preparing to claw their way through the duvet and into her. A stab of pain shot through her, radiating from her stomach and spreading outwards. She screamed, breaking her paralysis, feeling something hot and white, like anger, come surging out of her. It caught the figure, knocked it backwards, the hand falling away and the hood falling back. Caught her glass too, sending it tumbling away. A man's face glared at her. It was Seamus, their neighbour, the blood-red flecks in his eyes flashing. Jasmine screamed again.

She woke screaming, her heart pounding wildly, the farmer's face and the red of his eyes still with her. Almost immediately she heard a door open and the light from the landing flooded the room. Her mum dashed through the door, wide-eyed from a sudden wakening.

"Jas, what's going on? Are you OK?" she cried.

The room was quiet. Everything, but for the glass lying upturned on the ground and the puddle next to it, looked as normal.

"There was a man, in a hood—" Jasmine stopped, confused.

"Kate, what happened?" John was at the door, breathing heavily.

"A nightmare, I think," her mum said, leaning over and touching her forehead. "She's very hot."

"I'll get some water," he offered, turning to go.

"Can you get the paracetamol as well? Oh… wait… here."

Her mum crouched down and, picking up the fallen glass, handed it to him.

"I won't be long."

"Jas, how are you feeling?" her mum asked, perching on the side of the bed.

Her face was tense, her brow knotted.

"Rough," Jasmine admitted.

"Well, we'll see how you are tomorrow. You know what the doctor said in A & E; it's not concussion, but we should keep a close eye on you," she sighed. "You did give it a good whack. If you're no better in the morning, we'll call the doctor, just to be sure — oh, thanks John."

Taking the water and tablets from him, she handed them to Jasmine and waited for her to take them.

"I found this downstairs," John said suddenly, reaching into his dressing gown and pulling out the carving the carpenter had given her.

He placed it on top of the cabinet beside her bed.

"Oh, I forgot. I took it to school to show the girls."

"You'll be digging out her old 'Tinkywinky' next," her mum laughed, shaking her head at him.

She took the glass from Jasmine and stood up. "That should help. Now try and get some sleep."

"Night, Jasmine," she said as she followed John out the door, closing it behind her.

"Night," Jasmine murmured, snuggling down and closing her eyes.

*

It was late when she woke the next morning, lunchtime closer than breakfast. She lay there for a moment, remembering, catching the last of the night's dreams as they fluttered around the edges of her mind. And then they were gone, and she was throwing back the duvet and jumping out of bed. The lump on her head was still tender, but otherwise she felt fine. Better than fine; she felt energised, her body, her heart, bouncing and glowing as if she'd slept for a week. She went to the window. Opened the curtains to a grey, windy day, but somehow, after yesterday, nothing like that seemed to matter. A magpie swooped across the road, its wings lifting and tipping on the wind as she watched it for a moment. Imaged what it must be like, to soar on the wind. The exhilaration. The skin on her arms, her face, tingled suddenly, as if remembering a memory her mind had forgotten and for a moment…

…Jasmine stirred, absentmindedly rubbing her forehead. The lump was still sore. Outside, Bran appeared, sprinting out from under the trees overhanging the road. Seamus appeared next, pushing a wheelbarrow, carrying what looked like an enormous bottle of water. He glanced up at the house as he passed, his eyes seeming to rest on her bedroom window, but if he saw her he made no sign.

Chapter Six

Later, sat at her desk in front of the window, Jasmine clicked on her mouse, flicking idly from screen to screen as she took a sip of her Coke. It was nice to have the house to herself and a break from her mum and John's incessant fussing. Her homework lay on the desk in front of her, the half-written essay her brain refused to finish. It was impossible. The euphoria she'd woken up with was still there, still bubbling up inside her, urging her up and out, to do something and not just sit.

She'd just finished the last of her Coke when she heard the low throb of a tractor. She looked up just in time to see it appear through the trees, coming from the direction of Seamus' house. The driver was leant back, casual as he steered with one hand, his body bouncing furiously with the tractor's motion. It was Malachy. She watched him pass, waiting for him to look up and wave, but he was too engrossed. Sighing to herself, she turned back at her screen. The words of the website stared back at her, seemingly determined to make no sense. She rubbed her forehead again. She needed a break. *Fresh air's good for you.* The thought was all she needed. She switched off her laptop, grabbed her hoodie and went downstairs for her trainers.

*

Walking down the hill, following the direction of the tractor, it appeared suddenly, coming around a corner and heading straight for her. Spotting her, Malachy gave her a wave and a grin before veering suddenly off to the right. Turning into the field, he steered expertly between two gateposts. Even one-handed he didn't slow down.

"Poser!" she thought, even as she secretly admired his skill, his physicality.

Following him, she made for the entrance to the field, watching him over the top of the hedge as he turned the tractor in a slow, wide arc.

Stepping gingerly across the gravel and stone kesh, she joined Malachy as he stopped the tractor near the entrance of the field and jumped down.

"Hi, how the head?" he asked, grinning widely.

"How do you know?"

"Seamus. John told him this morning and he told—" He paused, made as if checking his watch, "—the whole village by now."

His face was serious, but she could see the glint in his eyes. "What I want to know is what state you left the stone ceiling in. I mean, it's a national monument. I hope you didn't damage it too much."

"Ha ha. Oh, very funny."

He laughed at that, and she couldn't help but smile. She couldn't blame him; walking into a stone ceiling, she'd handed him a gift, all wrapped up with a bow on top.

"So, what you doing?" she asked casually, changing the subject.

But he wasn't having it. "I can't believe John had to carry you out."

"He didn't have to carry me out! Who told you that?"

"But he got you out?" he snorted. "Rescued you."

"Yeah, OK."

"You have to admit, it's a bit ironic."

"Yeah, I suppose."

It was the only concession he was going to get. But it wasn't the irony that got her, it was remembering the look of fear on John's face, and then the relief. Malachy was saying something she didn't catch.

"What?"

"Are you OK?"

"Yeah, of course. Why?"

"You kind of disappeared back there."

"I'm OK."

Embarrassed, she looked at the ground.

"I didn't think they'd let you out."

"They're out shopping. Besides, fresh air's good for you."

"Yeah, it is."

There was a pause. "I'm putting the feed in here for the cattle. Then that's me done for the day."

It took her a moment to realise that he was finally answering her question.

"What, not got homework to do?".

"Not if I can help it." He paused, and it was his turn to look at the ground. "We've got Niamh and her family coming round for dinner."

"Oh, that's nice," she said lamely.

"Our dads are friends, from way back. They come round a lot. But you must've seen them."

"Once, but I thought that was because of, y'know…" she flapped her hand vaguely, "Niamh."

Malachy was staring at her, his blue eyes narrowed. She was beginning to wish she hadn't started this, but she'd so wanted to know. She tried again. "It must be nice for them, having their, er, children, for your dad. It being his friend's daughter, I mean."

"What about her?"

"The two of you." Another awkward flap of her hand. "Together."

"Together?" His eyes glinted. "Who told you we were together?"

"No one in particular, it's just—" she stopped.

Malachy's face was red; he looked furious.

"Just what?"

"Everyone at school says it," she finished weakly.

"Everyone at school should mind their own fucking business!"

"OK, sorry."

"You're the last one I'd thought would believe that shite."

"I don't. And it's not gossip. It's just the way Niamh is around you, the way she looks. Like a Rottweiler, like she wants to bite any girl that dares to speak to you." She paused, gathering her courage. "So it's not true?"

"Are yer serious?! Look, I've got to get on." Scowling, he turned away and stomped back to the tractor.

Dismayed, she watched him heave himself up.

"Fine. Well, I'll see you later then," she called as he started the engine.

He didn't answer. The tractor moved forward with a jerk, causing her to jump back hastily.

"Malachy!" she shouted, but he ignored her.

Anger swirled in the pit of her stomach, bringing with it a sudden wave of nausea. Swallowing it down, she trudged back to the lane. Behind her, Malachy was manoeuvring the tractor in next to the cattle feeder, pretending to be too engrossed in his work to notice her leaving.

"Tractor boy," she muttered, still smarting.

She climbed the hill, slowly. Disappearing as quickly as it had come, the nausea had left her with a strange lightheadedness that made her feel as if her head was floating. It was an effort to put one foot in front of the other. She hoped she hadn't done too much. Her mum would kill her if she knew. Her earlier euphoria, she noticed, had evaporated completely.

She was almost home. Around her the day was ending, the air cooling as late afternoon merged with evening, the sky streaking shades of red and orange as dusk approached. The colours were gorgeous, impossibly vibrant, like nothing she'd ever seen before. Moving over to the gate for a better look, she thought of her dad and wished he was here to see it too. But maybe, when he came home, she'd be able to show it to him. Slipping her hand in her pocket, she pulled out her phone. The battery was very low, but maybe she had enough for just one photo? She pressed the button, and the screen went blank.

"Damn!"

She pressed the on button, tapping it furiously with her thumb. Nothing happened. She pressed again, her stomach twisting. Another wave of nausea shot through her; she heaved, her stomach spasming, but nothing came up. Her phone vibrated suddenly, springing into life and the nausea receded again.

"Shit!" She stared down at the screen.

The battery symbol was still almost empty, was still flashing, but her phone, as she scrolled from screen to screen, seemed to be working fine. There must a slither of juice left inside, enough to take one photograph and then go back inside and rest. She went back to the camera, and lifting the phone, took a photograph. The phone clicked. *Maybe one more.* She turned to her right and, lining up her camera again, looked at the screen.

A man was stood at the far end of the field, staring her way. Shocked, she took a step back and lowered her phone. He was so still, looked so lifeless with his coat billowing slightly around him and his feet, ankles obscured by mud, that for one mad moment she thought he was a scarecrow, but then he began to walk towards her.

She watched him come closer. He was still so far away and yet there was something familiar about him. Something in the starkness between his clothes and the white of his face called to her. She froze. It was the man on the boat. And in the road looking up at her bedroom window, she'd thought him a trick of her eye. Still dressed in the same shabby black suit, the same heavy, grey coat far too big for his thin frame, he stared at her, his dark eyes fixed on hers.

He was already halfway across the field, his movements slow and oddly stiff. For a moment, she thought he had an injury and then she saw it. His upper body was completely still, with no swing in his arms, as though he had no need to balance himself, to make any effort as he walked through thick, wet clumps of mud. Or to look down either, to take his eyes from her, to check where his feet fell. As if the ground, the terrain meant nothing to him. Jasmine shivered, told herself that he was just one of the locals, the local eccentric maybe, and, forcing her body to move, to turn its back on him, crossed the road away from him.

Her garden gate was shut. The frame, old and rusted, had dropped and as usual it took her a moment to wretch it open, to push it, scraping, across the path. She glanced back. Impossibly, he was there, stood in the laneway, just a few paces from her. She jumped, her breath hissing out from between her teeth, her stomach flipping. His eyes, black circles on white, bored into her and she found herself gazing back, unable to look away. He took two more steps, lifted his hand towards her and she could feel the excitement vibrating through his body, the anticipation. Move! The word shot through her mind, a voice inside screaming it at her, but she couldn't; her legs wouldn't work. He began his last step, his foot shifting as his fingers stretched out towards her, their tips reaching, almost touching… she shuddered and he stopped, cocked his head to one side as if listening. But still he didn't take his eyes from her. "Jasmine! Jasmine!"

A voice was calling her, the caller real, not a voice inside her head, and coming closer. A dog, too, was barking, and she tried to turn her head to see, to shout back, but the eyes inches from her own wouldn't let her.

"Jasmine!"

The voice called again and then the dog was there, beside her. She caught a glimpse of black and white fur, of teeth bared, heard the menace in the growl and then the face was moving back and away. Her body slackened and she stumbled backwards, seeing Seamus limping towards them. His arms were swinging furiously, giving him impetus. Righting herself, she looked back. The lane was empty. The hedgerow too, the entrance to the field; he'd gone as quickly and as silently as he'd come. Bran was quiet now and standing next to her, seemed almost to be guarding her as he watched his master approach, the only sign that the man had ever been there.

"Jasmine, are you alright?"

"Yeah, I think so."

"You don't look it." One hand dropped, came to rest lightly, approvingly, on the dog's head,

"Good, Bran."

"Bran," Jasmine heard herself repeat.

Seamus studied her for a moment.

"Maybe we should get you inside," he said softly and, taking her arm, gently began to push her towards the house.

She allowed him to steer her through the gate, up the garden path and around the house. He chatted as they walked; she heard something about fence posts, but she wasn't really listening.

He stopped at the back door, gave the handle a tug.

"Have you a key?"

"What? Oh, er, yeah."

It was in the last pocket. Lifting it out, she unlocked the door, metal on metal scraping.

"Let me." Leaning past her, he opened the door and, nudging her inside, closed the door behind them.

"Here." Seamus propelled her to the nearest chair.

"Thanks."

He hovered for a moment, making sure she was alright, then pulled a chair out for himself and sat down opposite her.

"Now, I don't want you to worry about that man, Jasmine. He's no harm to you, or anybody else, but still you must take care. You would think coming here that this is farming land, and to those of us that live here, mostly farmers and descendants of farmers from way back, you'd be right. But for all the farming you see, this land was and always will be bog. Coming from London you won't have seen much bog and you won't know what a strange, haunted place it is. You've yet to see the mist rise slowly up this hill from the valley, creeping up over the fields of a morning, towards ye."

He paused, never taking his eyes from her.

"This place may seem nothing to the wild bleakness of Connemara or Donegal, but this is still the West of Ireland, the province of Connaught. The isolation of the place can be unbearable for the loneliest of us. Enough to send us mad: to send one of us mad."

He paused again, glanced at the kitchen window as if expecting to see someone.

"You're talking about that man. Who is he? Are you saying he's mad?" Jasmine asked, too busy with her questions to notice.

"There's one who would not mean to do you any harm, and it's easy for those of us that live here to know him, know his ways. But for someone new, he can be a little frightening."

"But who is he? Where does he live?"

"That one lives not far from here. And he's shy, doesn't like crowds, a lot of people, so it's best to stay together and not wander too far on your own."

"But—" she began.

"There's your parents," he interrupted her quickly, silencing her with a press of his hand.

A second later Jasmine's mum passed by the kitchen window.

The door handle jiggled, as if her mum was trying to open the door using her elbow and it kept slipping. Immediately Jasmine jumped up and ran to open it.

"Thanks, darling," her mum said breathlessly, bundling into the kitchen with two very heavy looking bags. "Oh, hi Seamus."

She let both bags slide to the floor. "God, they were heavy."

"You should've let John carry them," Seamus grinned.

"He's got the rest."

As if to illustrate her words, John appeared carrying four bags, two in each hand. Coming inside, he saw Seamus and his eyebrows lifted quizzically. "It's busy in here. How's it going, Seamus?"

"Grand. Except I can't remember what I came for."

John grinned. "You're getting old. It'll be the legs next."

"They went years ago," Seamus replied ruefully, getting slowly to his feet. "Well, I'd best be going. Wait now, I have it. John, I've been meaning to ask you where you got those posts for your garden from. I'm wondering if they'd be any good for me."

"Let me leave these down and I'll show you them on the way out. You can see for yourself."

Putting the bags with the rest, John left with Seamus. Jasmine took another sip of her drink, watching them go. Something about what Seamus had said was bothering her. Something that didn't quite make sense.

"Jas, put the kettle on will you while I put the shopping away."

Her mum delved into the shopping bags with both hands and began pulling things out.

"OK," Jasmine replied, still deep in thought.

She got up and, grabbing the kettle, moved over to the sink, began filling it all over again. She caught sight of John and Seamus through the window, stood at the very end of the garden, Bran milling around them. They were talking, their heads bent close. And then suddenly, Seamus' head snapped up and, glancing quickly back, he looked into the window and directly into Jasmine's face. He seemed to watch her for a moment and then, turning back to John, placed his hand on top of the post and gave it a shake, as if testing it.

"Don't overfill it."

"Shit." Jasmine quickly turned the tap off and poured a little of the water away.

It hit her as she put the kettle back, flipped the switch. What it was that had been bothering her. If Seamus was right, and the man she kept seeing was a well-known but harmless local eccentric, what on earth was he doing on the ferry?

Chapter Seven

"Are you going to eat that?" Fiona asked.

Jasmine looked up. Saw the look Fiona, Lisa and Rachel were sharing and flushed.

"Na, don't fancy it."

Ham poked out of one side of her sandwich. A tomato had made the bread soggy and it clung to the meat, the white stark against the pink, like pale flesh against the red of an open wound. Her stomach flipped and she quickly put it down.

"You didn't eat your sandwich yesterday," Lisa commented. "Or Monday. Are you feeling OK?"

"Yeah," she lied. "I'm just not hungry."

"And your head's OK? After the knock?" Fiona asked.

"Yeah, it's fine. Maybe I'm going off meat." Jasmine glanced at Rachel. "You know, after that film you persuaded us to watch."

"My master plan's working," Rachel grinned. "You'll never touch meat again by the time I'm finished."

"Yeah, after watching that I thought I never would," Lisa mugged.

"Until your mam cooked lasagne," Fiona laughed. "Or took you to Supermacs."

"Beef's different," Lisa protested. "Cattle have a grand life. They're in the fields most of the year, not like those poor battery hens, stuffed into the cages. Did you see the way they peck each other?"

"And sheep, they're out in the fields too—" Fiona began.

"Yeah, but it's lamb we eat," Rachel interrupted her crossly. "Little baby sheep ripped apart."

"I don't want to think about it," Lisa agreed. "They look so cute in the fields."

The three of them were talking, arguing, but Jasmine wasn't really listening. She was back at home seeing the man reaching for her, seeing Bran snap and snarl.

No matter which way she tried to turn it, she couldn't quite believe

Seamus' explanation of things. Couldn't quite reconcile the idea of a harmless local eccentric with the ferocity of Bran's defence, or her own certainty that it was the same man as on the boat. But three days later she hadn't seen him again. Maybe she was wrong, after all, and Seamus did know him and had talked to him, told him to keep away. Maybe.

"What do you think, Jas?"

It was Lisa. The three of them were looking at her.

"I think if everyone ate free range it'd be cheaper."

"What?" Lisa exclaimed. "Have you even been listening? We finished that ages ago."

"Oh, sorry," Jasmine flushed and they laughed.

"Actually, we were talking about you and Malachy Costello. I saw the look he gave you." Fiona gave her a speculative look. "What did we do?"

"Nothing." Jasmine shook her head. "It's me he's pissed off with; he barely spoke on the way to the bus."

"What did—?" Lisa began, but just then the bell rang for the afternoon lessons.

*

The teacher's voice droned. Jasmine rubbed her forehead and tried to focus. The nausea was back, this time bringing with it a headache, the pain sharp across both temples. Part of her knew she should tell her mum, but she didn't want the fuss. She'd had enough of that on Sunday. What she really wanted was for it to go away and for life to get back to normal.

Next to her, a frowning Rachel leant over and gave her arm a tap.

"I'm okay," she mouthed quickly.

The heat was on full blast and the classroom felt unbearably hot, stuffy. Jasmine rubbed her forehead again.

"Jas?"

Another prod, this time followed by a frown and jerk of the head towards the teacher. Rachel wasn't going to leave it. Sighing, Jasmine raised her hand.

Standing outside the classroom with the cool air on her face, she felt better. The nurse's office was to her right, down the corridor and past Pat the Baker's office, but she always made such a fuss, such a big deal when asked for painkillers. As if no one had ever taken them before. Jasmine turned left instead, headed off towards the toilets. With everyone else in lessons the corridor was eerily quiet, the only sounds the muffled words of teachers in the rooms she passed and her own footsteps as they echoed along the stone floor. She reached the toilet, lifting her hand to push the door open, but it swung back before she could touch it. Niamh, flying out and only seeing her at the last minute, twisted sideways and somehow managed not to bundle into her.

"Sorry, Niamh." Jasmine flushed as the two of them sidestepped one another.

Grey eyes stared coldly at her. Long, dark blonde hair floated, managing somehow to look as if every tress had been meticulously placed. Niamh, Jasmine decided, was just one of those people to whom normal rules didn't apply; dragged through a hedge backwards and she'd look photoshoot tousled, whereas Jasmine could spend hours getting ready and still manage to look as if she'd been the one dragged through the foliage.

"How's things?"

Niamh, already moving off, looked back. "OK, thanks. You don't look so good."

"Just a headache," Jasmine replied, giving her a weak smile before heading through the toilet door herself.

To her relief, there was no one else in there. Going straight to the sink, she let the tap run and began carefully to splash her face with ice-cold water. It made her gasp, but almost immediately she began to feel better.

Behind her the door swung open. Jasmine glanced up into the mirror and saw Niamh coming back in, through the doorway. Surprised, she quickly straightened and turned off the tap.

"It's OK, Niamh. I'm fine, really." Moving to the paper towel holder, she took two and began wiping her face.

"It's not that. I'd like a word."

Taken aback by her tone, Jasmine stared at Niamh's reflection in the mirror. She was standing just in front of the door, her arms folded and her shoulders upright, looking determined. Grabbing another paper towel, Jasmine used it to dry her hands.

"I want to know what's going on between you and Malachy."

"Me and Malachy?" Jasmine heard herself squeak.

"Yeah, ever since you came it's been different. He's not interested."

Jasmine threw the paper towels in the bin and slowly turned to face her, trying hard to ignore the nausea that was building inside her again.

"And I know you two have been seeing a lot of each other."

"Yeah, so?"

"You don't deny it?"

"We're friends, Niamh, friends that live near each other. That's what we do."

Niamh pursed her lips. "I don't believe you."

"Well, that's not my problem," Jasmine snorted irritably and then thought of the old saying about protesting too much and took a deep breath. "Look, we're just friends, OK? There's nothing else going on. What more can I say?"

"That you'll keep away from him. I told you, we were fine until you came here."

"Well, that's nothing to do with me. Don't you think you should be talking to Malachy about this?"

"So there really isn't anything going on between you two?"

Sighing heavily, Jasmine rubbed at her temple. "No there isn't, as I've already said, we're just friends."

"Good." Turning to go, Niamh stopped and looked back, "So you'll keep away from him?"

Jasmine's stomach churned, her irritation flaring into anger. "For fuck's sake, Niamh, are you even listening to me? I told you that there's nothing going on, that we're just friends. Not that it would have anything to do with you, even if we were!"

There was a silence. Jasmine's words echoed between them, stark against the pale grey walls, the white tiles and sinks.

"And what's that supposed to mean?" Niamh demanded, whirling.

It was too late to back out now, even if she wanted to. Jasmine held her ground.

"Well, you and Mal aren't actually going out, are you?"

"Who told you that?"

"Who d'you think?"

"I think you were right the first time; it is none of your business."

"And I think it's time you stopped pining over someone who doesn't give a shit about you!" Jasmine snapped, her temper finally giving way.

That did it.

"You——!" Niamh shouted, lifting her hand and swinging it hard in towards Jasmine's face.

There was little time to react. Without thinking Jasmine raised her own, blocking it and then the two of them were swaying together, tussling. Niamh was tall and surprisingly strong. She broke the deadlock, pushed Jasmine sideways into the sink. Hard. Jasmine clutched her side and her stomach spasmed, the anger spilling up into her throat and outwards, her ears singing with the rush of blood. Her head swam and she heard Niamh cry out, half saw her raise her arms as if to protect her face and then there was a loud crash from the wall behind her and piece of plastic bounced back towards them. For a moment they both stood there, frozen, staring at the floor, at the paper towel holder that lay in bits in front of them. And then simultaneously they turned to look at one another. Niamh moved first, her eyes suddenly huge in a pale face as she turned around and fled, the toilet door banging loudly behind her. Jasmine stared after her, looked again at the broken towel holder, at the hole left in the wall behind her. Bits of plaster lay on the floor, along with one long screw, as if the holder had been savagely ripped away. Her stomach spasmed again and this time the nausea was so bad that she retched. Dry, painful retches pulled at her body as she bent over the sink. They finished and Jasmine, straightening up, saw her reflection in the mirror, saw a face as pale as Niamh's.

Deep in thought, Jasmine wandered back to the classroom. Her headache had gone, the nausea too, the dry retches releasing, like a thunderstorm, something. But what? Maybe it was just a reaction to hitting her head. Stress, maybe. An image of the broken paper holder flashed through her mind. It must've come loose and fallen. But it had flown, gone clear across the room. Falling things didn't do that. Thrown things did that.

"Oh yeah, right, Jasmine," she told herself sourly, "And what do you think threw it, a poltergeist?"

Reaching the classroom, she grabbed the door handle and pushed just as the end of school bell sounded. Almost immediately, the stampede started. The teacher was shouting, trying to be heard over the din as Jasmine fought her way back to her desk. Rachel was waiting for her.

"Are you OK?" she asked, struggling into the coat.

"Yeah, much better."

"Jasmine, how are you feeling?"

Miss Glacken came towards them.

"Yeah, fine." Jasmine grabbed her coat and bag. "We'd better go.

Don't want to miss the bus."

*

Malachy was already on the bus when she got on, sitting with his mates in their usual place, all across the back seat. Flopping down on a seat near the front, she closed her eyes.

Someone slapped her shoulder. "You staying there?"

It was Malachy. She blinked, realised she'd fallen asleep and was about to miss their stop. He moved off and, still groggy, she got awkwardly to her feet and bundled down the bus after him.

They walked up the hill together.

"Late night?" Malachy asked, breaking the silence.

"No, not really."

They continued. Malachy was giving her sideways looks, as if trying to figure her out. He'd obviously forgiven her and was trying to make amends, but her quietness was discouraging him. She wanted to explain, to tell him they were OK and it wasn't him, it was what happened with Seamus and the man, and now with Niamh, but she couldn't. She didn't have the words.

"What is with everyone today?" he asked, as if speaking to no-one in particular.

She stared at the ground, watching as her feet ate the tarmac.

"You're as bad as Niamh. She went out in the last class and when she came back she was acting really weird."

"Really?" Looking up, she tried to sound how she thought she usually would; uninterested, but pretending not to be.

"Girls," Malachy muttered, again to no one in particular. "See you tomorrow."

They'd reached his house.

"Yeah, see you tomorrow," she replied, but he was already moving towards the drive; she was talking to his back.

Continuing alone, Jasmine kicked herself. Why hadn't she said anything? Maybe Malachy could've helped. He might know the man, and be able to confirm everything Seamus told her, or be able to explain what happened in the toilet. But she couldn't do that, not when it involved Niamh. He'd want to know what they were arguing about and if he knew that he'd definitely think they were fighting over him. As if she, Jasmine, would do a thing like that. Fight over a boy.

It was getting dark. It had been dull all day, the sun never quite managing to get going, and now even the grey light was fading.

Jasmine turned the corner, the brow of the hill and then home, just metres away. She looked left, over the top of the hedge, half expecting to see the man, but he wasn't there. Relieved, she glanced right. He was there. Stood in the middle of the field, his face turned unerringly towards her. She froze, for a moment unable to think what to do, but then she remembered Seamus and her mind began to whirl. He was a local, a harmless eccentric, but he was harmless. And she'd have to pass him to get home. Taking a deep breath, she set off again, walking as fast as she could. She thought of Seamus' advice and carefully kept her face averted, not wanting to encourage him.

Not far now. The words flew around her head like a litany as home came closer. She sped up, forcing her legs to go faster, faster, her back bending with the effort. Her heart thudded, felt like it was going to burst through her chest. She couldn't see the man, couldn't tell where he was; the hedgerow was too tall for her to see past and even without leaves the bushes were still thick, the branches grown into one another. *It's OK, you'd've passed him by now*, she told herself, willing it to be true, *he'll be way behind*. But she had to know. Up ahead, the steel bars of a farm gate gleamed dully and she threw herself towards it. Another step; she stretched, leaning forward. He was still there, stood in exactly the same place as before, watching her. And still ahead of her. But that wasn't right. He couldn't still be ahead, it was impossible. She must have got it wrong, she reassured herself quickly, mistaken exactly how far away he was. Pushing on, her right side began to protest, the start of a stitch, but she ignored it.

She reached another gap and couldn't help but look. He was standing close to the far hedge, almost, but not quite, under the reach of the trees metres from her house. Her stomach dropped and she stopped. He was still ahead of her. She could see it, see how far he'd moved, and yet, impossibly, he was perfectly still, his face turned towards her as if something had lifted him by the shoulders and deposited him further on. Her mind span, rejecting what she was seeing. It wasn't possible. No one, nothing, moved like that, in seconds, without any sign of effort. He lifted his left hand, swept it out and round in a wide arc, as if he were inviting her, telling her to come on, that the way was clear. With a sudden flash, she knew he was taunting her, playing with her, knowing there was nothing else she could do. She forced herself onwards, reached the lip of the hill, with the house only metres away and the man even closer. The hedgerow was thinner here and she could see the black and grey of his clothes, see them through the sticks and the branches. She drew level with him and she saw his coat sway and turn.

The bark of a dog made her spin. Bran was running towards her, coming from Seamus' house, his four legs leaping and stretching as he sprinted along the road. Instinctively she looked for Seamus, but there was no sign of him. She glanced back. The man was gone, the field empty through the hedgerow. Panicked, she ran towards the house. Bran slowed as she reached her gate, turned into a wide arc that took him to the other side of the road and began to run back the way he'd come. Surprised, confused and not knowing if Bran had been running to her or just running, she continued, desperate to get inside.

Chapter Eight

"Jasmine! Jasmine! Are you still in bed?"

Jasmine woke with a jump, realising that her mum was calling her, knocking at her bedroom door.

"No, I'm up."

Even half-asleep the lie was immediate, automatic. She glanced at her alarm clock, remembered vaguely turning it off and rolling over and sighed to herself.

"Well, hurry up then, it's gone seven."

"OK," Jasmine mumbled to herself, rubbing her eyes then throwing back the duvet.

Feeling something digging into her, she slipped one hand in behind her back and pulled. It was her player. She'd fallen asleep to it last night, used it to drown out thoughts of the man. *The man!* Her stomach sank at the thought of him, sending a wave of nausea upwards.

John and her mum were sat at the table, drinking coffee as she came into the kitchen.

"Is that mine?" Jasmine asked, flying past and grabbing a lunchbox off the sideboard.

"Of course. I've done you cheese and pickle."

"Oh, OK," she replied absently, stuffing it into her bag.

What she had in her sandwich seemed almost laughable compared to the thought that the man was stood in one of the fields outside, waiting for her.

"Sit down. I'll put some toast on for you."

Her mum drained the last of her coffee and stood up.

"I'm OK. I'm not very hungry. I'll get something later."

"Sit," her mum ordered, frowning as she waved one hand at a chair, "I'm not letting you go to school without eating something. That's a bad habit to get into."

Jasmine sighed, knew there was no point in arguing. Felt the first throb of a headache.

"OK, just one slice then." Plonking down on the chair, she placed her schoolbag on her knees.

"I'll do you two," her mum countered, dropping the bread into the slots.

Jasmine rubbed her head. Her mum and John were talking; she thought she heard her mum say something about her Aunt Becky, her mum's younger sister, about the baby that was due at Christmas, but they seemed so far away, their voices drowned by the voices in her own head. They'd been at it what seemed like all night, switching endlessly back and forth and pulling her with them. Her brain ached with them. Equally matched, they paralysed her, making it impossible to answer one simple question. Should she tell her mum and John about the man or not? Part of her was absolutely sure she should, despite what Seamus said; she couldn't feel the man was harmless, not after yesterday, the way he seemed to delight in scaring her, but the rest was just as sure she shouldn't. It would mean having to deal with their reaction, or rather, John's overreaction. And what if Seamus was right? And they called the guards? What would she say then? Suddenly, violently, she wished her dad was there. He'd know what to say, what to do.

"Jas, are you OK?" It was John, leaning forward, catching her unawares.

"What? Oh, yeah, I'm fine." Covering her confusion, she opened up her bag and looked inside, pretending to be searching for something.

"Lost something?" He watched her rummage.

"No, I don't… I don't know…" She was searching in earnest now. "I can't find my coursework… my blue folder… it should be here."

"Did you leave it upstairs?" her mum interjected.

"No, of course not. I put it in here last night," Jasmine snapped, feeling sick.

Her mum and John's heads lifted, like dogs sniffing the air.

"Sorry. It must be here." She began to take things out, piling them up on the table.

"Why don't you let me—?" her mum offered, reaching out one hand as she stepped forward.

"No, it's OK—" Jasmine said crossly, still searching and piling even though it was obvious that the folder wasn't there. Paper slipped sideways and she grabbed desperately at it, halting its fall. "Where is it?! I don't understand, it was here, I know it was. I have to find it. It's already late, Mr Taylor'll go mad."

"Late? Why didn't you take it in sooner?" John flashed her mum a knowing look. "Silly question, John."

Seeing that look Jasmine was furious, livid suddenly, her body throbbing with a fury so strong she could almost taste it. Her head thudded.

"Why don't you check upstairs and I'll put this lot awa——?"

"I can manage!" Jasmine all but howled.

Her mother's helpfulness was just making the whole thing worse. Desperate to get away, she used her wrist to drag everything off the table and drop it back into her bag. Her purse hit her leg and bounced, disappearing under her chair.

"Shit," she swore, leaning sideways and reaching down, beginning to feel for it.

"It's this side." Her mum leapt forward.

"I told you I can manage!"

"Jasmine, there's no need for that." John frowned. "If you weren't so stubborn——"

Her temper snapped. She jumped to her feet, sending her school things, her bag and the milk carton in the centre of the table flying.

"That's not my fault!" she shouted, as John quickly righted the carton and her mum went for a cloth. "It's your fault. You're always having a go at me, telling me what to do. I'm sick of it! You're not my dad and you never will be."

There was a silence, the room went very still and her mum and John were staring at her with shocked faces. Appalled at herself, at what she'd said, Jasmine fled.

She threw herself onto her bed, pressed her face into the pillow, her body shaking with the feelings that coursed through her. And then something broke inside her and a wave of grief flooded up through her, like nothing she'd ever felt before, and she cried and cried.

Her tears slowed then stopped and Jasmine sat up. She felt stupid, hysterical: a little girl crying for her dad, wanting him to sort everything for her. This was down to her, whatever it was. She touched her face. Her nose and sinuses were full, aching, and she felt as if she'd been crying for hours instead of a few minutes. She sniffed loudly, went over to her dressing table, grabbed a tissue and blew her nose. Her face in the mirror looked terrible, her eyes red and puffy and the skin of her face mottled from the tears. She couldn't go to school looking like that. She grabbed another tissue and scrubbed at her face before throwing it away. She turned back. Green eyes stared at her. She gasped, one hand pressing into the wall. It wasn't her face. Another woman gazed out at her. No, not one, three. Merged and yet not, with their features still distinct so that she could see every line and blemish, from the soft smoothness of youth of the first, the faint lines and creases of middle age of the second to the etched deep of the very old. Her stomach spasmed and then the nausea was back, rising up through her, and then she was bending over, ready to be sick. Nothing happened. She straightened, looked in the mirror again and saw her own pale face staring back at her. And then her stomach spasmed again and she was moving, tumbling out of her room and along the landing and into the bathroom.

She retched hard, but she couldn't be sick, couldn't get the relief from it. Staggering over to the sink, she turned on the tap and splashed water on her face. It seemed to help so she did it again. The throbbing in her head eased and, feeling better, she grabbed a towel and wiped her face, cautiously checking her reflection in the mirror. Her face stared back at her, reddened by the pressure of the towel and the tears, but at least it was her face. She put the towel down, stared at herself. What the hell was happening to her?

Water poured, the sound dragging Jasmine from her thoughts. She looked down and, seeing the water gushing, quickly turned the tap off. Studied herself again in the mirror and brown eyes, lined and heavy, stared back at her. She looked wrecked. It was too much, a voice inside her decided. The man, all these things… the nausea, in the toilet with Niamh, the strange face in the mirror… she couldn't make sense of it, couldn't deal with it alone. Anything was better than that. That thought did it; inside the deadlock broke, and feeling strangely calm, she knew then what she had to do. Steeling herself against the temptation to run, flee back to her room, she made her way out of the bathroom and slowly downstairs. Paused for a second on the last step and, taking a deep breath, tried to steady herself. John was talking, his voice low, and even from here she could hear the flatness, the weariness in his voice. It stopped her and she grabbed hold of the handrail, strained her ears to listen.

"I'm sorry Kate, but I can't help the way I feel. I don't know what to do. We talk and talk and it gets us, me, nowhere. I really thought this time I was getting somewhere and she was finally starting to accept me. And more than that, beginning to like me. We were getting on so well. But I've been kidding myself. I don't think anything will stop her resenting me."

"I know it's hard, but you can't give up," her mum's voice replied gently, sounding almost as if she was talking to a small, very fragile child. "Things are changing, I know. I've seen you together when you've been helping her with her homework and after Carrowkeel, but it's slow. Three steps forward and two back. But you know how close she and Justin were… are, how hard the divorce hit her, him leaving. And now to have nothing from him, not even a text, a postcard. And she still won't talk about it, not even to me. All those feelings bottled up can't be good."

"I know; that's why I worry about her so much. But it's not him, it's me. I just make everything worse. I know in London she thought I was too hard on her, that I fussed. But the way she used to hang around that park at night… it scared the shit out of me. Anything could've happened to her, anything. I just wanted her to realise."

"I know you did, we both did, do. It's not easy with a teenager, but we agreed after the divorce that she needed… stability, boundaries… it's not like Sarah was ever given any, and as for those boys—"

"I'd love to know who it was that got them alcohol. I'm sure it was more than that one time,"

John's voice said, sounding angry all over again.

There was a pause. Shocked that they knew about Sarah and the drinking, Jasmine sat down hard on the stairs. What else did they know about? Surely not that night with Ade's cousin Si from Manchester, when they'd gone much further than she'd intended?

"John, it could've been anyone. The ring leader, what's his name… Ade… I think he had an older brother. It could've been him. But it doesn't matter, she's away from them now and she seems to have got in with some lovely girls here. I don't know, John, I really don't."

Jasmine heard her mum sigh. "Maybe it's me that got it wrong. Maybe I've been a terrible mum, thinking it was y'know, the teenager thing. That she'd grow out of it, come to realise about you—"

"Do you regret marrying me, Kate?" John asked suddenly, interrupting her.

There was another pause. Jasmine heard her mum's chair move, heard it scrape the kitchen floor and heard the distress in her voice when she spoke.

"No, of course not. Why do you say that? Why would you even think it?"

"Because of this. Because your daughter is so unhappy living with me. Because maybe I don't blame her for hating me. If I hadn't come along you and Justin might have got back together."

"That was never going to happen! Me and Justin were over years ago, we just didn't know it. And she doesn't hate you. Don't look like that, I know my daughter, and I don't think she could ever hate anyone. Make their life a misery, maybe. She's well capable of that."

Jasmine heard John laugh, but her mum hadn't finished.

"You're the best thing that's ever happened to me. When I think of all those wasted years... but enough of that. Look, I know this was supposed to be a fresh start for all of us, but maybe we're expecting too much from her. She's still only sixteen and she's had a lot to deal with. We can't expect everything to be smooth all the time. God knows, I remember what I was like at her age!"

There was a pause and then when her mum spoke again Jasmine could hear the determination, the certainty in her voice.

"Look, we're only guessing. Anything could be bothering her... it could be something at school, with her friends, or Malachy even, and nothing to do with you at all."

"Maybe," John replied, his tone sounding thoughtful, considering.

Jasmine heard the scrape of a chair.

"I'm sorry, Kate, but I have to go or I'll be late."

"Don't worry. I won't say anything to her now, but when she gets home tonight I'll be asking her."

Jasmine heard footsteps and, fearing that John was coming into the hallway to get his coat, flew back up the stairs. She didn't know what to do with what she'd heard, but knew she couldn't say anything. Not now, not yet. She sat on the end of her bed, waited for John to leave for work. *Maybe tonight*, she told herself. When her mum asked her if anything was wrong, she'd tell her then. Maybe.

Chapter Nine

Jasmine walked along the empty road to the bus stop, checking the fields as she went, but there was no sign of the man. But for grass, weeds and cattle, the fields were empty. She reached the first bend, could see Malachy's house in the distance. She couldn't quite believe what she'd said to John. She'd thought it plenty of times, but to say it? And to see the look on his face, the shock and hurt. She felt terrible. A month ago, she'd have hardly cared, but now? She knew the effort he'd been making, and how scared he'd been at the tomb when he'd rescued her. How could she not feel that? No, she'd apologise to him tonight, tell them both everything. A blackbird shot out of the hedge just in front of her, its screech startled, wings flapping noisily as it headed out into the open field. Jasmine jumped and, before she realised what she was doing, she was running. Running down the hill, fast, like a fox with hounds and riders on its tail.

"Jasmine!"It was Malachy. She was almost at his house and here he was, coming fast along the drive. Her feet skidded on some loose stones as she tried to slow. One last skid and she came to a stop.

"Jas, what are you doing?" he called as he jogged towards her.

He'd only half put his coat on, she noticed obscurely, the left sleeve hanging almost to the ground.

She bent over, let her schoolbag slide off her shoulder and tried to catch her breath, but her lungs were having none of it. Her school shirt was sticking to the small of her back, the sweat trickling between her shoulder blades.

"Jas?" Malachy was next to her, touching her arm. "Is everything OK?"

"Give... me... a minute," she managed between each strained breath.

He looked away, flapped his arms impatiently, but nevertheless took a step back, waited.

"OK," she breathed finally, straightened up and looked past him, at the road, the hedgerow, checking the fields.

They were still empty.

"So?" Malachy asked impatiently.

She dragged her hand through her hair, saw and felt it shake and lowered it quickly.

"Why were you running like that?"

"I just fancied a run."

"Fancied a run?" Malachy snorted, openly disbelieving. "Running like that? Like there's a dog after you?"

"Why have you only got your coat half on?" she asked him abruptly, trying to deflect him.

"Why have I—?" he repeated, incredulous, then shook his head at her. "I was coming out and I saw you, saw the way you were running—"

He stopped, moved from foot to foot, flashed her a look of frustration.

"We'd better go, or we'll both miss the bus," he said eventually.

She nodded, picked up her bag and they set off, Malachy sliding his arm into his empty coat sleeve. Neither of them spoke.

Jasmine looked back twice as they walked, but the road remained empty. She was conscious of Malachy walking beside her, of the silence between them. Maybe she should tell him. He already knew something was up, and telling him would help prepare her to tell her mum and John. She glanced surreptitiously at him. He was staring at the road as he walked and didn't look up. But what if he didn't believe her, or thought she was losing it? She shook her head at herself, her doubts. But what if he did believe her? *That* thought was almost worse. It made it all real. *Come on Jasmine*, she told herself impatiently, *all you have to do is start. To open your mouth and say a couple of words and there'd be no going back.* She opened her mouth, closed it again. Pain shot through her left temple, her headache returning, and she rubbed at it. They turned a corner and the bottom of the hill came into view. The other kids had started to arrive; if she was going to say anything it had to be now. She glanced at Malachy again, but he was still looking down. She couldn't bear it, she had to tell someone. "Mal—" she began, stopped then pushed herself on again. "I'm sorry I lied, it's just… if I tell you, you mustn't tell anyone."

His head came up; she could see him thinking.

"OK."

"Promise?"

He sighed. "I promise."

"OK," she took a deep breath. "This sounds really mad, but I've been seeing this man."

"What?" He looked surprised, as this was the last thing he'd been expecting. "A man? A local?"

"I think so; Seamus knows him."

"Seamus knows? What about your mum and John?"

"No, I was scared what they'd say, or do. Y'know what John's like."

"I bet." He nodded wisely, looked away. "What does this have to do with you running?"

"I'm was coming to that. It's, er, it's difficult." She stopped again.

This wasn't going how she'd thought; Malachy wasn't reacting how she'd thought he would. He seemed, if anything, a bit put out.

"You say a man. How old is he exactly?" Malachy was asking now. "Only there's not many single men around here; most of them are old, really old. Wait a minute, you said you think he's a local? Don't you know?"

They were almost at the junction. The bus appeared in the distance, coming along the main road.

Watching it, for Jasmine, the penny dropped. "Hang on a minute—"

"He's not old is he, more than thirty?" Malachy interrupted her again.

"Do you think," she paused, flabbergasted, "I'm talking about *dating* someone?!"

"You said you've been seeing someone."

"Bloody hell, Malachy, I didn't mean it like that!" She cried, half-incredulous, half-exasperated.

The bus driver braked late and the bus shuddered to a stop. The other kids moved forward, Malachy following. "Well how was I to know? You said—" he said over his shoulder.

"I know what I said," she interrupted. "And I didn't mean that, I meant—"

"Look, it's too late now, let's talk about it tonight."

The other kids were filing on, and Malachy took another step forward. She didn't have long and now that she'd started to talk, to tell, the thought of having to wait was unbearable.

"Can't we meet at first break? Or lunchtime?" Her head was throbbing, her stomach beginning to churn; she could hardly think straight.

"No, I'm busy. Look Jas, I'll see you tonight, what's the problem?"

"Mal, please, wait." She held up her hand and he jerked backwards, almost knocking into her.

"Don't pull on me, you almost had me over!" he snapped, rounding on her.

"But I didn't—"

He shook his head impatiently. "Look, we'll talk tonight."

And then he was off, bounding up the steps and down the bus to his waiting friends. The driver gazed at her expectantly, his face forming the question his mouth didn't ask.

"I'm coming," she told him.

She swallowed hard and climbed aboard.

*

The day passed. She heard herself talking, answering her friends back, chatting and laughing, saw herself watching silently as her teachers drew diagrams, wrote words on the board, enthused and imparted, and watched as her pen flowed, her hand moving dutifully to copy and print. But it was like watching TV with the sound down, or having both ears blocked: nothing seemed real, connected.

"So, what are you wearing?" Lisa asked beside her, her voice booming as if Jasmine's ears had suddenly popped.

"What?"

Jasmine watched as another bus arrived and a group of kids swarmed forward. She glanced at Lisa's face and thought she saw irritation.

"Tomorrow night, Rachel's competition? You haven't said."

"Yeah, right, of course," Jasmine said quickly, remembering. "I haven't decided," she lied quickly. "You?"

"I'm not sure. It's only a local competition, but as a runner-up, Rachel'll have her photograph in the paper, and anyone with her will too." She shrugged. "I'll decide tonight."

Jasmine's bus pulled in behind the first.

"I'd better go, don't want to miss me bus. See you later."

Taking two steps, she turned and looked back.

"What time are we leaving again?"

Lisa rolled her eyes. "Fiona told us this morning. Her dad'll be at yours at six."

"OK, thanks. See you tomorrow."

The bus driver had opened the door and was letting the kids on.

"Text me when you know what you're wearing," she called to Lisa over her shoulder.

"OK."

Jasmine broke into a run.

*

The bus pulled out, cutting up a car going the same way. Sat on her own, in her usual seat three rows back, Jasmine's thoughts returned to Malachy. She knew he'd be expecting an explanation and with the urge to tell, to confess, long past, she was beginning to wish she'd never said anything. Because even if by a miracle he did believe, which she very much doubted, when one person knew… She pushed the thought away, looked out of the window. And wished suddenly, fervently that she'd never left London, had never come here and was back home in Muswell Hill, walking home from school with Sarah, discussing the same old boring things and listening to Sarah talking about Ade.

The bus turned sharply onto the main road, the driver accelerating quickly as he straightened up and left the last of the town behind. Jasmine sighed, rubbed her temple then leant her head against the window of the bus. The headaches were so frequent now she was beginning to forget what it was like without them. Outside the glass, the countryside flew by. The sun, low in the autumn sky, flashed through a row of trees, shining too brightly through the window and into her eyes. Irritated, she straightened up again. In front of her two girls chatted and laughed, the noise of their voices grating, making her irritation worse. The bus passed the familiar grey bungalow on the left and Brian opposite her switched off his iPod and began to stuff it in his bag as the bus began to slow ready for their stop. Jasmine levered herself upwards. Out of nowhere, the man appeared, slipping out of the hedgerow and stepping into the road just ahead of them, his face turned inevitably towards her. The driver gave a small shout and pulled on the wheel. The bus swerved, the wheels sliding violently, throwing Jasmine off her feet and hard against the window. She slipped down, fell half on to the seat, hearing shouts behind her. And then she was grabbing the headrest of the seat in front of her and holding on for dear life as the bus careered back and forth, the driver fighting to keep control. The bus slowed, the driver braking gently to avoid flipping but helpless to stop a long skid that threw everyone forward. Jasmine's stomach spasmed; fear, like fire, burned her throat and then she was hitting the seat in front of her. It was soft, enveloping her, protecting her, like a giant cushion. Wrapped inside it, a voice in her head was screaming at her, telling her that couldn't be right, but it was all happening too fast. There were more cries and then the bus slid to a slow yet merciful stop, half in and half out of the drainage ditch by the side of the road.

There was a moment of silence and then very slowly the bus began to tilt sideways and everyone on the bus seemed to shout with one voice. Jasmine brought her hands up to protect her head, but the bus shuddered suddenly and stopped. She lowered her hands. Then someone sobbed behind her and pandemonium broke out. The driver's voice rose above it, calling for people to get off, and some of the kids began to move, using the headrests to pull themselves upright; others, possibly afraid of the bus toppling further, or in shock or pain, stayed where they were. She thought she heard someone call her name, but she couldn't be sure. Her ears were ringing and she felt curiously detached from everything around her. She thought again of the softness of the seat, but then she heard her name again and immediately wondered about Malachy. She turned to look for him, tried to see past the kids to the back of the bus, but it was impossible to see. And then a new voice sounded, shouting from outside, telling the kids that had reached the exits to get out. She looked and saw arms, hands reaching up, helping to steady the kids as they clambered out.

"Jasmine! Jasmine!"

It was Malachy calling her; she saw the fear on his face as he moved down the bus towards her.

"Malachy, I'm here."

Using the seat in front to brace her body, she began to lift herself up and out. A hand appeared on the other side of the window, sliding along the glass as its owner moved back along the side of the bus. Jasmine recoiled in shock as the face of the man came into view. Seeing her looking, he continued to slide sideways until his face was exactly opposite, inches from her own. Without taking his eyes off her, he pressed his face hard against the glass, his black eyes glistening. He grinned, spite emanating from him, twisting his smile into something obscene. The window began to mist; she could see tiny drops of his breath trickle into one another, and then the glass between them began to shimmer and swirl. His lips closed; his face began to push and strain and then impossibly the glass was bending and stretching towards her as he forced his way through the window to get at her. She shrank back, as far as she could go.

"Jasmine, are you OK? What the—!"

Malachy was stood above her, his mouth open, voice trailing away as he stared at the face halfway through the window, the glass sliding across its cheeks and forehead. And then the head was through and, without taking his eyes from her, the man lifted his hands and pulled at the edges of the hole. Widened it enough to allow his shoulders and arms inside. Jasmine and Malachy watched transfixed as he stretched out his arms, his hands, reaching for her.

Chapter Ten

"Jasmine! Malachy!"

Seamus' voice cracked like a whip from the front of the bus. He called again, his face urgent as his hands gripped the top of the driver's seat. Jasmine turned back to the window, Malachy following suit. The man had gone, leaving the window smooth, unblemished.

"Did you see that?" Jasmine asked Malachy stupidly.

He didn't respond, turned back to look at Seamus who was beckoning to them.

"Are you alright to move?" he asked, not looking at her.

She nodded and began to lever herself out of the seat. Malachy placed his hands on either side of her waist, helping her up then supporting her weight as she clambered awkwardly down the aisle. Seamus stepped back to the top of the steps, giving her space to clamber over the driver's seat and out the door. Waiting hands eased her down to the ground. A middle-aged man dressed in a grey suit helped her to the grass verge by the side of the road and sat her down.

"Will you be alright? I need to get back and help." Anxious eyes gazed back towards the bus.

"Yes, I'm fine. Thanks."

He smiled briefly then hurried off. Feeling dazed, Jasmine looked about her.

There were people everywhere. Bruised and battered kids lined the verge, comforted by adults, the wailing of a Garda car cutting through the growing lines of traffic, but of the man there was no sign. Her stomach twisted suddenly and a wave of nausea rose up through her throat. She swallowed hard, holding her head in her hands until the feeling passed. A hand touched her shoulder lightly, making her jump, and she looked up to see Seamus gazing down at her. He squatted down beside her and squinted into her face.

"Are you alright? Are you hurt anywhere? Did he hurt you?"

"I'm OK. I just, feel, er, a bit weird. How's the other kids?"

He frowned. "I don't think anyone was seriously hurt. It looks like there's two who've broken something, but they're still on the bus."

He turned, looking at the bus for a moment then at the Garda car now parked alongside. Two Guards got out, one moving towards the traffic, then taking long quick strides towards the bus as he talked urgently into his radio. "The paramedics'll have to see them first, when they get there."

"Where's Malachy?"

She realised suddenly that he wasn't beside her. Couldn't see him among the people milling about, either. Seamus straightened up, his right knee clicking in protest.

"I don't know, I thought he was behind us. You're shivering. Take my coat, I'll go and check. Back in a minute."

She watched him go then, folding her arms onto her knees and resting her head on top, closed her eyes. She drifted, the noise around her fading. Abruptly, another siren sounded, its shrillness piercing the air. She opened her eyes and looked up. Malachy was coming towards her, his body slightly lopsided as if he was favouring his right side, a man's coat hanging loosely around his shoulders. He joined her on the verge, wincing in pain as he sat down next to her.

"Are you OK?" Jasmine asked, placing her hand lightly on his good arm.

He nodded, his face pale, but his eyes never left the bus. "Yeah, I knocked my arm in the crash. I didn't feel it at first. But I don't think it's serious, not like Liam."

Liam was his thirteen-year-old cousin. Jasmine looked at him in alarm.

"What's wrong with him?"

He sighed. "I don't know; I think it's his leg. I saw him when I was helping you off, tried to stay with him but the Guard wouldn't let me, made me go. He was awake though."

"Oh Mal, I'm really sorry."

An ambulance pulled up and a paramedic leapt out and ran towards the bus. They watched as the second one got out too, moved to the back of the ambulance and opened the door.

"It's not your fault." He still wouldn't look at her. "It was an accident."

She chose her words carefully, watched his face for his reaction. "Mal, do you remember what we were talking about this morning? About the man?"

"Jasmine, not now." His tone was even, but she caught the undercurrent of anger.

"But that was him, there. You saw him too."

A Guard came into view scanning the faces around him, spotting Malachy almost immediately and waving him over.

"That's Liam." Malachy swivelled round, finally looking at her, but refused to meet her eyes.

"But Mal, this is important." She touched his arm.

He flexed it, knocking her hand away. "I don't know what you're talking about. I didn't see anything on the bus."

He began to get up, moving awkwardly because of his arm.

"Mal, I hope Liam's OK, but you did see him, I know you did," she said softly.

On his feet, he leant over her suddenly, thrust his face towards hers, the anger she'd glimpsed bursting through.

"I don't know what you're talking about. You must be seeing things." He jabbed his finger at her. "Maybe you should get a doctor to look at that head of yours."

"I think it's time you went, Malachy Costello."

It was Seamus, his calm voice cold with disapproval. Malachy looked as if he was going to say something, but he changed his mind, shaking his head as he walked away. Seamus watched him go with a stony face.

"He'll be back," he remarked lightly and, bending awkwardly, placed the blanket he'd found around her shoulders.

She blinked, feeling tears close.

"I called your mum. She's on her way down. You should get yourself checked out after an accident like that. I said I'd drive you both to the hospital."

"But I'm OK," she protested, the tears retreating. "Really. I don't want to go to the hospital."

The Guards might be there. They might ask her questions, want to know what she saw. She just wanted to go home, to pretend that none of this was happening.

"I think your mum might have something to say about that." He grinned, touching her lightly on the shoulder.

He was looking at her as he talked, but she got the strangest feeling that he wasn't really listening, to her or himself, was talking to cover the fact that he was concentrating, focussing on something else entirely. Her stomach fluttered, the air seemed to almost vibrate around her, and she got the sense of… something… something unseen moving, shifting.

"You do seem fine."

Seamus was back, his eyes seeing her again, and he patted her arm. "Leave it to me. I'll talk to your mum for you."

He was true to his word, and to Jasmine's surprise her mum made no complaint as Seamus drove them up the hill to the house. He dropped them off but refused to come in, saying that he had cattle to sort. He waited until they had reached the far corner of the house then pulled off with a wave.

"Are you sure you're OK?" Her mum asked as soon as they stepped through the kitchen door.

"Yeah." Jasmine nodded.

"OK. Come here." Wrapping her arms around her, her mum held her close. "That could've been so much worse."

Snuggling in, Jasmine closed her eyes, for the barest of moments letting herself forget. But then the man's face was there, grinning as it pressed through the glass towards her. She opened them again. "I'm really OK, mum."

"I know you are." Her mum let her go. "Now, why don't you go for a lie down? Try and get some sleep."

"No." She shook her head vigorously. "I'm OK. I want to stay here."

"Then why don't you sit down and I'll make us both a drink." Her mum smiled. "Then afterwards you can help me make the dinner. You can do the veg at the table."

"Ok." Relieved, Jasmine sat down, watching as her mum filled the kettle.

"Mum, about this morning—"

"Oh, Jas, don't worry about that now." Flipping the switch, she flashed Jasmine a smile, "We can talk another day. All that matters is that you're OK." She opened a cupboard. "Now let's get you that drink."

*

Jasmine was cutting at a broccoli head at the kitchen table when the back door opened and John bounded in, his face pale, set. They both turned towards him in surprise, Jasmine realising she hadn't heard his car pull onto the drive.

"Are you OK? It was on the radio and then I just saw Seamus—"

John dashed over to the table, leaving the door open.

"She's fine," her mum replied soothingly as she moved to shut it behind him. "Just shock really. If you've spoken to Seamus I'm surprised he didn't say——"

"And why would I listen to Seamus? To anything that man has to say!" he snapped, rounding on her.

Shocked, Jasmine and her mum stared at one another.

"All I'm saying is that she should've gone to the hospital and got checked out," John continued, his tone defensive, but milder, as if he was already regretting what he'd just said.

"She didn't want to. Besides she wasn't hurt," her mum replied evenly, but Jasmine caught the edge to her voice.

"Then you should've made her! You'd be the first to shout if anything happened to her."

Her mum didn't say anything, for a moment just looked at him, then moved to the hob and turned down the potatoes that were threatening to boil over. And Jasmine, knowing that look, almost felt sorry for him.

"Sorry Kate, I didn't mean that," he apologised quickly, dragging his hand through his hair,

"I was worried, but I shouldn't take it out on you. It's the bus drivers I blame; they drive too fast along these roads. It was lucky no one was killed."

"We don't know if——"

The phone began to ring, and without another word, her mum disappeared down the hall to answer it.

There was a silence. Jasmine continued to hack at the broccoli, cutting off far more than was needed. She didn't like this John; he reminded her too much of the John in London. She found herself hoping that he'd go away, to the toilet or something. But he didn't.

"So, you're really OK?" he asked, sitting down next to her instead and leaning in.

"Yeah." She risked a glance at him.

He looked wrecked; with the grey in his hair and the lines on his face he looked suddenly old, worn. Her heart softened. She lowered the knife, preparing to reach out to him and try and comfort him.

"I think I should drive you to and from school from now on. I don't like the thought of you on that bus. It's not safe."

"What?!"

Shocked, she let the knife fall.

John was watching her, waiting for her to answer.

"I'm OK, and it's half-term next week," she mumbled.

Her heart sank. She was right; it was all starting up again.

He put his hand on her arm, stared intently at her. "It's not a problem, if you were worried or didn't feel safe."

"That was the head teacher." Her mum was coming back through the door. "We've a lot to thank the driver for. The Guards said that without his skill, his cool head, the crash could've been… well, a lot worse." She flashed John a look. "But he's in bits and Mr Corcoran said he won't be back at least until after the holiday. And as it's half-term next week he said for all the kids on the bus not to come in tomorrow. It's only one day."

John leant back, took his hand away. "That's good, but I was just saying to Jasmine that maybe I should drive her in anyway, permanently I mean."

"But what about work?"

"I can work round it. It wouldn't be a problem."

Her mum frowned. "It seems a bit extreme."

"But imagine getting on a bus after something like this."

"All the more reason to do it." Her mum paused, looked at Jasmine. "Jas, how do you feel about it?"

"I'll be OK." She looked down at her hands, wishing it would all just stop.

"There you go. But if she does find it difficult we can deal with it then. OK?"

There was another silence. Her mum and John were staring at one another, seemed almost to be sizing each other up, like two animals trying to decide whether to fight or not. Her mum won. John looked away.

"OK," he agreed quietly, but Jasmine could feel his anger simmering away beneath the surface.

"Good. I've got a dinner to finish. Why don't you go watch the news and I'll bring you in a coffee."

"OK." He stood up, glanced at Jasmine as he moved past her.

Pretending to be too busy with the broccoli to look up at him, she saw him leave out of the corner of her eye.

"Right," her mum said tightly, returning to the hob.

When dinner was ready, Jasmine went to call John and found him in the sitting room staring at the TV, at a fashion programme.

"I'll be there in a minute." But he didn't move.

"Fine, it's his problem if it's gone cold," was all her mum said when she told her.

"Kate, this looks delicious," John said, coming into the room two minutes later, his voice strained with false cheerfulness.

"I hope you like it."

Jasmine winced at their politeness. Wanting the dinner over, she ate too quickly, the sound of her own chewing loud in the silence of the kitchen.

"This is really good," he said, trying again.

"Good, I'm glad." Her smile was twisted.

There was another silence. Jasmine had already finished her chop and was starting on the potatoes.

"Kate." John put down his knife and fork and touched Jasmine's mum's arm. "I'm really sorry for what I said earlier. I wasn't blaming you, I was just — overreacting, as usual."

Her mum stopped eating and looked at him. Her face softened.

"That's not how it felt."

"I know, I'm sorry. It wasn't you, I was just mad at Seamus, at something he said."

She opened her mouth to speak, but he waved one hand. "It's nothing really... I'll sort it with him."

"Well, let's just forget it."

This time her mum's smile was genuine. Jasmine breathed a silent sigh of relief as John reached over and took her mum's hand, squeezing it gently.

"Of course, if it doesn't work out so well on the bus, just so you both know, the lift wouldn't be a problem," he continued airily, cutting into his second chop.

"What?"

Jasmine's mum put down her fork. "Now why did you have to say that? I thought we were going to leave it."

"I was just saying. What's wrong with that?"

"Because it means you still not getting what I'm saying. Jas says she's fine with the bus, I'm fine with it, so, why aren't you? You can't wrap them up in cotton wool, you know."

She glanced over at Jasmine. "Jas, slow down, there's no need to shovel it."

"I know that, I'm not trying to," John protested irritably. "I told you I was just worried."

"That's the trouble; when it comes to Jasmine you worry too much over nothing."

"Nothing? A bus crash is nothing?" He lowered his knife and fork, gave her a hard look. "You know I find this stepfather thing difficult—"

Jasmine's mum pushed her chair back, the legs scrapping loudly, and grabbed her plate, her hands visibly shaking. She paused, hovered over John for a moment.

"Y'know, John, you keep telling yourself that."

"What does that mean?"

"That I'm tired of the same old excuse. I'm tired of your overprotectiveness. It's not normal."

Moving to the bin, she lifted the lid and, angling her plate, tipped her dinner into it.

"Kate, what the hell are you doing?" John was on his feet, incredulous.

"I'm not hungry," her mum replied, leaving the plate to balance on the side and moving towards the back door.

"Where are you going?" John demanded, following her.

"Out, to get some air."

Her mum's hand was on the door handle.

"But it's freezing out there, and you don't have a coat."

Her mum ignored him, opened the door. But he was there behind her, reaching over her, pushing it shut.

"Kate, don't be stupid."

"John, let go of the door, you can't stop me."

She was shouting now, pulling on the handle. The door opened, but John pressed harder, closing it back up again.

"Kate!" he was saying, but her mum wasn't listening and, still pulling on the door, was still shouting at him to let go.

And then Jasmine too was on her feet and shouting at them both. "Stop it, stop fighting."

She was furious with them, furious, and hurt that somehow they were making this about themselves and not her. Just like Malachy. Her stomach churned and she felt sick. They weren't listening.

"Stop it!"

The plate shot off the side, span twice in midair then hit the wall above their heads. It shattered, the impetus sending shards of crockery over them and back across the room.

"Kate! Are you OK, did it hit you?" John took a step back, lowered his arms from when he'd raised them, instinctively, protectively, over her mum's head.

"No." Her mum shook her head; her eyes were wide, but she looked unhurt.

They held each other briefly and Jasmine, feeling her legs fall away beneath her, sank into the chair.

"What happened?" her mum asked as they pulled apart.

"The plate must've fallen." John shrugged.

He glanced at the side then over to the mark left on the wall. Jasmine, watching, followed his look, followed what had been the plate's trajectory. It took her a moment and then she realised that it had been rising, lifting upwards when it left the side, not falling. *It's not possible*, she told herself. But there was another voice inside her, another part of herself and it was telling her... she shook her head, shut her eyes against. Pushed, willed the voice away. She opened them again. John was looking at her; their eyes met for a split second and for one mad moment she thought he saw, thought he knew, and then he looked away.

"Jas, are you OK?" Her mum was moving across the kitchen towards her, stepping carefully to avoid pieces of plate.

"Yeah," she replied, feeling her heart beat beginning to return to normal.

"I'm sorry, I can't believe after everything you've been through today we have a row."

Her mum reached her and pulled her arms around her shoulders, squeezing her tight.

"It's OK." Jasmine gave her a crooked smile. "But I do feel a bit tired. I'm going to lie down."

"Maybe it's for the best." Her mum nodded.

John had stepped forward, was standing next to her mum looking worried.

"This is all my stupid fault. If I hadn't overreacted—"

It was too much hearing them both berating themselves, blaming themselves. Her thoughts whirled. It felt like she was disintegrating. She backed towards the door.

"It's OK, em, I think I just need to lie down, er, y'know, after... John, I'm sorry about this morning."

Mercifully, she was in the hallway, heading towards the stairs.

"I'll come up and check on you later," her mum called through the doorway.

Unable to answer, Jasmine continued, up the stairs and into her bedroom, closing the door behind her.

The sky outside was clear, and moonlight illuminated branches of the trees in the field opposite. Tinged them silver, ghostly. It wasn't them, it was her. The man, following her, crashing the bus and hurting Liam, and objects moving all by themselves. They all came back to her. She couldn't deny it anymore to herself. It wasn't them, it was her. She was the problem.

Chapter Eleven

Rain arrived halfway through the night and the wind driving it blew it sideways, lashing it against the house, the windows. It was still raining when Jasmine woke and, knowing she didn't have school, she pulled the duvet up over her head and buried herself, part of her wishing she could be like a dormouse and hibernate until the following spring.

It was after eleven when she got up. She'd gone back to sleep and to her surprise her mum hadn't bothered her. After her shower, she slipped into her worn trackie bottoms and an old sweatshirt. She wasn't going to go out, not after yesterday. The last thing she wanted was to go outside, today, tonight, or ever.

She ate breakfast in her room, checking her phone for messages. There were texts from the girls asking her how she was, and what had actually happened – there were so many rumours – but there was nothing from Malachy. She sighed, toying with the idea of texting him, but the way he'd been with her yesterday she wasn't sure if he'd even read it. She replied to the others instead and finished her toast. Her phone buzzed with more messages, but still nothing from Malachy. Annoyed now, she put her plate down, typed him a short message then read it back to herself. It was fine, what was she worrying about? She sent it and waited, sipping her tea. Ten minutes passed. Nothing. She replied to Fiona, and waited again. Still nothing. Sighing, dropping her phone down on the bed next to her, she picked up her laptop and opening it, turned it on. The motor whirled. She closed her eyes, but the plate was there, shattering above her mum's and John's heads, the toilet holder bouncing as it hit the wall, inches from Niamh. She opened them again. Her laptop was still loading, next to her, the phone's blank screen gazing upwards. Inside her head, an idea formed, a way to test the madness, the thought that somehow she could've done these things. Taking a deep breath, she pointed at her phone.

"Move," she ordered.

Nothing happened. The blank screen mocked her. Told her she

was a child playing at wizards, pretending her finger was a wand. She looked away. Part of her was tempted to try again, but she resisted, unwilling to make herself feel anymore foolish, and focussed on her laptop.

She was still surfing, still aimlessly clicking from screen to screen, when her mum knocked on the door.

"Yeah?" The alarm clock said a quarter to two.

The door opened just enough to allow her mum to poke her head round it. "John's just got home. They finished early today so we're going shopping today instead of tomorrow. Is there anything you want?"

"Na, thanks." She shook her head.

"See you later," her mum said breezily, her head disappearing.

Jasmine waited a few minutes then, scrambling up, went to the window. John was sat in the driver's seat, staring into space. The front door banged and then her mum appeared at the top of the drive, half running in the rain. She threw herself into the front seat and they kissed briefly. And then, putting the car into gear, John reversed out into the road. He pulled away, Jasmine watching as the car disappeared down the hill.

Jasmine scrolled. Her phone beeped on the bed next to her and she picked it up. It was Sarah. She'd met someone new, a boy called Max. Younger than Ade, he was nicer, more thoughtful. Delighted, Jasmine sent a quick text back then went downstairs for a drink, carrying her player in one hand. She was pleased for Sarah, pleased that she'd finally got over Ade, not that she had much choice after he'd ended it so callously. The kitchen was dark as she entered it; even on the brightest day there was never much light in it. Not that it mattered; she knew where the last can was, in the fridge, at the back. She'd spotted it earlier. Opening the fridge door, she bent down onto her haunches and reached inside. Her fingers caught the top of the can. What was that? One hand pulled out her earphones and she cocked her head, listening. The house was silent. It must be her imagination, she decided, reaching in again.

Something slipped past the kitchen window, casting a shadow. Jasmine was on her feet in an instant, the can forgotten. She imagined the man moving around the house and flew down the hall, into the sitting room. Her heart pounding, she slipped in behind the curtain. Holding it with one hand, peeked carefully out. The path was empty. Her phone, left upstairs, began to ring; she could just make out her ringtone. She thought of going to get it, but the idea that the man was still outside, waiting to see her move, stopped her. Maybe he'd been watching for a while, had seen her mum and John go out and knew she was on her own. *Oh, my God!* She took a deep breath, trying to calm herself. Maybe, it was nothing, the shadow of a darker cloud. How stupid would that make her? She straightened her shoulders. There was only one way to find out. Letting the curtain drop and not giving herself any chance to change her mind, to doubt the wisdom of what she was about to do, she marched back into the hallway, opened the front door and leant out, peering into the rain. A figure, dressed in a long, hooded coat came around the corner of the house. For a moment she thought she was going to scream and then the figure pulled the hood back, revealing its face. It was Malachy.

She didn't know whether to shout at him, laugh or cry.

"Jas, it's me," he said unnecessarily, coming towards her.

"Shit, Mal, you really scared me."

"Sorry."

He'd reached her. They stood in the rain and stared at one another in silence.

"Are you OK?" His eyes widened, "You didn't think I was—?"

He couldn't finish it.

"How's Liam?" she asked, changing the subject.

"Liam's OK. Enjoying all the attention, I think."

"That's good."

"Me arm's OK too." He lifted it up, flapped it at her.

"That's good," she repeated.

There was another silence.

"Jas, it's pouring, aren't you going to invite me in?"

"Why should I?" she retorted. "I called three times, texted you, but you never even answered."

"No, sorry." He sighed, looked at his feet. "I just couldn't handle it, what I saw. I just wanted to forget it."

She stared at his lowered head, the rain dripping off it. She noticed for the first time how wonky his parting was. She couldn't really blame him. If she were him, would she have come within a million miles of her? Then he lifted his head and she saw his eyes and realised how lost he was.

"But I can't forget what I saw. The glass—" He stopped, shook his head. "For fuck sake Jas, how is that even possible?"

"I don't know."

And yet, despite everything, he was standing outside her door, getting soaked in the rain.

"Come in." She stepped back to allow him inside.

*

"There's no way a person could do that," Malachy was saying, his voice muffled by the towel she'd given him. "So, if he's not a man, what is he?"

He stopped rubbing, lowered the towel and put it on the arm of the chair. "God, will you listen to me? I can't believe I'm saying this." His jaw tightened. "But I know what I saw.

But what is it I saw? What does it want? Have you told anyone else?"

"No." She thought of Seamus, but he hadn't known; he'd thought the man was just a local. "What would I say? Who'd believe me?"

"Yeah, I saw it and I didn't believe it. This is what you were trying to tell me yesterday."

"I thought you might know him. At first, I thought he was just some odd but harmless local, but it got worse—"

"Hang on a minute," Malachy interrupted her. "How would I know?"

"He said he was a local—" She stopped, remembering Seamus' words. "He didn't actually say that."

"He… that thing is no local. Who told you that?"

"Seamus."

"Seamus? Are you saying Seamus saw him?"

He stood up and, taking a few steps, began pacing. He moved back and forth across the hearth, as if it was suddenly too difficult to stay still.

"You said yesterday that Seamus knew. Are you sure he actually saw him?"

"Yes, no, I don't know. It was from a distance; he must've got it wrong and thought it was someone he knew."

"I guess, how close was he?" He stopped in mid-stride.

"I dunno." She shrugged. "A few feet?"

"A few feet?!" Malachy shook his head. "Seamus is too sharp for that. Or maybe he was just trying to reassure you?" He waved his hand in frustration. "Don't be stupid, Malachy, that doesn't make any sense. Why would he try to reassure you if he hadn't seen anything?"

He began to pace again, his body vibrating with excitement, thoughts racing through his head. She watched him move, found his energy unsettling, jarring, wished he'd stop.

"But why would Seamus lie? Unless he knew what this thing was? Maybe that's it. You know everyone goes to Seamus when they need advice, how to do something, about farming, the livestock, anything. He's like the wise man. But what if it's more than that. What if he knows stuff that no one else knows?"

Car lights appeared through the garden hedge.

"Mal—" Jasmine said warningly, seeing them slow.

"You know what we should do? We should go and see Seamus. Confront him. Right now," Malachy suggested, ignoring her.

"But mum and John are here. You have to go," she protested, her stomach fluttering.

The lights flashed through the window as the car swung into the drive and John parked.

Malachy looked over at her and she could see the worry in his face, around his eyes.

"Jas, this is serious; did you see the look on that thing's face when it was staring at you? Maybe they should know."

Her stomach dropped. She couldn't tell them. The way they'd reacted to the bus crash, the way John had reacted… What would he do if he knew? She thought quickly, the words tumbling out of her. "It wouldn't help. Even if they believed me, what could they do? Call the guards? Tell them a man made a hole in a glass window with his spit?"

"Yeah, OK, you've got a point there," Malachy agreed slowly. "But you can't stay inside forever and how can you go outside alone, knowing that's out there? You have to do something and they should know."

She knew he was right, she had to do something, but her mum and John would be coming in soon, and she couldn't trust him not to say anything.

"OK. Maybe you're right, we should talk to Seamus first." She moved to the door, trying to get him to follow. "We'll go together, tomorrow?"

The car lights went out. She heard a car door shut, saw John climb out. Heard the two of them talking. Malachy hadn't moved, seemingly determined to hold his ground.

"I don't know Jas, I still think you should tell them," he said, his voice earnest, coaxing. "I can stay, tell them that I saw him too. They'll have to believe the both of us."

"No, Mal." She shook her head at him, lying desperately, saying anything to get him to stop. "You're right, I will tell them, I promise, but just not now… not yet…"

She could feel the agitation building inside her and forced herself to keep calm. Her stomach flipped, sending up a wave of nausea.

"OK." Malachy frowned. "But we'll go and see Seamus tomorrow?"

"Yeah, tomorrow!" she agreed eagerly, stepping into the hallway.

This time Malachy followed her. She grabbed his coat, moved to the front door. She watched as he slipped his feet into his trainers.

"Hurry up, Mal."

He was too slow. Her mum and John's voices came closer, moved past the front door. Inches away from her. Her stomach spasmed. She was beginning to feel really bad, really nauseous. Like she had with Niamh, like she had last night, with the plate. Malachy needed to go. The kitchen door opened just as he straightened up, took his coat from her. She opened the front door, propelling him outside. She noticed vaguely that it had finally stopped raining.

"Jesus, Jas, wait a minute," he complained, reached out, holding the door open even as she tried to shut it on him.

"Mal," she groaned.

She could see her mum through the kitchen door, lifting a bag onto the side. She stepped outside with him, pulled the door to behind her.

He turned to face her. "I can't do it, Jas. I don't like this. I know they can't go to the guards, but I think they should still know. If only to protect you."

He grabbed her arm, began to push at her, trying to steer her back inside. "Let's go back, tell them together."

"No, Mal, please don't, please—" she began, trying to warn him, feeling the fear bubbling, turning to panic.

But he was still talking, still pushing at her, oblivious.

Fire exploded in her stomach, burned upwards. The power of it knocked her back and wrenched Malachy off her, flinging him backwards. She staggered to one side, her head spinning, her stomach convulsing. She began to retch, her body straining, aching with the violence of the effort, but nothing came up. She groaned, felt the spasms slowing and then they stopped altogether. Her skin felt clammy, her mouth wet with saliva and she wiped it with her sleeve, took a deep breath, then another, feeling better for it. For a moment, she could think of nothing beyond the needs of her own body and then she remembered Malachy.

He was lying where he had fallen, across the path. His arms were outstretched, his right hand touching grass, his body motionless. She dashed over to him, calling his name. His eyes were half-open; she could see them glistening but he didn't answer.

"Mal, are you alright? Mal, wake up," Crouching over him, she touched his face, shook his shoulder. "Mal, please."

"Yeah," he gasped finally, his voice thin and breathless. "Give me a minute."

He closed his eyes.

"Are you sure you're OK? Does it hurt anywhere?"

She pressed his coat, feeling him all over.

"Jas, I'm OK. Jas, get off." He opened his eyes in defeat. "OK, give me a hand."

She took his hand, and he pulled on her, levering himself up until he was sat.

"Mal, you're getting soaked."

"Hold on, just another minute," he said, breathing hard. "OK, ready."

He gathered up his strength and together they got him to his feet. Jasmine helped him down the path and over to the garden wall. He leant against it, his chest still heaving.

"That's better, I just needed to catch my breath."

His voice was getting stronger and, relieved, she moved in next to him and waited.

"What happened?" he asked eventually, turning his head to look at her.

"I don't know."

The lie was immediate, reflexive; this time there was no room for doubt. Malachy was frowning, looked as if he was trying to piece it all together.

"You pushed me. No, you didn't."

He straightened up, took a step away from her, still staring. "What did you do? How did you—?"

He was moving around her now, keeping her firmly in his vision as he backed towards the garden gate. And now it was her turn to reach out to him.

"Mal, please—"

"You're like that thing. What the fuck are you?"

"Malachy!"

It was John, stood next to the house, his face twisted with fury. Malachy flushed.

"I've got to go," he mumbled, shimmying through the half open gate.

John watched him as he disappeared down the lane at a half run.

"You two had a fight?"

"Yeah," Jasmine replied, not knowing what else to say.

She felt empty inside, as if Malachy had kicked a hole straight through the centre of her.

"Well, I'm sure you'll sort it out." He gave her a rueful smile, a smile that told her he knew what it was like. "We've lost a jar of coffee. Your mum thinks it's in the car." He pressed the car fob and the lock clicked.

"Oh, OK." She walked towards the still open front door.

"Let's hope it's there—" John's voice disappeared as he bent over and began to rummage under the back seat, but she wasn't really listening.

Back inside she thought of how Malachy had looked at her, at what he'd said. He was right: what the hell was she?

*

She was still asking herself that an hour later when her phone buzzed. She would've ignored the text if it hadn't been for the thought that it could be Malachy. She picked it up. It was him.

"Sorry I idiot found something important u MUST come convent by lake ASAP."

Sitting up, she called him straight back, but his phone went straight to voicemail.

"Damn!" she muttered, thinking it through.

It didn't take long. The man was still out there somewhere, but Malachy had obviously thought things through and if there was the slightest chance he knew something, could tell her what was happening to her, she had to take it. She texted him back, letting him know she was on her way, then tiptoed out of her bedroom and down the stairs. Putting on her coat and shoes, she carefully turned the latch on the door, before slipping out of the house and over to the shed. Being as quiet as she could, she manoeuvred her bike out through the shed door and wheeled it out onto the lane. Climbing on, her heart pounding, she rode away, pedalling as fast as she could, as fast as her legs would go.

The road down to and through the village was deserted, the houses quiet, like a ghost town. She reached the wood, saw the white top of the convent come into view through the trees. Below it, the high, ornate gates gleamed faintly in the afternoon light. It was dark under the thick canopy, the air a few degrees colder. The avenue up to the house came into view and she slowed, freewheeling her bike to a gentle stop just in front of the gates. There was no sign of Malachy and there was nothing to do but wait, so, straddling her bike, she waddled awkwardly to the grass verge and stood there studying the convent, or the little of it she could see through the trees. It looked in pretty good condition. Malachy had told her once that a property developer owned it, was trying to ride out the recession, to wait and turn it into a luxury hotel. Looking at it now she suspected that he'd have a very long wait. She glanced at her watch; almost ten minutes and still no Malachy. She sighed to herself as she placed her elbows onto the handlebars, rested her head on her hands and tried to make herself comfortable.

A bird flew across the sky in the direction of the convent. Jasmine lifted her head, watched it disappear then checked her watch again. Five more minutes gone. She tried Malachy again and this time, when it went to voicemail, she left a message. Her phone back in her pocket, she wondered irritably if the whole thing was a joke after all. It was cold standing here; she hadn't thought to put on her winter coat, but then she hadn't thought she'd be left waiting. She grabbed the bottom of her coat, preparing to zip it up when a thought stopped her. What if she'd got it wrong, that Malachy meant for her to meet him in the actual convent grounds? Or near the house? He could be there inside, waiting for her just as she was waiting for him, only unable to tell her because he couldn't get a signal through the trees. There was only one way to find out, she decided, hopping off her bike and dragging it onto the grass verge before leaning it against the trunk of a tree. The entrance gates were iron and rusty, held by an equally rusty padlock, but they both held firm when she tugged at them. She looked about her, trying to find another way in, and spotted an old stone stile half hidden by the overgrown shrubbery, long-forgotten. She pushed the shrubbery away, broke off the tougher, more resistant branches to create a space big enough to squeeze through, then hopped over the stile. It was even darker the other side and hard to see. The ground was rough and uneven, littered with loose objects that slipped away as she stepped. Twice she tripped and almost fell. By the time she'd reached the avenue her face and hands were scratched, and she was breathing heavily. She stopped for a minute to catch her breath then started along the avenue towards the convent.

The avenue was silent as she walked slowly along it. The grass came up to her ankles; she guessed someone had cut it during the summer, but it was the only sign that anyone had been there for a very long time. Halfway along and the trees were beginning to thin, making it easier to see, and then the avenue curved slightly to the left and the convent came fully into view. Up close it was in a worse condition than she'd first thought; the plaster had long been flaking and huge chunks had fallen away altogether. Very few of the windows remained and what was left of the frames had been boarded up with strips of plywood. Abruptly, the avenue ended, widening out into a square courtyard, with the house to her right and stone, half-crumbled stables to her left. A chapel lay to the far side of the house, recognisable by the gold coloured cross she'd missed last time, and the dark, vaulted windows, but of Malachy there was no sign. She looked back. Through the foliage, she could just make out the end of one of the gates. It seemed very far away. The convent was far more isolated than she'd realised, but at least she wasn't on her own, she reassured herself quickly. Malachy was somewhere here, waiting for her. Turning back, she began to cross the courtyard, taking care not to trip over the cracked, uneven concrete. She passed the house and spotted a small passageway. Sat in shadow, it separated the house and the chapel and halfway down it a door, leading back into the house, lay open. Jasmine shivered, rubbed her arms through the sleeves of her coat. Malachy must've opened it and was inside, waiting for her. She grimaced, hoped he didn't think this was some kind of joke. Steeling herself against the urge to turn back, to run back along the avenue to her bike, she moved into the passageway and down into the shadow of the building. At the door, she paused, still unsure, then stepped across the threshold.

Chapter Twelve

Jasmine moved into a corridor. It was narrow with a high ceiling, shadows in the dim light creeping along both walls. Metal lamps on long cords hung from the ceiling, equally spaced along the hall. The place was a mess, the plaster on the walls disintegrating with neglect, the floors covered with filth, rubbish and encroaching vegetation. She had to step carefully, watching where she went. There were rows of doors down both sides and she realised she was passing through a dormitory. Some of the rooms were completely empty and others contained pieces of rotting furniture, wardrobes and chairs; in one a rusting iron bed had fallen flat to the ground at one end, two of its legs collapsed beneath it. Jasmine passed under an arch and found herself in a wide, high reception room. Old newspapers, leaflets and envelopes littered the floor, but here and there she saw patches of the original Victorian tiled flooring, the colours just visible through the dirt. Opposite her, a second corridor, a mirror image to the one she'd just left, disappeared into the distance. To her right the last of the day's light streamed through the dusty windows that framed the front door. She moved forward. Left, a grand staircase swung wide and high up to the next level, the mahogany wood thick with dirt and dust. She stopped, noticing a thick wooden door underneath the staircase, lying slightly ajar.

"Malachy, are you there?" she called, unwilling to go any further. There was no answer, so she tried again. "Malachy, this isn't funny, where are you?"

She strained her ears in the silence. There was something there. The noise was too low, too indistinct for her to make out, but even as she listened it got stronger and stronger. Sounded almost like someone tapping. She leant forward, realising with a flip of her stomach that it was coming from behind the wooden door. She shivered, her neck prickling with fear, her stomach churning, but she ignored it. Walking over to the door, she pushed at it, and it opened, creaking. The room was dark, much darker than the front entrance. She couldn't see.

"Malachy?"

Something shifted; she heard the rustle. Taking a deep breath, she stepped inside, her footsteps echoing as if she'd entered a huge empty space.

"Malachy?" She stopped.

Her eyes were beginning to adjust to the lack of light, the room gradually taking shape around her, the lines of the walls, floor and windows becoming stronger, more distinct. It was, she realised, what had once been the main hall. The windows all along the far wall reached from floor to ceiling. It looked as if they'd been boarded up years ago, the wood rotten, the planks splintered and broken. Light seeped in through the gaps and fell to the floor in fine rays, illuminating the dirt and the dust, making it look like a silver mist or stardust, dropping slowly to Earth and coating the floor. And then she spotted him, standing in front of the windows with his back to her. Malachy.

Relieved, she rushed forward.

"Malachy, you git, you scared me half to death!"

His neck swivelled, his head turning, and something in the way he held himself made her slow to a stop. He faced her. It was him, the man, his face deathly white, stark against the dark in the room, the familiar black eyes rolling as they searched for her own. He took a step towards her, then another and another, his eyes never leaving hers. She willed herself to move but she couldn't, was frozen to the spot, just like before. He paused, tilting his head to one side as if he enjoyed toying with her, then his eyes narrowed, his head straightened and he was moving again, his body lithe, delicate, stalking like a cat as he stepped closer and closer. She watched him come, her body shrinking away from him, her voice shouting at herself in her own head, but she was powerless to move. He was only a few feet away. She wanted to scream, to call for help, for Malachy, for anyone, but when she opened her mouth nothing came out. And then he stopped again and, shifting slightly, he lifted and half turned his head away from her, as if he'd heard someone coming. His eyes left hers only for a split second but it was enough to release her and, stumbling backwards, she turned and ran, back towards the door. She was almost there, the handle almost within reach when she glanced back, checking where he was. He hadn't moved and was calmly watching her. She turned away, bit back a scream. Impossibly, he was there, right in front of her, his back to the door. She skidded, trying to stop, but her momentum carried her forward and, desperate, she threw herself to one side, out of his path. She hit the wall hard, her shoulder crunching. She had barely time to straighten and he was next to her, his body inches from her own, his face pressed close to hers. Terrified, she watched, helpless, as his black eyes examined her face, studying the contours, then his lips parted and he licked at them as he raised his hand to her face. She flinched, thinking he was going to touch her and, seeing it, he smiled, before lowering his hand and slowly, deliberately, tracing the outline of her body, millimetres from her clothes. She shrank away, pressing her body hard into the wall. His hand reached her stomach. She watched his fingers spread, splaying wide, as they hovered over her belly button. Slowly they inched closer, the tips touching her top, flexing, and beginning to press. She gasped, and his smile widened as he pressed harder and harder, pushing his hand into her stomach, making her cry out in pain. Her stomach began to blur and shimmer, just as the window on the bus had done, and she watched in horror as he slid his hand into her. He opened his mouth and from inside his throat came a low, deep sound. For a moment she could feel him, feel his fingers, his nails as they moved inwards, towards the centre of her. Then the pain started and it was excruciating and she screamed and screamed.

For what seemed like forever there was only the pain and then from somewhere very far away she heard a loud bang, like a door being violently thrown off its hinges and across a floor. With a huge effort, Jasmine raised her head, looked past the figure and saw that the room had lightened. Saw Malachy running across the room, followed by a slower Seamus. She blinked and the pain in her stomach lessened: the man was gone.

"Jesus Christ! What was it doing to you?" Malachy, his face pale, was the first to reach her.

He was stood over her and she realised she'd slid down the wall and was half lying, half sitting on the floor. She looked up at him, but she couldn't speak. It had all happened too fast, was too much for her. He knelt down beside her, looking almost as if he wanted to throw his arms around her.

"It's OK Jas, he's gone," he said instead. "You're safe now."

She nodded, her breath coming out in one long gasp. She hadn't known she'd been holding it. And now Seamus was there too, squatting beside Malachy, his face deep in frown as he scrutinised her.

"Are you alright?" he asked quietly looking deep into her eyes.

"I think so." She was surprised how dry her voice sounded, hoarse. "My stomach—" She couldn't finish, just fluttered her hand in its general direction.

Seamus' eyes flashed, their soft brown tone taking on a reddish hue, and the lines across his face tightened. Without a word, he gently lifted her top and began folding it, revealing her midriff.

"Seamus?" Malachy asked uneasily, but a swift look silenced him.

Too busy looking down at what the man had done to her, Jasmine ignored them. Lying at the very centre of her stomach were five small cuts, each one matching perfectly the spread of a finger. The area around them, about the size of a hand, was beginning to darken into the purple and black of a livid bruise. Malachy leaned forward.

"What the hell did that?" he exclaimed, his voice thick with disgust.

"Fingernails," Seamus replied grimly.

He reached out towards her and she flinched.

"Is it sore?"

She nodded. She felt very strange, as if her head was stuffed full with cotton wool, or her ears were filled with water.

"Hold very still."

He lowered his hand and very gently placed it across her stomach. Watching, Malachy's eyes met hers and she felt, sensed something in the air change, shift. Just like after the bus crash when she'd refused to go to the hospital and Seamus had put his hand on her. Her stomach began to tingle; she could feel her skin growing warmer and warmer and then the heat was spreading through her, getting hotter and hotter, radiating out from underneath Seamus' hand. For a moment, it was so hot she thought it was going to burn; then abruptly Seamus stopped and lifted his hand.

"Shit. How did you do that?" Malachy, still leaning in, swore in disbelief.

Jasmine looked down. The cuts had closed, looked as if they were halfway to being healed, and the bruising gone completely. She looked back at Seamus, not believing what she was seeing. He laughed at her, at the expression on her face. A bark that echoed loudly across the hall, then almost immediately he became serious again.

"I think it's time for me to explain a few things. But not here. We'll go to my house. Malachy, she's still in shock; take that arm."

His voice crackled with authority and Malachy obeyed without question, each of them taking one arm and lifting.

Back on her feet Jasmine swayed slightly and Malachy tightened his grip, worried she was going to fall. She smiled to reassure him and allowed them to lead her across the floor to the back of the hall. They had to tread carefully as there were pieces of board and loose nails everywhere; it looked as they'd been ripped apart in a storm. They reached the end window, or what was left of it: a frame with a few jagged ends of wood clinging stubbornly to it, the remnants of the boards that now lay all across the floor. Seamus moved sideways, preparing to lead the three of them through, but Jasmine shook her head at him.

"I'm OK now."

He gave her a doubtful look, "Are you sure?"

She nodded again and he left them then, stepping through the window frame. Jasmine came next, followed by Malachy. And then Seamus was leading them away from the convent, through what had once been an ornamental garden, but was now overgrown and choking with weeds. They squeezed through a gap in the hedge then stepped out onto a dirt track. Seamus' car lay just ahead of them.

"I'll get in the back," Jasmine said, moving towards the back door as Seamus put the key in the lock and turned it.

The car was filthy, the polar opposite of John's immaculately clean upholstery. Climbing in, Jasmine caught the stale scent of dog, and something else even less pleasant, farmery, from cattle, the farmyard, and wondered idly what else Seamus carried in here. Malachy slipped into the front, turned and flashed her a grin, letting her know that the front was better, that in a farmer's car the front was almost always better.

They passed Jasmine's house on their way. It looked quiet, inviting, the lights shining through the curtains, and she wondered if her mum and John had noticed that she wasn't there, or thought she was still in her room, surfing the net. The clock on Seamus' dashboard said four forty-three, less than an hour since she'd left. It seemed like a lifetime ago. The car stopped; they were outside Seamus' house.

"I think we all could do with a drink," Seamus turned off the engine and, opening his door, began to climb awkwardly out.

He led them up the path to his house. A traditional cottage, he'd painted it the traditional way, white and black, with thick stone walls and a low-slung roof. It looked tiny, just enough for one, but as Seamus unlocked the door and ushered them inside, Jasmine realised it was much bigger than it looked.

"Sit down, you two. I'll be back in a minute." He led them into the sitting room, indicating a small sofa placed along one wall.

He disappeared through a door towards the back of the house and, with a look at one another, she and Malachy sat. There was very little furniture in the room, very little decoration. Just a sofa, one deep armchair and a small Formica kitchen table and two chairs under the window. But still the room felt warm, cosy, with a huge iron stove in the alcove opposite them, burning brightly, blasting out heat. The two baskets either side of it were filled to the brim with logs and turf.

"Here you go." Seamus returned with three glasses in one hand and a half-empty bottle of whiskey in the other.

He placed them on the table, poured three generous measures and handed one first to Malachy then to Jasmine.

"I know it's early, but this will help." Grabbing the last glass for himself, he moved over to the armchair and sat down.

Taking a large gulp of his drink, he swished it around his mouth before swallowing then left it on the floor next to him.

"You'll have a lot of questions, but I would ask you to be patient and I will try and explain this to you as simply as I can." Leaning back, he pulled a tin of tobacco out of his pocket and, peeling a paper from its packet, began rolling himself a cigarette.

Jasmine and Malachy looked at one another again.

"You and I, Jasmine, are the same, or rather, have the same."

He'd finished rolling his cigarette and paused long enough to light it. She opened her mouth, but he lifted his hand, anticipating her.

"Wait. Before you ask who it was that attacked you, you should know the reason he attacked you. We have what you would think of as magic, but I call a power. In Irish, it's called Iomlan and in English it means whole, complete, although the meaning is not exactly the same. The druids had it, but it doesn't come from them. It's not related to any one race or creed, or time. As long as there have been humans there has been Iomlan."

He paused again, took a drag of his cigarette and Jasmine felt Malachy beside her shift impatiently. Seamus' eyes flicked in his direction, but he made no comment. After a few moments, he continued.

"It helps to think of Iomlan as a seed inside us. A seed without soil or water, inert, dormant. There are certain places that for us are like soil. I won't go into that now, but if the conditions are right, Iomlan will come alive and begin to grow."

"Like a baby?" Malachy asked quickly.

Seamus shook his head. "It sounds very like it. But an egg is made to grow into a separate, distinct thing. A creature that will live outside the mother or shell. Iomlan doesn't do that; it grows into us, becomes part of us. Like ivy, it remains distinct, but unlike ivy, as we join together we become something more than either of us, something whole. We cannot be separated. Any attempt to do so would kill us both. But in the time before that, in the time before the joining, when Iomlan has started to grow, it can be removed, harvested."

Seamus looked down at his cigarette, saw that it was mostly burnt-out, and reached over to the hearth. He picked up the ashtray lying there and stubbed it out. There was a silence.

"Jasmine has this power, this Iom… Iomlan," Malachy said slowly, eventually. "You said it was like magic, so what does it do?"

"Many things." Seamus waved his hand. "The easiest, the quickest thing we learn is to move things."

Malachy leant forward, his eyes wide. "Or knock things, people, over?"

Seamus laughed. "We try not to, but yes, we can."

Malachy turned to look at her; their eyes met and she knew instantly what he was thinking. It explained everything, and yet it couldn't be. But hadn't she thought the same thing herself?

"And that's what that… that… thing wanted… to harvest Jasmine's power?"

"You've yer mam's quick mind, Malachy," Seamus said drily. "It's a shame you don't use it in school a bit more."

Grinning stupidly, Malachy took a sip of his whiskey. Jasmine looked down at her own, still untouched. Listening to Seamus, she heard everything he said, but it made no sense, as if her mind was like a gear slipping, refusing to connect. All she could think was this wasn't happening, it wasn't real, it couldn't be. But she knew it was.

"That's exactly what he wants," Seamus continued, oblivious. "He can sense her. We can sense one another, but for him an unjoined Iomlan is very strong. He can sense to the changes in Iomlan, when the joining is close."

"So he's the same, he has Io… Iomlan like you two?"

"He was once, but not now. Ellyllon was a druid."

"A druid?!" Malachy asked, incredulous.

The sofa jiggled as he leant forward again, but Jasmine didn't look up.

"Yes." Seamus nodded, his face serious. "All druids followed something called Druid Law. It was like a code dictating how druids should live, use their power. Here in Ireland, the druids were more individual, acting like shamans, healers, moral guides for the clans, the clan leaders, but in Britain they were organised, followed a strict hierarchy. A hierarchy that enforced the law. Ellyllon misused his power, used it for his own ends, and as punishment the hierarchy took it from him."

"But how could they take it from him? I thought you just said that you couldn't be separated?"

"To tell you the truth, Malachy, I don't know, but I believe that the druids had a power, a knowledge that we've lost. It wouldn't be so surprising. For centuries after the druids those suspected of what was called magic were systematically demonised, tortured and killed. Our kind learnt to keep themselves hidden, and apart, even from one another, except, of course, at this time, when there is another who's joining and there is the need for the older to guide the young. To give back. When you know Iomlan better you'll understand how important that is." Reaching down, he grabbed his glass and took an even larger gulp. "Aahh, that's good." He smacked his lips. "But we were talking of Ellyllon. I was told that even the hierarchy didn't foresee what would happen. Maybe he was just too powerful and they failed to take Ellyllon's power completely, leaving the faintest remnant behind. And over the centuries he used that remnant to steal the power of others, and in turn used that to sustain him, to help him live far beyond a human lifespan. But after centuries of feeding, I think anything that was human in him has long gone, that he has become little more than an animal, running on instinct and his urge to stay alive, to feed, to consume."

To feed, to consume. The words echoed around the room, magnified by the sudden silence. Jasmine, feeling cold despite the heat of the room, shivered, using one hand to pull her coat tighter around her. She looked up at Seamus, but he was too deep in his conversation with Malachy.

"If you're saying he was from Britain and Jas said she saw him on the ferry, do you think he must've followed her here?"

Seamus started. "You saw him on the ferry?" he asked Jasmine sharply

"I—" she began, her voice croaking. She tried again, "I… think so."

He frowned but made no comment and began to roll another cigarette.

"He'll go wherever he can feed," he said in between licks of the paper. "His name is Welsh originally."

He held the cigarette in one hand and, reaching into his pocket with the other, brought out a lighter.

"I knew another like us; his name was Patrick. My mentor mentored us both. Patrick's joining was slower than mine. Ellyllon found us before his was complete." He paused, placed the cigarette in his mouth and, giving the lighter a flick, dragged deeply on it. "I was there, but I couldn't stop him, couldn't stop what he did to Patrick. I was young then, inexperienced, but don't underestimate Ellyllon. He may be more animal than man, but he's fast and strong and, according to legend, cannot be killed by our power. If anything, using Iomlan on him risks making him stronger." He turned his cigarette sideways, examining the tip. "No, we were lucky today."

"But I don't understand. Why did he go for Jasmine there?" Malachy said then, placing his hand on his stomach. His eyes widened. "Shit!"

"What?" Roused finally by his tone, Jasmine looked from one to the other, then down to where Malachy's hand was still pressed to his stomach. "Oh my God, it's in my stomach?!" she cried, her voice shrill. "He was trying to rip it out of me!"

"Here, take some whiskey, you've hardly touched it," Seamus replied quickly, lifting half out of his seat. "That's it, that's it... slowly now."

She coughed, the alcohol catching in her throat.

"Take another one. Better?"

The burn was fading, leaving inside, a deep, warm glow. She nodded, her head clearing.

"Good, I didn't mean to scare you." He sat back.

"It's not that, it's just I can still feel him, his hand, *inside* me." She shuddered. "It was horrible, like he was in the centre of me."

A shadow flitted across Seamus face.

"In a way he was, but I checked and you and Iomlan are fine. In time, this memory will fade." His voice hardened. "And you're safe here; he wouldn't dare face me."

"But what about out there?" Malachy interjected, nodding at the window, the darkness outside.

"I have something that will help. It will hurt him to come close. It might stop him for a time, but not forever. Like all animals, eventually his hunger, his desperation to reach you before you join, will overcome his own caution. But we've a ways to go before that. This is a waiting game, keeping you safe until the danger passes. Another thing; don't be on yer own, keep with other people, make his instinct to stay hidden work for you."

He looked at his watch then stubbed out what was left of his cigarette. "You should go, it's getting late and your parents will start to wonder where you are."

Jasmine glanced at her watch. It was half five. *Shit, Rachel's ceremony!*

"I have to go." She stood up.

"Wait a minute, I must get your protection. And there's one more thing. You can't tell anyone."

"What, no one?" Jasmine asked in surprise.

Seamus shook his head. "No one. Can you imagine what would happen if this got out? You can't tell anyone, not even your parents," He flashed Malachy a meaningful look, "You too, Malachy. Now, I'm not saying this will be easy, but you'll need to pretend that everything's normal."

"And what about Iom… this power? I think it's getting stronger, it feels—"

"And harder to control? It will. Which is why I'll be want you back here tomorrow morning, around nine. For your first lesson."

He grinned, his eyes twinkling, as if he enjoyed the look of surprise on their faces. "You too, Malachy, if Jasmine doesn't mind."

Relief flooded through her. "No…it's… great."

"Grand. I'll be back in a minute." Darting into the hall, he turned right and disappeared into the back of the house.

Full of teeth, the grin Malachy flashed at her stretched from one side of his face to the other.

"What are you looking so smug about?" she asked tartly, and then she got it. "OK, you were right," she conceded, rolling her eyes at him. "We should've talked to Seamus."

His grin, if possible, widened. "I was, wasn't I?"

She laughed, and he laughed too and suddenly they were both laughing as if it were the funniest thing they'd ever heard.

"What's so funny?" Stood in the doorway, Seamus was staring at them as if he couldn't believe his eyes.

"Nothing." Jasmine sobered, catching sight of the cloth sachets dangling from each hand. Each had a leather cord fastened to them, fixed in a loop, like a necklace.

"Here, these will help to keep Ellyllon from you." Coming inside, he passed one to Jasmine and the other to Malachy.

"What's in them?" Jasmine looked at hers curiously.

Next to her Malachy took a sniff of his.

"Jesus Christ!" he swore, jerking his nose away and pulling a face. "That'll keep everyone away. Couldn't you make it smell any better? Y'know, make it less obvious?"

Seamus smiled. "It won't smell so bad under your clothes. Don't frown, Malachy, it works best next to your skin." Malachy opened his mouth to speak, but Seamus anticipated him, "And it can't hurt for the both of you to be wearing it. Just in case."

He watched as they put the sachets on over their heads. Jasmine suppressed a cough as she folded hers under her clothes. Malachy was right, it smelt foul.

"Now, I'll see ye at nine tomorrow. And make sure you walk here together."

He led them back to the hallway and out, towards the front door.

"My bike!" Jasmine exclaimed, remembering it suddenly.

"I'll go back and get it for ye, tonight. I don't want you going back there." He opened the front door, stepping aside to allow them out.

"Are you sure?" Jasmine paused, hovering on the doorstep. "But what if he's there?"

"Oh, he won't go bothering me," Seamus replied serenely. "Now, don't forget nine o'clock. Off ye go."

He waited for Malachy to join her and then, without another word, closed the door firmly behind them. They looked at one another.

"Come on." Malachy cocked his head and moved past her and, after a brief, doubtful look at the house, she followed him.

Chapter Thirteen

It was late, gone one, and still Jasmine couldn't sleep. She'd thrown herself into Rachel's award ceremony, desperate to leave Seamus, Iomlan and the thing he called Ellyllon behind her and have things normal again, if only for a few hours. But back home, in the overly bright glow of her bedside lamp, with the grey and black shadows behind it, it was impossible not to think of Ellyllon. To feel his hand as it slipped slowly into the centre of her, to imagine him outside her house, his eyes turned upwards, staring at her window. She turned up her player and closed her eyes, letting the music wash over her, crushing her like a giant wave, and sending Ellyllon crashing.

*

The next morning, Malachy was there, waiting for her inside the garden gate, just as they'd arranged. He looked so normal, stood in the early sunshine, his head turned away, but she knew different. He was watching the hedgerow, the road and fields, knowing Ellyllon was still out there, waiting for her to appear, unseen. But Seamus was waiting too, wanting to help, to guide her. If it hadn't been for him and Malachy, she'd be dead by now. She'd been so lucky to find Seamus; it was amazing, really, but even then, without Malachy… She smiled at the thought and just then, Malachy turned around.

"Hi." Solemn, his forehead frowning, he didn't smile back.

"Hi."

They looked at one another and then Malachy shook himself.

"Are you wearing your, y'know what?" He waved vaguely at his chest and neck, his voice light, casual.

"Yeah, you?"

"Yeah." He nodded. "It still smells terrible."

"Yeah."

They went through the gate and turned right.

"Did you sleep much?"

"Not really."

Walking under the trees, imagining Ellyllon watching them from behind a trunk, his face pressed tight to the rough bark, Jasmine tried very hard not to look, to check.

"Did you use Iomlan?" Malachy was asking.

"No." She shook her head. "I was at Rachel's ceremony. And then, afterwards, I was too scared."

"Maybe that's a good thing."

"Maybe."

She could feel his eyes on her.

"Are you nervous?"

"A bit," she admitted.

"A bit? Is that all?" Malachy exclaimed, incredulous. "And there's me shitting myself."

Jasmine laughed at that, a loud bark of surprise. Then Malachy was laughing too, his eyes sparkling and suddenly, fiercely, she was glad, more than anything, to have him with her, because, like last night, he always made everything seem alright. And in that moment, she felt invincible, as if nothing, not even Ellyllon, could really hurt her.

They reached Seamus' house. Malachy had just put his hand on the gate when Seamus came around the side of the house.

"Come round." He ducked his head and without another word went back the way he came. They followed.

At the back of the house was a huge, wrought iron hay barn. It was the kind used by almost every farmer in the area, but Seamus had had all the sides filled in with breeze blocks and built a doorway, creating a huge, watertight space.

"After ye." He opened the door and stood back.

Jasmine, not quite sure what to expect, went in first, Malachy close behind.

The inside was enormous, the metal ceiling so high it seemed to reach up into the sky. It was empty apart from two old chairs placed slightly apart in the centre of the room, a pile of rusting farm machinery in one corner and two round hay bales covered in plastic in the other. Jasmine and Malachy looked at one another. She wasn't sure what she'd been expecting, but it wasn't this… ordinariness. "Help yerselves to a chair." Seamus closed the door.

With another look at each other, Jasmine and Malachy did as he said. He waited for them to sit then looked down at his feet, appeared to be thinking.

"Now," he said abruptly, lifting his head, "I'm thinking you'll need to understand a little bit more about Iomlan before we start. And the first thing you have to understand is how Iomlan works inside us, how it responds to us."

He began to pace, nodding his head as he talked, ticking off each point. "Iomlan is led by us, and what are we led by? Mostly, it's our feelings. So, if we want to control Iomlan we have to be able to control our feelings, to merge our heads and our hearts, our desire to our will. This sounds simple,, but believe me, it's not. I'll give you an example. Anger. We've all felt the urge to lash out, to hit something, shout or hurt someone when we've been angry. But what if you could do that with a thought? Anger is one of the hardest feelings to control; it's strong, primeval. And it's why Iomlan often shows itself first when we're angry."

It makes sense, Jasmine thought to herself, remembering what happened with Niamh, her mum and John, Malachy and how she'd felt, the fear that she wouldn't be able to stop it.

"How, er, long does the joining take?" she said after a moment.

"It depends. Weeks, months, years even, but mostly it's weeks. But that's no bad thing; it gives the person time to adjust, to learn how to control Iomlan before they gain their full power. For some the joining never ever fully happens and the potential, the power, is lost. With you, Jasmine, the joining seems to be happening much quicker than usual."

"But with this Ellyllon hanging about that's a good thing, surely?" Malachy asked.

"Possibly. Sure, the danger will pass more quickly, but it'll come more quickly too as Ellyllon gets more desperate. And that means we'll have less time to help Jasmine learn to control her power. We'll have to work very fast."

He stopped pacing and looked over at Jasmine. "I won't lie to yer, I'm going to be pushing you and yer going to have to work hard." He smiled. "Are you ready?"

No, part of her wanted to scream at him, to jump to her feet and run and run and keep running until she was back home, in London and among cars and crowds, concrete and shops, where the most she had to worry about was her studies and what topping to have on her pizza.

"I think so," she said instead, taking a breath like a diver preparing to plunge.

"Grand." His smile broadened.

"Now Jasmine, close your eyes. I want you to try and relax." He breathed, his tone deepening and softening. "That's it. Malachy, I want you to stay where you are and keep quiet. And don't speak until I say it's OK, whatever you see. She needs to concentrate."

She could hear Seamus moving in front of her, sense Malachy to her left.

"I want you to think back to the tomb at Carrowkeel."

She started, opened her eyes in surprise. Seamus was looking at her, smiling gently, and she knew that this was some sort of test. She thought back, remembered being inside, getting sick, how everything seemed to start after that…

"It was the tomb! It's one of those places you talked about, that start it off. I wasn't sick at all."

Seamus nodded, his eyes glowing with approval. "No, you weren't. It was just yer body adjusting. Sometimes I think its nature's way of preparing us for what comes next."

His face became serious. "Again. Close your eyes. That's it, keep them closed this time." His voice deepened even further. "Imagine you're in the tomb. You're high on the hill and you can hear the wind howling outside, feel the dampness of the stone beneath you and smell it in the air around you. And yet there is no cold; you feel warm, snug almost, protected from the elements. This is an old place, an ancient place that calls to you through the memories of your ancestors. You feel a tingling in the pit of your stomach, a tingling that stretches and turns and you're spinning, your stomach churning. But then you open your eyes and you see that it's the tomb that is turning and it's spinning wildly out of control."

His voice was almost hypnotic and she became lost in her remembering, remembering how her stomach had lurched and span, turning faster and faster until she was no longer just remembering but feeling it here and now. She put her hands to the ground to stop herself falling, groaning with the effort.

"Jasmine, what are you feeling?"

To her ears Seamus' voice sounded suddenly very close and she could feel him in front of her, his face level with hers.

"I feel… sick," she replied thickly, her throat full of nausea.

"That's good, you're almost there. You're fighting the spinning, resisting Iomlan. That's why you feel sick. The spinning is Iomlan's heartbeat; it has a rhythm and you have to find it, feel it. Each time your stomach spins follow it, push into it, not against it. It's like sawing wood, you have to push into it with your whole body. You feel the rhythm of each stroke. That's it, keep going, you're getting it."

She was. She could feel it, the nausea beginning to lessen and her body becoming lighter, energised. She let go of the ground and a feeling of power surged up through her, lifting her up until she felt like she was floating. She laughed; it was intoxicating.

"That's it, Jasmine! You've got it!" Seamus' voice was full of glee.

Malachy's voice cut across the barn, thin with excitement. "Oh my God, Seamus! How is she doing that?"

Doing what? She asked herself then opened her eyes to look. She was floating up high, at the very top of the barn. Far below Malachy was looking up at her, his eyes wide. She hung there for a moment, suspended, and then her body fell, plummeting towards the ground. She shrieked and Seamus leapt forward, his gaze a study in concentration. A metre from the ground her body jerked heavily and then slowly and gently was lowered back to earth.

Seamus came over to her, breathing heavy. "Are you OK?"

Jasmine felt down her right side, where Seamus had jerked her. "I think so."

She levered herself into a sitting position. "What about you?"

"I'm grand." He was breathing a little easier already. "You were harder to stop than I thought… a little heavier than I was expecting."

Slightly offended, Jasmine opened her mouth to protest but at that moment Malachy touched her shoulder.

"What happened? Are you alright?"

She looked up at him and grinned, feeling slightly dizzy with the movesment of her head.

"Yeah, I'm fine. Did you see what I did?"

"What made you fall?"

"You did. You broke her concentration doing exactly what I asked you not to."

Malachy ran his fingers through his hair. "Shit, sorry. I didn't think."

Seamus sighed. "No harm done. It's my fault; I forgot what it's like the first time you see it."

Jasmine was gazing up at Malachy, still grinning. "Mal, I was floating."

Malachy looked at Seamus.

"It's the energy. She'll get used to it," Seamus said drily. "She has good instincts though, a feel for Iomlan."

"Why did she float? Did she mean to?"

Seamus looked down at her and laughed. "I don't think so, Mal. When you've no focus and you tap into Iomlan it just follows how you're feeling. She was relaxed and peaceful and that's what it meant to her, so she floated."

Once again Jasmine thought of Niamh. "So I could really hurt someone, without meaning to?"

"Of course." Seamus gave her a shrewd look. "Has something happened?"

"Yes. No." She sighed. "I had an argument with a girl at school. It was in the toilet, I didn't mean to but I think I… Iomlan pulled a towel holder off the wall. It almost hit her."

She stole a glance at Malachy. He was staring at her with a strange expression on his face.

"You're going to have to be very careful, Jasmine, until you get the knack. Iomlan gives us power others do not have. Our deepest, darkest urges, our most childish of whims can be made real."

She was looking at him now and his gaze as he looked back was intense, "The best of us, our motives of love, compassion, pity can turn bad in front of our very eyes, so what of hatred, envy, greed, pettiness, hurt? What can these emotions do with Iomlan behind them? Iomlan *is*. It is neither good nor bad; it cannot corrupt you, but if you use it to satisfy your emotions, to feed only yourself, your wishes and whims, you will corrupt yourself. With me, you will begin to understand not just Iomlan but also yerself. Discipline, if you will. When you can have power over others, there's a reason for it."

He looked at her for a few seconds, as if assessing her reaction. "We'll come back to this. More than you'd like, but now it's time to try again. We know you can lift yourself, let's try you with something or someone… else."

He rolled his eyes towards Malachy and grinned. "Malachy, I want you to stand here, in front of Jasmine."

"Shit, me?" Malachy breathed in surprise, but he did as Seamus said.

"That's it Malachy, right there. And this time I want you to stay very still and keep quiet and do exactly as I say." Seamus' mouth twitched. "We don't want Jasmine to drop you."

Malachy's eyes widened but he kept his mouth firmly closed.

"Now, Jasmine, again. Close your eyes and focus on your breathing.

That's it. Nice and slow. Concentrate and remember the feeling."

Once more she did as Seamus told her, following his voice. The spinning returned and then her stomach lurched and the familiar feeling of nausea rose within her. But this time the knowledge that she'd controlled it before gave her confidence and, with Seamus' voice to guide her, she found the rhythm of the spin. There was the same feeling of lightness, of her body becoming energised and the same urge to let go, but Seamus' voice cut across her.

"Jasmine, don't let go, keep hold of it. I know every fibre of you wants to let go, but don't, keep control. That's it, good, you've got it. Can you feel the ground beneath you?"

"Yes," she whispered, working to keep her focus.

"Now, staying with it, I want you to think of Malachy. I want you to imagine him very slowly and very gently lifting off the ground. And you'll want to be bracing yourself; he's a heavy lad from all that farm work."

Jasmine stifled a laugh. She couldn't help it, the way he'd said it, the thought of lifting Malachy off the ground… it sounded so stupid, so ridiculous. Another wave of laughter bubbled up through her and she clamped her lips together tightly, trying to fight the urge.

"Jasmine, focus!" Seamus' voice cracked, sharp, echoing across the barn and killing her laughter instantly.

She was only just in time; the spinning inside was already turning off-kilter, like a top just before it falls away, but her renewed focus righted it. She breathed deeply.

"That's it, now concentrate, see it in your mind, feel it in your guts, your will."

In her mind's eye, she imagined Malachy lifting up into the air until he was poised about four feet from the ground.

"That's really good, Jasmine. Now slowly, and keeping your focus, I want you to open your eyes."

Jasmine did as she was told, seeing Malachy suspended in midair in front of her, his eyes even wider as he looked at the ground.

"Keep your eyes open and slowly lower him back to the ground."

She concentrated, but nothing happened. She tried again and this time Malachy's body began to shake and bob, moving up and down as if caught between two air currents, his face twisting in alarm.

Seamus interjected quickly. "Jasmine, you're losing it. Close your eyes and focus. Bring him down, slowly, slowly, that's it. He's down now. You can open your eyes."

She opened her eyes just as Malachy dashed over to her, his eyes shining.

"Jesus, Jas, that was amazing. I can't believe you did that." Unable to keep still, he hopped from foot to foot, his body jigging. It was as if the energy she'd used had somehow transferred to him. "I was shitting myself when you first lifted me up, but then I got used to it and it was — incredible."

Seamus joined them. "After only two attempts your control is improving. I was right; you do have good instincts."

Jasmine's head was clearing. "But why couldn't I do it with my eyes open?"

"It's easier to concentrate and visualise with your eyes closed, easier to shut out any influences."

He moved back. "Don't worry, it'll come with practice. But it's time you took a break. We've been at it for a while. Go get some lunch and come better later."

"But…" Jasmine began, glancing down at her watch.

It was almost one.

"I didn't realise," she said softly, almost to herself.

"You need a break and we don't want your parents getting suspicious. Let's keep things as normal as we can," Seamus said as he moved over to the barn door and opened it. "Back here by two."

He waited for them to step outside then closed the door behind them without another word.

"He's right," Malachy said as they walked across the yard. "And I am starving."

"How can you even think about…?" Jasmine began then changed her mind. "I'm starving too."

They moved around the side of the house, down the path.

"I'm not surprised you're hungry," Malachy said with a grin and a sideways look at her. "All that energy. No wonder you knocked me off my feet. I didn't know it, but you were like my dad's old boiler… you could've blown at any time."

"Yeah, thanks Mal, likening me to an old boiler."

His grin widened. "I think your ego can take it, oh powerful one."

She laughed at that. Tried to think of a suitable retort but nothing came to mind. They reached the trees.

"So, who was this fight with? The one at school?" he asked suddenly.

"Oh, just one of the girls in my class," she replied casually, not looking at him.

"What did you fight about?"

"I forget. Nothing important," she lied, feeling a blush beginning to spread across both cheeks.

Her house coming closer, but not close enough. She could feel Malachy's eyes on her.

"Oh, so it has nothing to do with Niamh acting weird?"

"I need the loo," she said, saying the first thing that came to mind. "I'll run on. I'll meet you after lunch."

Before he could say anything, she was gone, through her garden gate and up the path.

The afternoon was more of the same.

At Seamus' insistence, over and over. Practice was the only way to improve her control, he said, to get a true feel for Iomlan, the way it worked. But it was hard to stay focussed; the slightest distraction and she lost the rhythm and as the afternoon wore on and she began to tire, the harder it got to concentrate.

"Enough," Seamus decided, checking his watch a little after four. "Go home and rest, watch TV or summat. We'll continue tomorrow."

"Tomorrow?" Jasmine echoed in surprise.

"Jas, it's half-term," Malachy interjected, sitting up and stretching.

"Oh, yeah." She'd forgotten.

"Come back at nine." He waved his hand, dismissing them.

They moved to the door, Malachy pushing it open and stepping through and Jasmine following. She looked back at Seamus, but he was staring up into space as if thinking and then Malachy closed the door, shutting them out.

Chapter Fourteen

Jasmine woke suddenly. Her bedroom was still in darkness and, disorientated, it took her a moment to realise that the phone was ringing, the sound echoing up the stairs. Light flooded the landing and she heard the heavy fast footsteps of someone running awkwardly to get it. It stopped, she heard her mum's voice murmuring and then she was turning over and drifting back off to sleep.

Her alarm clock said eight when she woke again and it was the raining; she could hear the raindrops falling on the roof above her. The house was quiet as she got ready. John, she guessed, had already left for work. Of her mum there was no sign, no sound.

Her mum was sat at the table when Jasmine entered the kitchen.

"Morning, love," she said, looking up from her laptop.

She pressed a button. "There, sent."

"Whatcha doing?"

"Sending an attachment to John so he can print it out for me." She gave her an odd look. "Jas, sit down for me, will you?"

"O-kay." Sitting, she leant forward. "Mum, what's wrong? Is it dad?"

Her mum lowered the lid of the laptop and sighed.

"No, it's not your dad. I had a phone call from your Uncle Alex this morning. It's your Aunt Becky."

"Aunt Becky?!"

"You know the pain she was having the night before the bus accident? She went to the hospital and they checked her out and said everything was fine."

Jasmine's mind whirled; she remembered that morning, her mum talking, saying something about Aunt Becky but she wasn't really listening, and now…

"Becky's fine. She's had the baby, but it was early, far too early."

She paused, her face solemn. Jasmine's stomach dropped, causing Iomlan to churn, but she controlled it with an effort.

"He's on an incubator. He's OK, doing well they say. I know they can do wonders now, but he's so early. There are no guarantees."

She sighed again. "Becky's in bits, but mum can't get there straight away. She has to sort out about Dad, so I said I'd go over until then. Of course, Alex's mother is coming over from Marseilles, but it's natural for Becky to want her own mum there. Or sister."

"When will you go?" Jasmine asked, thinking of the images she'd seen on TV, tiny babies with tubes running into them, encased in clear, rigid plastic, and tried to imagine how he looked; her first and only cousin.

"Today, this afternoon. I've just booked the flight. I'll get a taxi to the airport. But it means I'm leaving you and John." She shifted uncomfortably. "I know things haven't always been easy—"

"Mum," Jasmine interrupted her quickly. "We'll be fine,"

"I know but—"

"We'll be fine. This is more important."

Her mum smiled then, her relief obvious. "You haven't asked."

"What?"

"His name. They've called him Hugo."

"Hugo?" Jasmine scoffed then said the name in her head, with the French accent of his dad. "No, actually I like it: Hugo."

There was another pause.

"I won't have time to get him anything."

"Don't worry; I'll get a little something for him at the airport. Y'know, a teddy in an Ireland t-shirt, something like that. We can buy him something proper if, no, *when* he comes home. Maybe we could go over together?"

Jasmine nodded and her mum gave her an affectionate look. "Y'know you're getting as soft as your old mum."

"Yeah, but still twice as clever," she responded automatically.

She couldn't remember the last time they'd shared that joke. They smiled at one another, and, getting impulsively to her feet, Jasmine slid around the table and gave her mum a huge hug.

After breakfast, Jasmine's mum went upstairs to sort the laundry, leaving Jasmine to finish the clearing up. She was just putting the breakfast bowls away, stacking them neatly in the way her mum liked, when Malachy's head appeared, coming past the kitchen window. Anticipating him, she opened the back door.

"You ready?" He gave her an appraising look.

"I've just got to finish this."

He joined her inside, closing the door behind him.

"I'm not sure I can go this morning."

Malachy's face fell.

"It's just me mum has to fly home – to London. There's a family crisis and I'm thinking maybe I should stay until she goes."

"What about your lesson?"

"Hello, Malachy," her mum said brightly, coming into the room with an armful of laundry. A purple bra, the cups lined with black lace, protruded from the pile. "Jasmine didn't say you were coming round. How's your mum and dad?"

"They're grand." Staring at the bra, Malachy shifted awkwardly.

She dropped the pile at the washing machine.

"Leave that Jas, I take it the two of you are going out?"

"We were, but now—"

"Don't be silly, you two go on." She waved a hand. "I'll see you at lunchtime."

*

As soon as they arrived, Seamus set her to work, going over everything they'd done yesterday, seeing what she'd learned. To her surprise, Iomlan was flowing better now, easier. She was, she realised, getting the knack.

"I think we'll stop there," Seamus said suddenly, looking at his watch. "You've been at it for over an hour. Ya need a break."

"But I'm not tired!"

"That may well be, but I am. I need caffeine." He flashed her a smile. "You're doing well. Better than I'd hoped. Now, who wants coffee and who wants tea?"

He brought iced queen cakes back with the drinks and they ate in silence, each busy with their own thoughts. Sitting sideways from Seamus, Jasmine found herself studying his face. Relaxed, the lines looked even deeper, as if life's hardness, its sorrows and its pains, surfaced when he was at rest. It matched her feeling that, under the softness, his aura of calm, was a toughness, a ruthlessness almost, as if part of him was permanently on guard, waiting for an attack. He finished his cigarette and, dropping it on the floor, ground it with one heel. He was a strange man, she decided, full of contradictions. He had a power and knowledge beyond anything most people could imagine, could do anything, be anything or have anything he wanted, and yet here he was, living quietly in the middle of nowhere, eking out a living with only a handful of cattle and not enough land to bother with a tractor. Of course he had to keep Iomlan hidden, but there were so many good things he could do, lives he could save, if he were careful. She looked down at her mug and realised she'd hardly touched it. She took a drink then made a face. It'd gone cold.

"So, after yesterday, have you any questions for me?" Seamus said suddenly.

She looked up to see him staring at her. How did he do it? Read her mind like that.

"Who are you? Sorry, I mean, you're not just a farmer, are you?"

"Who is anyone?" he answered cryptically. "But I was beginning to wonder when you'd ask."

He settled himself further into the chair. Jasmine glanced over at Malachy and they shared a look.

"It was me mam who gave me my name, after her father. He was a farmer too, from here. But my father was a fisherman from Sligo. They met at a fair in Sligo and some might say it was destiny, but I don't believe such things. Anyway, they saw each other just the once and a week later they were married. She was only young, barely old enough to allow marry, but she was an amazing woman. Went into a house with four men as well as her husband (my grandmother had died the year previous) and lorded it over them. My grandfather was a tough man, to be a fisherman you had to be, but he adored me mam, loved her like his own." His gaze turned inwards. "And so, it was by the sea that I was born and raised. In a place called Aughris Head. It's a small village on the coast. And although there's not much there, just a few small houses and the jetty, it is beautiful. In the warm haze of a summer's evening the Atlantic shimmers silver and the Donegal mountains across the bay turn blue. When I was young I had the need for wildness with the restlessness of the ocean in my blood, but I am well named and as I became older it was towards the earth I yearned. So I came here, to the land of the grandfather I never knew. And here I stayed,"

His eyes flicked back to Jasmine. "You're young, but as you become older you'll begin to see that people are always so much more than any one of us sees. Seamus the farmer is not a pretence. He is me, just not the whole of me. Just as the Jasmine I see before me is not the whole of you." He paused. "I was given a name by my mentor, a nickname if you will, but a name that spoke to him of the joining between me and Iomlan. He called me Madra Rua."

"Madra Rua?" she repeated, surprised.

He smiled. "Yes, he said I had the quick wit of the fox. I think he meant the craftiness, its boldness."

"But the man in Sligo gave me a carving of a fox, he called it Madra—?!" She tailed off; it couldn't be coincidence.

"Michael." He nodded, smiled again. "He's Croi. It's Irish for heart. For that's what he does, he captures the heart of a thing in wood. It's a gift not many of us have. Sometimes with Iomlan, when a person has a particular talent, like carpentry, Iomlan follows it."

"I don't understand."

"Michael is a talented carpenter, so Iomlan magnifies that talent. Don't forget that this is a joining. We, our bodies, are more than a just a host for Iomlan. We give Iomlan as much as it gives us."

Jasmine nodded as if she understood, but she didn't really. She couldn't see what she brought to the joining that could in any way match the power of Iomlan.

"The carving he made holds an image of me and so the carving helps give the protection I would give."

"What?" Her mind span. "But John told him, told him it was my favourite animal. How—?" She tried again, "Does John *know?*"

Of course not!" Seamus snorted. "John mentioned that he was taking you and your mother there to get a present for her and I intervened."

"Intervened?"

He flushed. "Yes. Just a little." He sat up. "Look, I'm not saying this is a good thing. Mostly, I try not to use it. I don't like it." His mouth twisted. "But sometimes it's necessary. Now, with Iomlan it's possible to change a person's mind, to have limited control over what they say and do. It's more of a nudge than a push; we can't actually make someone do something they don't want to. It's called Tionchar, or in English, Influence."

"But, I don't—"

"Seamus, what else can Iomlan do?" Malachy asked suddenly, interrupting her.

"Other than move things? It's hard to say exactly; we've lost so much knowledge through the centuries. We can float, obviously," he said, flashing Jasmine a grin, "propel ourselves in a number of ways. Sense things. Use it like an energy to, er, heat things up."

"Heat things up? Why would you want to do that?"

Seamus gave him a dirty look. "If you got caught out in the rain you could use it to warm and dry yerself."

"To dry yourself?" Malachy laughed. "What, instead of a towel? Or changing your clothes?"

"There must be other things," Jasmine interceded quickly, her lips twitching.

Seamus scowled. "There's a good many things, but they take time and experience to master. But I suppose you could say that what Iomlan can do is limited by what we know how to do or what we can imagine."

"I can imagine walking on water," Jasmine said dreamily.

"Or changing shape," Malachy grinned, joining in. "Y'know become an animal, someone else. What you call them, shape shifters."

"I'd imagine it wouldn't be too difficult to give at least the illusion of walking on water. But as for shape shifting?" Seamus shook his head, looking doubtful. "The druids were meant to be able to shape shift, but I don't believe it. There's no science to it. I think it was Tionchar. When people believed in fairies and the like, it wouldn't take much to convince them of anything."

He paused, gave Jasmine a mischievous look.

"So, you'd like to try something different, would ye?" He cocked his head. "Come outside."

They followed him out and over to the fence leading to his back field.

"You won't be able to do much, but this'll give ya a taster. A glimpse of what is the best part of Iomlan." He grinned suddenly, his eyes sparkling. "At least, I've always thought so. Now, Jasmine, I want you to follow me voice and focus. First, gather Iomlan. That's it." His voice slowed and deepened. "Now, I want to imagine you're an animal searching. All your senses are attuned: your eyes, ears, nose and tongue even. You're a hunter. You feel, sense, everything. Now, go!"

She let fly, and Iomlan streamed across the field. It tipped the grass, tore between the blades, the soft strands of delicate green and caught the scent, the tracks of last night's animals; rat, fox and badger, and the tiny movements of a vole as it scurried back to its hole, its cone-shaped nose twitching. She gasped, but already Iomlan was moving on, swooping upwards, curling around the trunk of Seamus' old horse chestnut, feeling the beat of the Earth as it throbbed its way up through the roots and into the centre of the tree. She felt its life in the centre of her being. It was too much; she lost the rhythm and Iomlan slipped away from her. Reluctantly, she opened her eyes. Seamus was smiling down at her.

"You saw."

She couldn't speak, barely managed a nod. Nothing had prepared her for this. It was as if she'd never really seen the world before. Life had been going on around her in all its brilliance, and she'd been oblivious.

"Don't question it, or try to think too much about it, ye'll drive yerself mad. Just accept it," Seamus told her, placing one hand lightly on her shoulder. "Think of it like Christmas."

She smiled. It was exactly how she felt, all twinkly inside, glowing, like Christmas lights. She glanced across at Malachy, saw the quizzical look on his face and wished more than anything she could show him what she'd seen and felt.

"Maybe one day, you'll be able to use Iomlan to show himself," Seamus murmured softly, reading her mind for the second time that day.

They went back inside.

"Jasmine, let's run through things again," Seamus said, moving the mugs and plates aside. "As I said before, practice is everything; it hones and refines the skill. Let's try and lift that chair."

She focussed and Iomlan flowed. It tore past the chair, slipped effortlessly under the door, and escaped outside. She felt the cold drops of rain, smelt the deep wet of the grass, leaf and bark, and then Iomlan was leading her on, across the field and through the hedge. Something stirred. Dressed in black, its face pale against black, glittering eyes, she knew instantly who it was and tried to pull away. Too late, she felt him, his body, his skin, his dark, endless hunger, and then there was only pain. It drove into her, threatened to rip her in two. She screamed and then Iomlan was falling away and she was going with it.

"Jasmine! Jasmine!"

She opened her eyes, feelings tears wetting her face.

"What happened?!" Seamus peered anxiously down at her.

She shook her head. "I can't."

More tears welled. Reaching down, Seamus pulled her to him and she sobbed into his shoulder. He waited for the worst to pass then held her at arm's length so that he could see her face.

"What happened?"

She swallowed, "It just went. I couldn't stop it. I was outside. I could feel everything, the rain and then—"

"What?"

It burst from her. "It was him, Ellyllon. I felt him, his body, and...
and, there was this pain. It was terrible. I thought I was going to die."

Seamus frowned. "This pain, do you know what is was?"

"I'm not sure." Her eyes widened; she pulled herself away, out of
his arms and upright. "It was him, his pain. I felt his pain." She shook
her head, wondering. "It's worse even than his hunger. It drives him."

"It drives him," Seamus repeated softly. "Like a wounded animal,
full of hunger and pain."

His eyes refocussed. "I think that's enough for today. I'm sorry,
Jasmine, we shouldn't have tried that. It opened you up; it's obviously
too advanced for you."

That stung, although she tried hard not to show it. Seamus got to
his feet, didn't seem to notice. Behind him, Malachy was staring at
her, his face pale with shock.

"Will you be alright? You can come back tomorrow. Iomlan just
needs some time – to settle."

Distracted, he moved over to the mugs and plates and began
stacking them, ready to carry them in. Jasmine scrambled to her feet.

"Bye then." She and Malachy looked at one another.

"Come back tomorrow, in the morning," Seamus repeated, not
looking up.

Not knowing what else to do, she and Malachy left without another
word.

Malachy insisted on walking her all the way to the back door.

"I'll call for you tomorrow," he said as he left, seeming as distracted
as Seamus.

Opening the door, she stepped into the empty kitchen, feeling like
she'd just been in the centre of a violent explosion.

"You're back," her mum called from the hallway, bending over a
small suitcase.

She straightened. "How about some lunch?"

Her mum left about an hour later, promising to be back in a few of
days. She waved her mother's beeping car off then came back inside
to a house that was too quiet. It felt empty, brittle, as if the heart had
been ripped from it. John wouldn't be back for a few hours. She was
on her own. Just what Ellyllon wanted. She shivered, remembering
the feel of him. It had been like stepping into a pool of thick, black,
slime, feeling its slippery cling across her feet, her ankles. Flying to the
back door, she turned the key, locking it. That felt better. Grabbing a
can of Coke out of the fridge, she went upstairs, turned on her music

and her PC and waited for John to come home.

Listening to music, lost in the comfort of it, she didn't hear the car. She only realised he was home when he banged on her bedroom door and poked his head through the gap. She took off her headphones.

"Jas, I'm back. Why did you lock the back door? I had to come through the front. It's lucky I had a key."

"Oh, I forgot. Mum told me to," she lied, hoping he wouldn't check.

"Oh, have you heard from her? Has she arrived?"

"No, not yet."

"Are you hungry?"

"Not really."

"Then you won't want the takeaway I bought, will you? It's curry." His head disappeared.

"Curry?!" Turning off her player, she scrambled after him.

They ate it in the sitting room in front of the TV, Jasmine with her feet curled up under her and her plate balanced in one hand. She dipped a piece of naan bread into her curry, scooped up chicken, onion and sauce and dropped it whole into her mouth. For the first time she could remember, they were coconspirators, eating curry on the new grey sofa while her mum's back was turned, and was mildly surprised to find that she was enjoying herself.

"I'd got the day off work for a dentist appointment on Thursday, but they've cancelled it," John was saying, chomping on a poppadum. "I thought rather than try and change it, I wondered if you'd like to go out for the day? There's a castle near Sligo I thought you might like to see."

She swallowed her mouthful.

"Maybe you could ask Malachy as well?" John continued, talking fast. "It's just a thought, but maybe you have plans—?"

"No, I'd like to. I'll ask Malachy." *And Seamus*, she thought to herself.

"Well, just let me know," he said casually, but he looked pleased. "And we can grab lunch out."

There was a silence. Jasmine put down her plate.

"John—"

It was her turn to be nervous.

"What I said before, erm, I didn't mean it. I was just, er, upset, but I know, I shouldn't've have said it. I'm sorry."

His eyes widened, and then he grinned. "Forget it. I know you were only thinking of your dad." He put down his fork. "You know I never wanted him to leave. I can't say I didn't want any of this, being with your mum, you, having a family. Your mum has always been very special to me, even from the first time I met her. But your dad was my best friend. And in those days, they were so happy. They seemed surrounded by sunshine." He smiled sadly, his eyes glowing with memories. "Or maybe that's just how you remember it." He sighed. "Y'know, despite everything that's happened, all I ever wanted was for us all to be friends. But I guess that was stupid of me, naive. Life doesn't work like that. And loving your mother the way I do, if I'd been your dad I'd probably have done exactly the same thing."

"Do you think he'll ever come back?"

"Of course he will," John smiled. "I don't think he means to hurt you, he just needs some space and time to sort himself out. I think your mum was his rock; she grounded him in life and when she went it hit him more than he'd ever thought. Once he finds his feet again, he'll be back."

"Yeah," she agreed thoughtfully and, feeling better, picked up her plate again.

*

Later that night, under a half-moon hung low in the dark sky, a figure slipped from the dark of the road into the pale light in front of the house. It stopped a few feet from the garden gate and looked upwards, towards the window of Jasmine's bedroom. Her bedroom light could be seen through a slight crack in the pull of the curtains and the figure stared at it intently. The hedgerow rustled suddenly and he turned to look, his head cocked to one side, but all was still and silent. Ellyllon waited for a moment then turned back, towards the window and lifted his hand absentmindedly to his face. He began to caress his lips with it, breathing in the faint smell of Jasmine's skin on his fingertips. Her scent soothed him, pacifying a hunger that was getting harder to ignore.

Chapter Fifteen

Thursday morning, and Jasmine, Malachy and John were on their way to a castle. It was a beautiful autumn day, the sun making the reds, oranges and yellows glow.

"I think Sligo will be the team to watch next year," John was saying, turning through a sharp bend.

"No way," Malachy disagreed. "Cork's too strong."

"Yeah, but they're losing their best players to the Premiership."

Bored, Jasmine turned her head and watched the countryside fly by. It was good to get away, even for a few hours. The last few days with Seamus had been intense, and yet it seemed as if there was still so much she had to learn. There had been no sign of Ellyllon, no sense that he was even close. It didn't make sense. Every day brought her a step closer to the joining and him further away from his prize. What was he up to? The car passed a small wood, and the autumn sun flashed. Sitting low in the sky, its glare magnified by the glass, it hurt her eyes and she closed them against it.

"Jasmine, Jasmine, wake up. We're here." John's voice woke her and she opened her eyes reluctantly, blinking hard. "We're here. You've slept the whole way."

Her mouth was dry; she swallowed, lubricating it with spit.

"I feel terrible," she complained, sitting up. "I can't believe I slept so long."

"You must've been really tired. Up all night online, I suppose," John teased, opening his door and climbing out.

Ignoring that, she opened her own door and climbed out herself. "So, where's the castle?"

It wasn't there; beyond the car park was nothing but trees. Standing in front of a light blue car, Malachy was studying a wooden board with a map on it.

"We drove to the castle, but its closed for renovation so we turned round. You didn't even stir," John explained. "This is Dooney Rock, on the other side of the lake. I thought you might like a walk and the views are pretty good from the top. We could go to Strandhill for some lunch — it's by the sea, there's a promenade and amazing views of Knocknarea and Benbulbin. What do you think?"

"Yeah, it sounds nice."

They joined Malachy.

"I think if we follow that track up there, that will take us to the rock then down there to the lakeshore," he said, tracing the red path then pointing to a track to their left. It disappeared under the trees, rising steeply as it led up the hill in front of them.

"That sounds familiar; let's do that," John nodded, and Malachy led the way.

The track was steep and narrow and they had to walk in single file, but it wasn't far and within a few minutes they'd reached the summit. John was right; the views were stunning and they could see clear across the lake (shining a smooth blue platinum in the sun) to the long, gently undulating heights of Benbulbin.

"I should've brought my camera. Your mum would've loved this," John enthused. "We must bring her. Damn!"

He began searching frantically through his pocket.

"What the matter?"

"I've left my phone in the car. I said I'd keep it with me in case she phoned and sod's law she'll phone the one time I've forgotten it."

He started back the way they'd come, calling over his shoulder. "You two stay here, I won't be long, just a few minutes. Wait for me."

He disappeared and they stared at the view in silence.

"C'mon, he'll catch us up, it's not like we can get lost if we follow the trail. Let's go and look at the lake," Malachy suggested with a grin.

They followed the path, walking side by side as they moved along the top of Dooney Rock and then falling back into single file, Malachy in front, as it began to descend down towards the lake.

"When's your mam coming home?"

"I'm not sure. She rang again last night saying Hugo's doing really well. They're even talking about bringing him home. But it depends on my nan, when she can get there."

"Oh."

The path gave way suddenly, the soil eroded by the wind and rain and leaving a knot of tree roots that was wider and deeper than a comfortable stride. Malachy stepped over it and turned back to

Jasmine, holding out his hand to help her balance.

"Thanks." She took his hand and plumped for a series of small, quick steps through the roots. They continued.

"So, we're going to Strandhill after this. What else is there?"

"Not much," he said over his shoulder. "The strand, a beach, the surf school, the airport."

"An airport? By the beach?"

"It's only small," he glanced back at her. "There's a place you'd love. I went there once, years ago. It's out past the runway I think. It used to be a village called Killaspugbrone, but it got overtaken by sand. There's all these huge sand dunes everywhere. All that's left is a ruined church and churchyard, rising up out of the sand."

"Like a horror movie. I want to see it; it must look so creepy."

"Told you, weird."

The slope eased, the path widening enough to allow them to walk side by side. They reached the bottom and stepped onto a second path. This path went both ways, skirting the edge of the lake and overhung with the branches of the trees that grew both inside and outside the water.

"Left?" Malachy asked with a tilt of his head. She nodded.

They walked in silence for a few minutes and then the trees thinned out completely, revealing the remains of an old stone jetty. To their left was a huge wall of rock, the base of Dooney Rock, the hill they'd stood on earlier.

"Is that the castle?" Jasmine exclaimed, darting towards the lake.

Stood on the far side of the lake, she could just make out the square stone tower.

"Yeah."

"It's smaller than I thought." She gazed at the lake and the hills beyond. "It's almost like an Arthurian legend here. Y'know, the Lady of the Lake, Excalibur."

Malachy grinned suddenly, gave her a soft nudge, "You remember what you said you wanted to do with Iomlan?"

"Walk on water."

He cocked his head. "Shame you can't use it."

"It is," she agreed, her eyes shining.

They grinned at one another.

*

"Malachy, are you sure you don't want to have another go now I've got the hang of it?" She called, trying desperately not to laugh, or smile even.

"No, you're grand. I'm not sure I trust you."

Hopping on one foot as he peeled off his wet sock and placed his foot on the cold ground, he winced loudly.

"I didn't do it on purpose. You should've let me go first."

He ignored that.

"Besides, this was your idea."

"Don't remind me. Any chance you could dry these for me?" Taking off his second sock, he waved them at her. "It's freezing in bare feet."

"I'm not a hundred per cent sure how, but I can try," she offered as she walked carefully up and down.

"Don't bother, you'll probably end up setting them alight!" he grumbled to himself. "I suppose this serves me right for laughing at Seamus."

He slid his feet into his wet trainers and pulled a face. Jasmine, he noticed, had walked even further out.

"Don't go too far out. You'll get very wet if you lose it."

"Yeah, yeah. How do I look?" She flashed a smile at him over her shoulder, her features luminous.

"Feckin' brilliant, Queen of the Lake!" He couldn't help but smile back. He watched her for a moment then wandered off, looking for a sunny spot to dry his socks in.

Jasmine looked back; she'd got carried away and gone out much further than she'd intended. It was hard not to. Iomlan was singing inside her, mirroring and intensifying the elation she was feeling. It was unbelievable… she was actually walking on water. It made her want to dance and sing and shout: *look at me, look at what I'm doing!* It was so much easier than she thought it would be, almost effortless. It needed the minimum of focus. She imagined herself walking clear across the lake and the look on the tourists' faces on the river cruise when they saw her. She giggled. Her right food dipped and freezing cold water submerged her toes. It sobered her; quickly she refocused and her toes lifted. Conscious now of the risks she was running, especially if she was seen, she headed back for the shore. At the water's edge, she concentrated again and the trees around her creaked and groaned as they bent to one side to give her passage. And then her feet touched earth, and she looked up to see Malachy standing with his back to Dooney Rock, watching her. She joined him, feeling the wet on her shoes and the bottom of her jeans. Inside she was still glowing; she couldn't believe how in less than a week, Iomlan was bending to her will, her desire.

"I think that was the best thing ever."

"You've got so good so quickly," he said softly, "Amazingly quickly."

The back of her neck prickled. She looked at him uncertainly, and he seemed to realise, for he smiled, his face relaxing.

"That was a good idea of mine, wasn't it?"

"The best," she agreed, relaxing herself.

"Now, what do I get for such a good idea?"

"I dunno, what would you like?" Jasmine replied archly.

Stepping away from the rock, he circled her. She turned with him, leaving her back to the rock. He leant forward, his neck bent slightly so that she had to lean backwards to look at him.

"Hmmm, I'll have to have a think," he murmured, "What shall I ask of a girl who can walk on water? What would she be willing to give me?"

"Dry socks?" she quipped, her pulse quickening.

Iomlan fluttered inside her, like a bird trapped, mirroring her anticipation. She watched his lips part, felt the sudden stillness in his body and he lowered his face again. His eyes gazed into hers, their darkness eating into the usual blue and then he kissed her and she was kissing him back. She pressed her body to his as his hands stroked her hair, slid across her shoulders, then down her sides to her waist. Pressing back, he pushed his body into hers, pushed her back into the rock. Hard. Too hard.

"Ow!" she exclaimed, breaking off. "That hurt."

"Sorry." His head tilted, the gesture strangely familiar.

He bent in again, let his hand play gently across her stomach as his mouth moved for another kiss, but Iomlan stirred again, and this time it felt wrong, off. She pulled away and, placing one hand on his chest, held him back.

"Mal, what's happening here?"

He smiled a smile that was almost teeth gritted in pain. "I think it's pretty obvious."

Flexing, his fingers began to press.

"I'm not sure — Mal, not so hard."

He ignored her.

"Mal, what are you doing?" He was hurting her.

"Mal, let go of me!" She grabbed at his hand and tried to push it away, but it wouldn't move. He watched her, his dark eyes glittering.

"Malachy, let go of me!" she cried again, this time in real fear, and Iomlan burst upwards through her. "Get off me!"

He was ripped from her, the force of her fear sending him flying across the path to the edge of the lake. To her right she heard running footsteps and her first thought was of John. She turned to look just as Malachy appeared, coming around the corner. Seeing her, he slowed then stopped.

"Jas, I heard you shouting. Is… Shit!" His mouth hung open.

The other Malachy climbed to his feet. They stared at one another and then, in a blink of an eye, the Malachy by the lake disappeared, leaving Ellyllon in his place. Jasmine gave a cry, her hand flying to her mouth as she realised who it was she'd kissed. Ellyllon saw the gesture and smiled, his eyes hard and malicious. And then Malachy, the real Malachy, was moving and in two rapid strides he was beside her, grabbing her arm and pulling her close to him. Ellyllon watched, unconcerned, as he span around and with a wild yell pulled her into a run.

They ran hard, their feet pounding, Malachy half dragging her along with him as she struggled to match his speed. She itched to look back and check how close Ellyllon was, but the ground was uneven with stones and tree roots and it took all her concentration to keep upright. They came to a fork in the path and Jasmine recognised the way they had come earlier. They stopped, breathing heavily.

"Mal, which way should we go?" Jasmine managed between breaths.

"That's the way back." He nodded towards the right fork. "But it's uphill." He looked at her critically. "Straight on'll be longer, but it should take us back. Hopefully."

Jasmine glanced over her shoulder. Ellyllon appeared, coming around the last corner, less than fifty yards away.

"Mal, he's coming!"

"Shit!" he cursed. "Come on."

He went straight ahead, pulling Jasmine after him.

They ran on. Jasmine's legs were starting to thicken, but fear kept her going. Up ahead they could see the path narrowing and Malachy pushed her in front of him, keeping her in sight. It was darker here; the trees had grown closer together, letting in less sun, and twice Jasmine slipped through wet mud and almost fell. The path veered again to the left, taking them very close to the water's edge, and suddenly it fell away all together into the boggy ground of an inlet. She tried to stop, but her momentum carried her forward and she had just enough time to shout a warning to Malachy before she jumped. Covering the gap, she hit the ground and skidded before toppling straight into the side of a tree. Behind her, Malachy shouted.

"Mal, are you alright?" Scrambling up, she went back to where he was struggling to get to his feet.

"I think I've hurt my ankle." His face, like hers, was bathed in sweat. "Help me up."

She grabbed his arm and he used her to lever himself up. Upright, he let her go and gingerly placed his foot on the ground, testing his weight. He grimaced in pain.

"It's not broken, but I don't think I'm going to get very far on it. You go on, get back to the car."

She shook her head. "I'm not leaving you. Besides, how the hell do I get out of here?"

He followed her gaze. The land beyond the tree had been reclaimed by the lake long ago and the only other possible exit was a steep bank to the right. Rising above their heads and topped by a barbed wire fence, it was too high to climb. Seamus' face flashed through her mind and she wanted suddenly, desperately, for him to be there. Something cracked behind them. They whirled and Ellyllon appeared, coming around the corner. He stopped when he saw them, taking in their situation in one swift look, and then slowly, his eyes gleaming, moved towards them.

Chapter Sixteen

They watched, frozen to the spot, as he crept towards them. Malachy's neck swivelled; he gazed at the bank as if seeing it for the first time.

"Shit, Jas," he swore, tugging her arm and making her jump. "Use Iomlan! To lift us up the bank."

"Oh, my God!" She couldn't believe she'd forgotten it. "Take my hand," she told him quickly, closing her eyes.

She dug deep within herself, trying to ignore the pounding of her heart in her ears, but it was like trying to find calm in a maelstrom. She couldn't focus. Malachy shouted and she knew Ellyllon had reached them and her stomach turned to ice. She opened her eyes. Ellyllon was stood at the very edge of the path, towering over them. With agonising slowness, he lowered first one foot and then the other, joining them on the boggy ground below.

"Jas," Malachy whispered, and without hesitation pushed her behind him.

That did it. Closing her eyes, she forced herself to focus, cutting ruthlessly through her fear to where Iomlan waited. It surged too late; Malachy was pulled from her. She heard him yell and opened her eyes as the rhythm tumbled away. She gasped. Malachy was stood about a foot in front of her, his body rigid, stretched taut as if he was straining on tiptoes. A high-pitched scream sounded, setting her whole body on edge, and it took a moment for her to realise that it was Malachy screaming in pain. Just above his waist, the left side of his back began to shimmer and very slowly five small black marks appeared. Five more appeared opposite. As she watched they grew, becoming more distinct, and with horror she realised that they were fingernails. Fingernails that were growing, lengthening into fingers and then white, bony hands, wrists. It was Ellyllon, reaching for her through Malachy, pushing into him, ripping his skin and tearing through flesh and bone as if he was nothing.

"Get out!" she shouted, her whole body vibrating with disgust at what was being done to him. "Get out of him, you bastard!"

Iomlan erupted from her, its fury wrenching Ellyllon from Malachy in an instant and leaving his body to drop like a stone. Without thinking, she leapt over him, facing Ellyllon as he swung around towards her. Iomlan surged again, catching Ellyllon across the chest and throwing him back almost twenty feet. In a flash he was up, his faced twisted, his body uninjured. She hit him again, lifting him high into the air and sending him crashing into a tree further up the path. She followed, waited for him to stagger to his feet, then hit him again. His body caught a rotten branch, shattering the wood and showering him with splinters. He cried out, the sound like an animal in pain, but it only fuelled her anger. Remorseless, she threw him again, sending him spinning over and over. Iomlan coursing through her, mingled with the satisfaction she felt every time his body hit wood, darkening it like a stain. She forgot Malachy, forgot his body, lying still and crumpled, far behind her.

Ellyllon staggered to his feet. He looked unhurt, but exhausted, beaten, and she knew it was time to finish it. A low branch on the oak tree behind him had broken off, leaving behind a raw, jagged stump. She studied it for a moment, and then, slowly lifting him up, held him, dangling, helpless, inches from the ground. Ellyllon followed her gaze and then his white neck swivelled and his dark eyes bored into hers, as if daring her to do it. She smiled and, gathering herself, let Iomlan go. Ellyllon's body jerked, caught by the impetus, like a wave, and then hurtled towards the tree, the stump trained on his chest. He twisted, turning sideways, impaling his shoulder instead of his chest. She heard the sound, the suck as flesh gave way to wood. He hung there for a moment, his shoulder taking his weight, his legs bent under him. Then he found his feet and slowly inched forward, dragging his shoulder off the stump. She watched him dispassionately, noticing there was no blood, no torn flesh or skin hanging loose. It didn't make sense, but it hardly seemed to matter. Too strong, the power running through her drove out all other thoughts.

"Have you had enough yet?" she asked him.

He studied her, his head cocked to one side as if she'd surprised him, and then in a blink of an eye he was gone. Stunned, Jasmine stared at the space he'd left, not quite believing it. She glanced up and down the trail, half expecting him to reappear, but the path was empty. He'd gone. She'd beaten him. Iomlan was still singing inside her with an elation that made her head swim. For a moment, she felt more alive than she ever had, as if she'd become truly herself, whole, complete, and then she remembered Malachy.

She flew, running as hard as she could, fear cold and hard in the pit of the stomach. She didn't notice the uneven ground, the stones and bits of branches that caught at her feet, or the breath that whistled through her chest, her cramping lungs. Malachy was lying where she left him, unmoving. She scrambled over to him and, with shaking hands, she rolled him over. He was breathing, but his face was deathly pale. She pulled at his jumper and t-shirt, lifting them up to take a look at his torso.

"Jesus!"

Mottled red, purple and black, Ellyllon's work was imprinted on his skin. Very gently, carefully, she reached out and traced the area with her fingers. There were no cuts where Ellyllon had clawed his way into him. The skin wasn't even broken. It was just very badly bruised. She shook her head. *How was that possible?* She pushed the thought away. It was useless; what mattered was healing it. *But how?* She touched it again, lightly with her fingertips. If only Seamus was here, he'd know what to do. But he wasn't. She took a deep breath and reached a decision. Scrambling to her feet, she gathered Iomlan and slowly, carefully, lifted Malachy into the air. Bringing him with her, she clambered back onto the path, and then, frowning with concentration, retraced her steps. But for the sound of a breeze, the gentle rustle of leaves on the trees, the forest was silent. She walked slowly, afraid that she'd lose concentration and Malachy would fall. Voices murmured, coming from up ahead, and she froze. Immediately Malachy dipped and, quickly refocussing, she lowered him to the ground. Kneeling beside him, she lifted her arms to protect him as the figures of two men came around the corner.

It was John and, to her amazement, Seamus. They stopped in mid-stride, staring at her, and then John rushed over to her. She just had time to get to her feet when he was grabbing her, holding her in a fierce hug. For a moment, she let herself be held and then she thought again of Malachy and began to pull away. He let her go, but not completely, his hands sliding down to her wrists, holding her at arm's length so that he could examine her face.

"Jasmine, what happened? I've been calling your phone, looking for you for ages."

He caught sight of Malachy's body on the ground, "What the hell happened?"

"We were mucking about and he fell. He landed on his front. I think his chest and ankle are hurt, but I can't wake him." She looked away, ashamed of her lies, the way they tumbled out so easily.

"Did he hit his head?"

"No."

Seamus was bent over Malachy, checking his torso and legs with swift, gentle hands.

"Are you sure? It's important, Jas?!"

"I'm certain."

He let her go and looked at Seamus. "How is he?"

"Give me a minute," Seamus replied, twisting sideways and obstructing their view.

There was a small surge and Jasmine felt the air around her warm slightly.

He stood up. "He'll be grand in a while. Best get him home, though."

John moved to Malachy's side, Jasmine close behind.

"We should try and wake him," he said, kneeling.

"No," Seamus shook his head. "It's better to leave him be. He needs rest."

Malachy eyes flickered; for a moment she thought he was going to wake, but they closed again. She glanced at Seamus but he pressed a finger to his lips.

"I'll call for an ambulance." John took out his phone. "He should go to hospital."

"No need," Seamus countered. "It'll be quicker to take him."

John frowned. "But if we have to carry him back, we could do more harm than good, especially if that ankle's broken!"

"I'll put money on it just being a sprain. The main thing he needs is rest, but you're right, we should get it checked."

John got to his feet and the two of them stared at one another.

"John," Seamus said softly. "We should go."

There was a pause, and then John put his phone back in pocket.

"OK, we'll try it your way. I'll go under his left shoulder and you take the right."

Lifting him carefully by the arms, they turned and slipped in under his shoulders.

"Right." John looked at Jasmine. "You go first. Just follow the path; it'll take us all the way back to the car park."

She led them back. She knew she had to trust Seamus, that he, out of everyone, would know the harm Ellyllon had done. But what if he'd got it wrong or missed something and Malachy was seriously hurt? But John trusted him, she reminded herself, he must do to listen to him the way he did. It didn't really help. How could it, when John had no idea what was happening? The path widened, the gap in the trees all too familiar. They'd reached Dooney Rock. There was the jetty, where she'd walked on water, and the patch of the rock where she'd flirted with Ellyllon, let him stroke her hair, responded to his kiss. Feeling sick, she looked away.

"It's not far," John grunted.

They skirted around the rock, turned a corner.

"Oh, no," Jasmine groaned, seeing the car park.

If only they'd run the other way! It was so close. And there were people here, milling about, chatting, preparing for their walk. They stared at them as they made their way to John's car. Two women bent their heads together, muttering.

"Jasmine, you get in the back with Malachy and mind him," Seamus ordered as he and John laid Malachy across the back seat.

"Seamus, have you got Malachy's dad's number? I feel I should be the one to phone him, given that Malachy was out with us."

Seamus found the number as Jasmine climbed inside. "Here."

John dialled as he read it out and then walked off, waiting for the phone to answer.

"What happened?" Seamus asked as John began to talk.

"It was Ellyllon. Malachy stood in front of me, protected me, and Ellyllon just pushed his way through him. His hands—" Her voice choked. "They were out Mal's back!"

"He's a brave lad. And don't worry, he'll be fine. It's shock mostly, he'll be grand when he wakes."

"But he went through him, how can that be fine?"

"Because it is." He glanced quickly at her. "Ellyllon doesn't need to disturb the flesh; he can move through it."

"But, but, what about me? I had cuts."

Seamus sighed. "I think because he was too eager, he was careless. This is my fault. I shouldn't've let you come. I should've known this was too risky. Look." He nudged her. "John's finished. We'll talk later." He raised his voice, "Did you get through to him?"

"Yeah, he's on his way to the hospital, will meet us there. Let's get going."

Tucking herself in further around Malachy, Jasmine moved his head. His eyes flicked open.

"Mal, Mal, it's me, Jasmine. Are you OK?"

His eyes focussed on her briefly; he murmured something she didn't catch and then closed them again.

"He woke up!"

"He did," John agreed. "Thank God. Let's go."

*

John drove straight to the A & E entrance.

"Wait there," Seamus said, jumping out.

He was back in a few minutes with an orderly and a wheelchair. Lifting Malachy gently into it, they disappeared, leaving John and Jasmine to go park the car. Desperate to get back, with John following, she ran through the car parks and up the steep steps around the side of the hospital.

A & E was quiet, with just a few people sitting dotted amongst the rows of chairs.

"Wait here," he said, leading her to a pair of empty seats near the back.

"But I want to see him!"

"I need to see what's happening first. None of us might be able to see him."

She didn't move, so he tried again. "Please Jas, just sit down. I'll go and ask what's happening and I promise I'll come straight back."

"OK," she relented, sitting.

"Thanks, I'll be back in a minute." Flashing her a smile, he walked over to the reception desk and began talking to the woman behind the counter.

Exhausted suddenly, Jasmine rested her face on her hand and closed her eyes. Immediately, she was back at the lake, Malachy in front of her, Ellyllon's hands pushing through his back, while he screamed over and over. She opened her eyes with a start and, lifting her head, rubbed at them. John was still talking, so she looked out of the window instead, trying to get the image of Malachy out of her mind. Iomlan moved restlessly inside her, matching her agitation. She thought of Ellyllon, what she'd done to him, and hoped he was lying in a ditch somewhere, driven half-mad with pain.

"Jas."

It was John, his hand on her shoulder as he slipped into chair next to her. She sat up.

"How is he?"

"I don't know." He rubbed his face. "Luckily it's quiet, so the doctor's in with him now. They've told us to wait."

"OK." She didn't know what else to say.

He took her hand and gave it a squeeze.

Twenty minutes later, Seamus appeared through a side door.

"How is he?" John asked quickly, getting to his feet.

"He's fine," Seamus said reassuringly. "He's awake and talking and just waiting for his x-ray —ahh, here's Martin and Pauline. I'd better go."

He went over to them. Jasmine watched him hug Malachy's mum and then he was talking to them, explaining, she guessed, what happened. Malachy's dad gave them a brief look, dismissing them, and then Seamus was leading them through the door to Malachy.

"I think we'd best go. There's nothing more we can do," Seamus said as he rejoined them.

John nodded and the three of them walked in silence back to the car.

*

Jasmine stared out of the window. In the front, John and Seamus talked quietly together. Twin wind turbines turned lazily in the distance. They were almost home.

"Who's that?" John asked as he pulled up towards the house.

A strange car, new and immaculately clean, was parked in front of the house.

"Looks like a hired car," Seamus remarked, craning his head to look.

John turned into the driveway and the three of them got out.

"Well, I best be going," Seamus said, and without waiting for an answer darted off.

"We'd better go and see who and where our visitor is."

They walked around the side of the house to the back, but the garden was empty. Jasmine looked in through the kitchen window; it was empty too. They stood together at the back door.

"I dunno where they are," John frowned. "Maybe they're not for us, they're just using the space to park. Let's get inside."

Lifting out his key, he placed it in the lock and tried to turn it.

"It's not locked."

A shadow moved across the kitchen window.

"John!" she hissed, grabbing his arm. Inside her Iomlan swirled. Stiffening, she stifled it with an effort.

"Right." Giving her a grim look, he pressed down hard on the handle and flung the door open.

"Kate!"

The next moment he was through the door and into her mother's arms.

"Mum!" Open mouthed, she watched them kiss. "You're back so soon. Why didn't you call?"

"Mum arrived, finally, and with Alex's mum there was too many of us; we were tripping over ourselves and I wanted to surprise you both, but I got an even bigger surprise at the airport."

Something moved inside. Looking over her mum's shoulder, John started and pulled away.

"Shit!"

"There's someone here to see you." Her mum smiled as she stepped to one side, pulling a frozen John with her.

Jasmine's heart thumped. A hand appeared, a hip and shoulder and finally, the face. He grinned at her, as if he'd never been away, his smile, white in a deeply tanned face, as dazzling as ever.

"Hello Jas. How about a hug for your old dad?"

Chapter Seventeen

Jasmine stared at her father. She opened her mouth to speak, but nothing came out. A scar ran across his left forehead, disappearing above his left ear. His face looked thinner, older, the lines around his eyes deeper, more pronounced. His hair was longer and streaked with small touches of grey. Her breath caught, and to her horror, she burst into tears. He was to her in an instant, his arms around her, holding her tight.

"Dad." It slipped from her, mingled with spit, as she sobbed into his shoulder.

The sobs eased and they broke apart. Jasmine wiped her eyes and face with her hand, feeling Iomlan churn. She pushed it down, stamped on it, not wanting it to ruin the moment.

"I can't believe how much you've grown since I last saw you," her dad was saying, his eyes wide. "It's been so long. You're almost a woman."

"Oh, Dad!" She paused, embarrassed. "You've got older too."

"It happens." He touched his hair. "Going grey makes me look distinguished, don't you think? The ladies love it." He grinned roguishly.

"Dad!" She paused. "Where have you been? Why didn't you call?"

His face became serious. "I was in an accident in Canada. In the north - no, it's OK," He touched his scar, ran two fingers along its length. "I was in a coma for a while, but I'm fine now. They fixed me up."

"But why didn't they let us know? I'd have come over."

"You'll never believe this, but I didn't have any ID on me. I'd been mugged the day before and hadn't had chance to get it sorted."

"But surely there was some way they could have found out who you were?"

"I'd been travelling around." He waved one hand airily, "By bus, using cash, so there was no way they could know."

"But you had a phone, surely, everyone has—"

"That was stolen too." His voice rose.

"But we'd tried to find you, Grandad spoke to the police, how could—"

"It happens, OK?! Now, please, Jas, will you leave it!"

There was a silence. Hurt, Jasmine stared at the ground.

"I'm sorry." He sighed. "I didn't mean to shout. They did everything they could, honestly, they did. It was my fault, there were things… look, sorry, but I don't like to think about that time. Can we leave it there?"

She didn't answer. Her mum stepped forward.

"Justin, we talked about this, remember? On the way from the airport. You have to realise it's confusing for us. We had no idea what had happened, you just disappeared, and there's been nothing, no sign of you, for over a year. As far as Jasmine knew she was never going to see you again."

"You're right, I'm sorry." He rubbed irritably at his scar. "I'm sorry darling, I didn't mean to sound cross. This is hard, but sometimes, I… I can't always control it… the doctors warned me there would be some long-term effects. You'll have to bear with me; being in a coma for so long, it changes you. But I can't bear to think of you not knowing what had happened and thinking I'd just abandoned you." Impulsively, he held out his hand. "It was the thought of seeing my beautiful daughter again that kept me going."

"Dad." Taking his hand, she looked up.

"Thank you," he mouthed, giving it a squeeze.

"I just wish I'd been there."

"We're here now, together."

They smiled at one another.

"Why don't we go inside?" Jasmine's mum said suddenly. "I'll put the kettle on. I think we could all to with a drink."

"I'll do it," John offered before disappearing inside.

"You've got him well-trained!" Jasmine's dad laughed, trying to lighten the mood.

"I wish," her mum replied lightly but her eyes flashed. "But I can't take credit for the fact that he doesn't see pulling his weight around the house as a challenge to his manhood."

"Ouch. I think that was aimed at me."

"I think it was," Jasmine couldn't help but grin.

"And totally deserved." He lowered his head contritely, but the eyes he slid towards Jasmine were bright with mischief.

She couldn't stop herself, the loud bark of laughter, as they followed her mum into the kitchen.

Jasmine and her dad sat as her mum readied the table and John made the tea. She still had so many questions, but she had to be careful. There were things he obviously didn't want her to know, or maybe he just didn't want to remember.

"Why didn't you call to let us know you were coming?" That seemed safer.

"I wanted to surprise you."

"How did you know where we were?"

"That was easy. I went to your Nan's as soon as I got to London."

"How long are you here for?"

"I'm not sure, I hadn't thought that far ahead." John passed him his cup of tea. "Thanks John, I needed that,"

John looked at him for a moment, as if surprised by his tone, then smiled back awkwardly.

"Are you hungry, can I get you something?"

"No thanks." Jasmine's dad shook his head. "I don't seem to have the same appetite as I used to."

"Where are you staying?"

"I'm in a hotel, it's not far. At least I don't think it is. I booked it online before I came." He took a sip.

"If you want to stay here, we've plenty of room," John offered. Next to him, Jasmine's mum started, but he ignored her. "It's no trouble."

"No, it's better I stay at the hotel. I still get pretty tired, and the doctors told me not to push it and make sure I rest when I need to."

John drained his cup. "Excuse me, Justin, but I need to chop wood for the fire. The nights get pretty cold here. Maybe see you later?"

"Yeah." Her dad nodded vigorously. "Thanks again for the tea."

He left, closing the back door firmly behind him.

"And while John's doing that, I'd better go unpack."

"OK, Kate, I'll see you later."

They waited for her to leave.

"So, it's just you and me." Her dad grinned. "Not very subtle, are they?"

*

It was getting dark, late afternoon turning towards evening. Jasmine checked the kitchen clock; five thirty. They'd talked for over an hour. Aside from passing through the kitchen, her mum and John had left them to it.

"So, tell me more about these new friends of yours."

"The girls? They're great." She shrugged, not quite sure what to say.

Her dad rubbed his forehead, near his scar, and looked suddenly old, his face lined and grey.

"And what about boys? Anyone special?"

Flushing, she looked away. "Of course not."

There was a pause. She looked back. One hand cupped his face, shading his eyes.

"Dad, are you alright?!"

"Huh?" He lowered his hand.

His eyes were blank and empty.

"Dad!"

"What, what?" His eyes focussed. "I'm sorry, Jas." He ran his fingers through his hair. "I disappeared, didn't I? That means I should rest. I'd better go."

"Oh, OK. Are you sure you're OK to drive?"

He nodded. "Yeah, it's not far."

Pushing the chair back, he stood up. "But you could walk me out, if you want."

They walked in silence around the house. The front door opened as they came around and Jasmine's mum poked her head out.

"You off?"

Her dad nodded. "I need to rest."

"You look shattered. Will you be OK to drive? You can lie down upstairs if you need to."

"No, I'm fine. But I'll come back tomorrow, if that's OK."

"Of course it is. You're welcome any time."

"Thanks. I won't be here very early. I have sleeping tablets… otherwise I'm awake all night then asleep all day."

"Well, take care, won't you?" Her mum's head withdrew and the door closed.

"Are you really OK to drive?" Jasmine repeated as they stopped next to the car.

"I'll be fine. All I need is a good rest." He gave her a knowing look. "I'll call you after I've had a sleep. I don't want you worrying."

They hugged. Jasmine shut her eyes, feeling tears close. Again, Iomlan churned, and for a moment she wished she'd never heard of it. That she was just a normal girl happy at having her dad back.

"Right, I'd better go." He broke away first and, unlocking the car, climbed inside. "I'll call you later."

"OK," she agreed, sniffing.

Holding herself, she watched as he pulled away, tooting. She waved until he was out of sight, and then, wiping her eyes with her sleeve, she walked slowly back inside.

Her mum and John were in the kitchen; they stopped talking when she opened the door and turned to look at her, their faces serious.

"Are you OK?" her mum asked softly.

"Yeah," she sighed as she came inside, turning to close the door behind her.

"Don't close it. I'm going out — leave you both to it." Jumping forward, John took the door from her.

"John, thank you. For, er, y'know, me dad."

Lifting up, she kissed him lightly on the cheek.

"No bother." Grinning foolishly, he darted outside, quickly closing the door after him.

"You know, for some reason, he really does care." Her mum grinned, her eyes soft.

"I can't believe I was so horrible to him."

"It was a difficult time, for all of us. And with hindsight I think we all would've done things very differently." Her mum paused. "And while we're talking about things, about your dad, we need to talk. Come and sit down."

They sat, and Jasmine waited, her heart in her mouth, for her mum to continue.

"You know what your dad said about the long-term effects of his accident?" Unable to speak, Jasmine nodded. "What he didn't say, what he couldn't explain, was exactly how bad the accident was. It took months of work, of rehabilitation, to get him to where he is now."

"But he's better, isn't he? I mean, I know he gets tired, but he looks—"

"Jas, this isn't easy, but you have to know if you're going to understand how... to be. Your dad has what's called an acquired brain injury. Do you know what that is?"

"I suppose it's when the brain gets injured, hurt."

"That's exactly it. And sometimes, when the brain gets hurt, there is some lasting damage. Now, with your dad, most of the time you won't even notice, and the people he meets won't realise, but there'll always be things he finds hard to do. He can do them, but it takes him a bit longer than everyone else: he has to concentrate and that concentration wears him out. But it's not just doing things, it's understanding things. Maybe someone will tell him something and he won't really get it. It's like he can't make the connections that you or I might make, if you see what I mean?"

Jasmine nodded, thinking she understood. But they were just words, the description of a condition suffered by a stranger. They had nothing to do with her dad.

"There's something else. This is the hardest thing and your dad is going to need all our love and support. You know that our brains make up who we are, our personalities, and sometimes, when the brain's damaged, the person's personality changes." She sighed. "I don't want to worry you, but there might be times when your dad says or does things that aren't him at all. And I want you to know that it's nothing to do with you, that if he gets cross or frustrated, he's not cross or upset with you. Or when he doesn't remember something from the past, about your childhood, it's not because he doesn't care. He doesn't mean it." Her mum touched her arm. "Jas, are you OK?"

"I don't know." She shook her head. "But he's still the same person. We were talking, and he was fine."

"You're right, he is the same person, and he's still your dad. It's just – every so often, you'll notice things, small things, but it doesn't change who he is. After a while you'll get used them and you probably won't even notice."

"But why, why didn't he tell me himself?"

Her mum sighed again, retracted her hand. "He couldn't bear to. I think he was worried about how you'd react. You saw how he reacted when you said the authorities in Canada should've contacted us. Well, the doctors knew who he was as soon as he woke. He was in a coma for three weeks, but after that, he didn't want anyone to know."

"But why?" Jasmine asked, appalled.

"I don't know. Maybe, if we all knew, it would become real. Maybe it was too much for your dad to face. Maybe he hoped he'd get better and we'd never know what had happened. But he's still your dad and he loves you very much, more than anything. He just needs us to understand, to accept him as he is, and maybe he'll start to accept it himself."

"Is that why John offered—?"

"No, he didn't know, then. I just don't think he's ever forgiven himself for what happened with your dad, the way he left and what that did to you. We were just so tied up in ourselves, and looking back I was just so angry with your dad. With the way he reacted, his holier than thou attitude after the way he'd behaved all those years. We've never actually talked about it, but you know, don't you, about the other women?"

Jasmine made a face. "I guess. I always knew he flirted, but then, one night, I heard you arguing."

Her mum tutted. "Oh, bloody hell! I'm so sorry, you should've had to find out like that. You always think you're doing the right thing, telling yourself that you're putting your kids first, but you're kidding yourself." She shook her head. "But this changes everything. Whatever happens, we pull together, all of us. For you as well as your dad. Agreed?"

"Agreed." Her voice broke, and wrapping her arms around her, her mum held her tight.

Just as he promised, her dad texted her later that night and straight away she copied his number into her phone. She thought of Malachy, of how easily Seamus had healed the bruises Ellyllon had given him and her own cuts, and wondered how easy it was to repair an injury to the brain.

Chapter Eighteen

The next morning, Jasmine left early to go and see Seamus, wanting to be back before her dad arrived. Deep in thought, she wandered along the road, careless of Ellyllon. After yesterday, she guessed she'd seen the last of him. He'd hardly be stupid enough to try again after she'd beaten him into submission, and even if he was, she'd simply do the same thing to him again. She smiled to herself, imaging the look on Seamus' face when she told him what she'd done. The amazement and, maybe, a little bit of pride at the prowess of his pupil. After that she'd go and check on Malachy, and then she'd be free to focus on her dad. For if there was no danger from Ellyllon, there was surely no need to rush her lessons with Seamus? Except, of course, there was one thing she really needed him to teach her.

Seamus was stood in his doorway. With an almost finished cigarette in one hand, it looked as if he'd been there a while, waiting for her.

"Morning, Jasmine."

Straightening up, he tossed it away as she came up the garden path then ushered her inside.

"I texted Malachy but he hasn't replied. Is he OK?" she asked immediately.

He nodded. "He's fine. I spoke to his dad earlier. It wasn't even a sprain, just a twist. The hospital told him to rest it, but it's not so bad."

"So he's really OK?"

"Of course. It was mostly shock, and sleep and rest is the best thing for it." He waved her towards the sofa then sat in his usual chair by the stove. "So, your father's here; that was his car yesterday."

"Yeah, I can't believe it." She frowned, wondering how he knew.

"I was passing your house earlier and John told me."

"Oh." He was reading her mind, again.

She rubbed at the knee of her jeans. What else had John told him?

"Seamus?"

"Yes?"

"You healed me and Malachy. But they were small things. Can Iomlan heal worse things? I mean, bigger injuries, like a broken bone, or a damaged organ?" She paused, made as if she were scrambling around for examples, plucking ideas from the air. "Like the heart, or the brain, maybe?"

Seamus sighed. "John told me about yer father's injury."

"Oh." She tried to look repentant, but gave up almost immediately. "But can we?"

"Heal the brain?" He shook his head. "To be honest I've no idea. I've never had the need to try and, not knowing what you're doing, you'd likely just make everything worse," He smiled sadly at her. "But I think if a doctor or surgeon couldn't do it then neither could Iomlan. I'm sorry, Jasmine. I know it's not what you wanted to hear."

There was a pause. Jasmine stared at the floor. Seamus might be right, but she wasn't ready to give up just yet. If she couldn't do the really important stuff with her power, like heal her dad, what was the point of it?

"Now, I need you tell me properly what happened at the lake," Seamus said softly. "And leave nothing out."

She did as he asked. Pictured it in her mind's eye so that she caught all the detail. Occasionally, Seamus asked a question, but mostly he was silent. Only the tilt of his head showed he was listening. When she'd finished, he stood up without a word and began to pace around the room, rolling another cigarette as he went. She watched him nervously. This wasn't the reaction she'd been expecting. She'd never seen him so agitated, not even that first day, when he'd rescued her from Ellyllon. Lighting his cigarette, Seamus took one, long drag and stopped in front of her. He bent over her, his face looming.

"Do you mind if I check Iomlan?"

It wasn't a question. She had just enough time to nod before he was reaching down and touching her stomach. His fingers pressed, his touch so light, so brief, they were gone before she realised. Abruptly, he turned away.

"Seamus, what is it?!" she asked with real concern.

He didn't answer.

"What's wrong?"

"You've joined."

Stunned, she stared at his back.

"But that's good, isn't it? That means Ellyllon's gone for good?"

Again, he didn't answer. As she watched, he returned to his chair and sat down heavily.

"I don't know." He sighed. "I should be happy, relieved, but I'm not. I'm…" He took another deep drag of his cigarette. "It feels wrong. It's hard to explain, but this is just too quick, too easy."

He sat back and then, changing his mind, leant forward again. "Did you feel any different, notice anything different at the lake yesterday?"

"No, I would've said." She thought back. "There was one thing. By the end of it, using Iomlan, it was easier, smoother. Like there was no gap between what I wanted to do and doing it."

"That would be it." His cigarette froze halfway to his mouth. "Are you sure you told me everything that happened yesterday?" His eyes stared intently into hers. "There's nothing else, no matter how small?"

She reddened and looked away.

"Whatever it is, you must tell me. It could be important."

"It was something Ellyllon did. I don't think it can be important, it was just another one of his tricks. It was just so horrible, I didn't think it mattered, and it makes me cringe just thinking about it."

She paused for breath. Seamus was watching her, his face expectant. She wished she'd never said anything, but it was too late now.

"Jasmine?" Leaning sideways, he picked up his old, discoloured metal ashtray and stubbed out his cigarette.

She took a deep breath, and began.

*

"You and Malachy?" was the first thing he said when she'd finished.

"No, we're just friends," she said quickly, flushing all over again.

Seamus stood up and went over to the window and looked out. The house was so quiet she could hear the clock ticking on the mantelpiece. It sounded like a heartbeat. Outside, the sun went behind a cloud and the room darkened. Still, Seamus didn't move. Jasmine rubbed her forehead. Something creaked in the hallway, making her jump.

"This can't be right!" Seamus said suddenly, spinning. "Has he ever done anything like this before? Taken the form of anybody else?"

"No, I don't think so." An unpleasant thought occurred to her, "But how would I know?"

Seamus didn't seem to hear.

"I always thought of him as like an animal. A cunning animal, with the uncanny instinct of a hunter, a tracker, but without the purpose of real, sentient intelligence. But this? This shows not only power, but intelligence."

He returned to his seat. "I need you to think very carefully about him. Forget everything I've told you. What's your sense of him? Of who he is?"

She thought back, not just to yesterday, but each time she'd seen him.

"Sometimes it's felt like he's been playing with me. Like he enjoyed scaring me, making me suffer, but I guess I thought he was like a cat, the way they play with their prey. But yesterday it was like he knew exactly what he was doing and wanted to hurt me. It felt malicious, deliberate."

Seamus shook his head, his eyes flashing. "I'm going soft!" he accused himself angrily. "Lazy. I should've listened to you with more care. Asked more questions, but I was too certain of myself, my knowledge." He calmed himself with a visible effort. "And if I've misjudged the nature of him, what else have I misjudged?"

"But why does it matter? It's too late; he can't take Iomlan now. Maybe that's why he left at the lake; he sensed we'd joined. It's over."

Seamus frowned. "But Jasmine, ask yerself, if Ellyllon is so clever and has so much power that he can change shape, how is it that he failed so easily? Even it was Influence he used, the thing is, he still has power and the wit to use it."

Lifting out his tobacco packet, he changed his mind and put it away again.

"It's a filthy habit. I should've stopped long ago," he complained.

"Maybe he got caught out? Maybe he thought he had longer."

"Possibly," he replied thoughtfully. "It was fast." He went still. "Tell me again why you went to the convent?"

"Because Malachy sent me a text. Why?"

"But Malachy didn't send you one!" he exclaimed angrily, slapping the arm of the chair. "How could I have missed that? Ellyllon sent the text. It was there, all the time, staring me in the face. He set a trap for you."

"But how?"

Seamus frowned. "I don't know, but it has to be." He stared at her, his eyes fierce, intense. "We were almost too late. A few seconds more. Why did he stop when he could've had what he wanted? Or maybe it's not Iomlan he's after? What if it's something else? Something more valuable to him? But what else is there?"

He rubbed his face. "I'm still missing something. I need time to think, but before you go, there's one thing we can do. I want to see you and Iomlan together."

He took her to the barn.

"Let's start at the beginning," he said as he closed the door behind them. "Let's see how you lift. Try the chair."

She did as he said and immediately noticed the difference. It was just as it had been by the lake. The chair hovered six feet in the air, unmoving.

"And now, that tyre." Seamus pointed. "Together."

Iomlan surged again. The tyre joined the chair.

"Make them turn," Seamus ordered.

She started with the chair, turning it so that it flipped over and over. Then brought in the tyre, whirling, spinning crazily, like a top. Iomlan flowed through her. She wanted to cry with the feeling, as if it were just another part of her, like a hand or a leg, moving in perfect symmetry.

"That's enough."

Stopping only reluctantly, she lowered them gently back to earth

"You've stopped closing your eyes," Seamus commented, his face unreadable.

"Have I? I hadn't noticed." Inside, the ghost of Iomlan was still singing, making her feel like she could do anything, be anything.

"And your control is excellent. There's almost no gap between your will and Iomlan's action."

"Almost?" She grinned.

Seamus tutted. "Don't get too confident. You have skill all right, but you've a lot to learn and with more power than most, it can easily slip away from yer. We have to be careful and keep our wits about us. No matter what, I don't want you using Iomlan anywhere, except here, with me, in our lessons. You have to be supervised."

"What?" Her face fell. "Are you serious?"

"Very." He gave her a stern look. "This is all just a little too convenient. And I'm thinking to myself, what if this is what Ellyllon wanted, you and Iomlan joined?"

"He wanted—? I don't understand, why would he want that? It doesn't make sense."

"I don't understand either," he admitted. "But power and inexperience are a dangerous mix. And until you're more experienced, and until we know better what Ellyllon's planning, limiting your use of Iomlan is the best we can do."

"But, it's not fair!"

It wasn't what she wanted to say. Earlier, she'd been happy to put Iomlan to one side to spend time with her dad. But now, feeling the euphoria again and knowing Iomlan was now fully, irretrievably part of her, her very being, to be told she couldn't use it was too much. No, couldn't use it *unsupervised*, she reminded herself, as if she were a child and not someone who'd already seen Ellyllon off. And all for an old man's feeling he didn't even understand himself.

Coming over, Seamus put one hand on her shoulder. "Jasmine, I know you think I'm fussing, but you have to trust me. Is it really so much to ask? You'd hardly be using it anyway."

That was true. Even without Ellyllon, she had to be careful no one found out. And it was impossible to argue with his logic without proving his point that she still had so much to learn.

"No," she admitted quietly, finally.

"Then promise me you'll do as I ask."

She nodded.

"That's not enough. Your question about your father shows me how much you've yet to learn. You know what they say about good intentions and you, Jasmine, have a good heart. Don't let it be yer undoing." His grip on her shoulder tightened, squeezing her skin through her jumper. "I need to hear you say it. I need your vow. Now, promise me you won't use Iomlan without me."

"Ow, Seamus, I promise!"

He let her go. "I think we should leave it there for today. Come back tomorrow, in the morning."

She looked at the floor. "OK."

"I'll walk with you."

They walked in silence back to her house. Even if Jasmine had wanted to talk, she wouldn't've known what to say. Other than to say that this was wrong, Seamus was wrong. She and Iomlan were joined, Ellyllon was gone and it was over.

"That yer dad's car?" Seamus asked, with a nod.

His car was sat in front of the house. He was early.

"Yeah. It's a hire car."

Coming out from under the trees, they stopped next to it.

"I imagine he's eager to see you. I won't keep ya."

"OK, bye then." She took a step.

"Jasmine." He stopped her with an outstretched hand. "If you see Ellyllon, or have any doubt, think of me with Iomlan and I'll come."

He gave her a tentative smile, "Whenever you need me, I'll be there. I hope you know that."

He looked so unhappy, as if this was hurting him as much as it was her. Her heart melted.

"I know." She smiled. "Thank you."

Patting her arm, he lowered his hand, "Be careful and I'll see you tomorrow."

She left him and, looking back once, from the back corner of the house, saw him continuing on in the direction of Malachy's house.

*

Inside, her mum was stood, leaning over one end of the kitchen table, her back to the door. Her dad was sat in the chair at the opposite end, drinking coffee.

"Jas!" he greeted her, with his huge, heart-stopping smile.

"What do you think of my flowers?" Her mum said, half turning and pointing to a huge pile of flowers pulled out of their wrapping and left on top.

"They're lovely. Big."

"They are." Her mum laughed. "I'm not sure I've got enough vases for all these."

She grabbed the flowers and, leaving them next to the sink, went over to the corner cupboard and got down on her knees to pull different things out.

"What's your hotel like?" Jasmine asked as her dad got to his feet.

"OK. I didn't take much notice. Was too busy sleeping."

They hugged and he sat down again. At his feet were two plastic bags.

"It's very quiet here. Lovely, but quiet. Don't you miss London? All that noise, that excitement?"

She thought of Seamus walking down towards Malachy's. "Not really," she replied ironically, sitting down opposite him.

Her mum had given up pulling things out of the cupboard and was reaching instead. Her stretch wasn't long enough, so she moved further in, her head and shoulders disappearing.

"Now where did I put it?" she muttered to herself, the cupboard muffling her voice.

Jasmine's dad laughed, tilting his head so he could get a better look at her bottom poking out.

"Aha!" She reappeared, holding the vase up in triumph.

Scrambling awkwardly to her feet, she filled it with water and began placing the flowers carefully inside it.

"They're so beautiful, Justin," she gushed.

Jasmine shifted in her seat. She knew her dad wasn't well, but her mum was wildly overdoing it.

Her dad said something, cutting across her thoughts.

"Jas, this is for you. To make up for the lost birthdays." Bending down, he grabbed one of the bags and swung it across the table at her.

She took it from him awkwardly. "Thanks Dad, you didn't have to."

He smiled. "Of course I did. I'm your dad. Now open them."

She pulled two presents out of the bag, both immaculately wrapped.

"Leave that one until last." He pointed to the smallest one. "That came all the way from Canada with me and it's very special, one of a kind."

He watched, his eyes bright, as she ripped the paper off.

"Shit! It's an iPhone, and the latest one. Shit, Dad, how much did that cost?"

"Language, Jas." Her mum tutted, leaning in for a look. "Nice."

"It doesn't matter." He beamed. "I told you, I have three birthdays to catch up with, not to mention Christmases."

She gave him a hug, trying to ignore the fact that he'd missed two birthdays not three.

"Go on, open that one," her dad said eagerly, oblivious.

She did as he said. Inside the paper was a handmade cardboard box, the top painted with a symbol she'd never seen before, all swirls and intricate colours. Iomlan fluttered, caught by her anticipation, but she ignored it and focussed on the box instead. The fit of the lid was tight and it took her a moment to wiggle it off.

"Oh dad, it's beautiful!" she breathed, seeing what lay nestled between the layers of red tissue paper.

It was a necklace made of bright, sparkling silver. Lifting it out, she placed the pendant carefully in the palm of her hand, letting the chain, long and stylish, drape across the back. It shone, bright against her skin. Round, with a face etched deep into the metal, it was basic, primitive, the silverwork deliberately rough, the eyes, nose and mouth barely more than holes, but yet it had a strange beauty to it. Iomlan fluttered again and this time she pushed it down, swatting it away like an annoying fly.

"What is it?"

"It's a traditional symbol from a Canadian Inuit tribe. It's from a jewellery gallery in Quebec. I knew the artist."

Holding a flower poised in midair, her mum turned to look.

"It wasn't a female artist, by any chance?"

"Yeah it was actually. She was very talented."

"I bet," she snorted, turning back to the vase.

Ignoring them, Jasmine lifted the necklace high to look at it and was surprised at the weight of it. The pendant spun lazily, the eyes coming around to look at her.

"Let me put it on," her dad offered quickly.

She gave it to him and, standing up, he placed it, with great ceremony, over her head.

"There. A special gift for my special girl. To keep her close: always."

He stepped back and looked at her, his eyes shining.

"Thanks, dad."

She lifted up the pendant to look at it. Upside down, the face with its heavy, empty eyes took on a sinister look. She let it go. Behind her, the kitchen door opened and, stepping inside, John began to wipe his boots against the mat.

"Hi, how's it going?"

"Good, just opening presents." Her dad grinned.

"John, look what me dad got me." Wanting to include him, she jumped and held it out to him.

He reached out. Millimetres from the metal, his fingers froze. He let his hand drop. "Very nice, er, and, er, very unusual."

"It's art," she said defensively, glancing at her dad.

"It's beautiful, really," John reassured her quickly. "And as it's art it's one of a kind, which makes it even more special." Placated, she smiled at him.

"I'll make you a drink," her mum offered, moving her vase to the window ledge and leaning back to examine it. "Anyone else want one?"

It was her dad who answered.

"Not for me, Kate." He got to his feet. "I was wondering if Jasmine would like to go for a walk, show me around."

"There's not much—" Jasmine stopped, catching the look her mum gave her. "OK, dad, we'll do the loop."

"Before you go," said John, putting out a hand to stop them, "Justin, you will stay for dinner, won't you? I know Jasmine would like you to, and so would we. I know things weren't easy before, but after what happened, let's just say life's too short. It would mean a lot to me if we could be friends again."

"I dunno," Jasmine's dad replied slowly, coming forward. "At Uni, we weren't so much friends as you were my annoying good angel, trying to keep me on the straight and narrow."

"As if anyone could do that!" John grinned. They clutched hands then went in for a brief, manly hug. "You know what your trouble was, you were always too good-looking. One flash of that smile and everyone just rolled over."

"Still do, mate, still do."

They laughed. Behind them, her mum wiped at her eyes.

"Tell me about your Uni days together!" Jasmine demanded, so happy she could've hugged herself.

"Maybe later, after dinner." Her dad smiled, touching her lightly on the head. "But it's not half as interesting as it sounds."

*

What Jasmine called the loop took them past Seamus' house to the crossroads, then down the hill to the main road and along the main road back to where the bus stopped. It wasn't long before they were turning off the main road and onto the last lap of the loop, following the road uphill towards Malachy's house. Slowing against the gradient, her dad's breath began to catch. Automatically, she slowed too, matching his gait. It seemed to help. They ambled past Malachy's house, her dad puffing, and she couldn't help but look, but the house was quiet.

Malachy was probably still in bed, she thought, smiling to herself. He wouldn't need much excuse to stay there.

Almost home, they reached the top of the slope. Her dad wasn't looking so good; his face had gone a deep, dark red and his ragged breathing whistled.

"I can't." He stopped, and leaning forward, pressed his hand on her shoulder.

He gulped, taking in loud, shaky gulps of air.

"Are you OK, Dad?"

"Give… me… a… minute."

She waited. His breathing was beginning to steady as he took slow, exaggerated breaths, in out, in out, his chest heaving.

"That's… better." Letting her go, he cocked his head. "Let's look at the view. It'll give me time… before we go inside."

Together they walked to the nearby farm gate and, resting their arms across it, looked out across the valley.

"I saw you looking at the house as we came up. A friend of yours live there?"

"Yeah, it's a boy, Malachy. He had an accident, so I was a bit worried about him. He's OK, though."

"A boy?" He cocked his head. "Malachy. Nice, is he?"

She flushed. "He's a friend."

"Of course he is." He nodded wisely, his lips twitching.

"Shut up, dad." She swiped at his arm and they laughed.

Above them, the cloud parted suddenly. The sun caught the valley, sent a golden glow sweeping across the hillside opposite.

"Hmm, it is lovely," her dad murmured. "I can see why you like it here." He paused, then leaning back, gave her an assessing look. "You do like it, don't you?"

"Yeah, course. I didn't at first. I didn't even want to come, but now…" She shrugged.

"But what if you had the chance to go home, to London?"

"London?!" She had to think, "No, I don't think so. Maybe when I'm older. I could study there."

"But what if I was there?" He persisted, his face intent.

"So, you're staying in London?"

"I never should've left it. Obviously I'll live with your Nan and Granddad for a while, until I get myself sorted. I'll need somewhere to live and a job, but I've the insurance money from the accident. But I was wondering, when I'm all sorted, if you wanted to come and live with me. You're old enough to decide for yourself now."

Jasmine looked away. Six months, six weeks ago even, she'd have bitten his hand off.

"Thanks, dad," she mumbled. "It's just that I'm in the middle of my course and—"

"And you've settled," he finished for her. "I understand."

There was silence for a moment, and then he touched her arm gently.

"I won't be so far away. I'll come over regularly and you'll come to me too. Your Nan and Grandad would love it; I know they miss you. And if, y'know, if you decide to go to university, London's a great place to study."

"OK, thanks Dad." Impulsively, she tucked her head into his shoulder. "I'd love to come over. Maybe at Christmas, it's not long."

He slipped his arm around her. "Yeah, we could go into town, see the lights and wander around Leicester Square or Convent Garden or Camden even. Take in a show, anything you'd like."

Chapter Nineteen

Jasmine texted Malachy that evening, but he didn't reply. She tried him again, just before going to bed, but still nothing. He didn't reply until the following morning, just as she was getting ready to go to Seamus'. He was on his own he said, come as soon as. She frowned, glancing at her watch. She really wanted to see him. But then, Seamus hadn't said a time, and her dad probably wouldn't be here for a couple of hours. If she was quick, maybe she could fit in both. Charging downstairs, she knocked into John at the bottom and almost sent the two mugs of hot tea he was carrying flying.

"Sorry!" she called over her shoulder as she dashed for the back door.

It was raining again, so she zipped her coat up and put on her hood. Dragging her bike from the shed, she wheeled it around the house and jumped on. The wind caught her as she pedalled downhill, took her hood and flattened it across her back. By the time she'd reached Malachy's, her hair and face were soaked.

Knocking, she waited. She wiped a wet wrist across her wet face, unwittingly sliding her fringe into a tuft. The door opened. It was Malachy. Without thinking, she threw her arms around him and held him tight. He leant his head in towards her neck; she felt his hair soft against her cheek and closed her eyes.

"Ugh, Jas, yer all wet!" he exclaimed, pulling away.

"Sorry." She grinned stupidly. "How ya feeling?"

"Fine. Bored more than anything, and now wet." He gave her a sour look. "You been busy?"

"Actually I did text you twice yesterday, but you didn't answer. And, yes, I have been busy. A lot's happened."

"Then I'd better sit down." Turning around, he hobbled off.

"Oh, Jasmine, do come in!" she muttered sarcastically, closing the door and shutting out the rain.

Following him into the sitting room, she watched as he edged awkwardly around the coffee table then flopped heavily onto the sofa.

"Where is everyone?" she asked, perching on the end.

"Mam's at my sister's and Dad and Finn's out in the fields."

He lifted his leg awkwardly onto a cushion left on the table. Sliding slightly, it knocked into a pile of empty Coke and Fanta cans.

"Me mum would go mad if she saw that."

"Tell me about it," he replied gloomily, then perked up. "So, give."

He listened, his face intent, as she told him about returning home and finding her dad there.

"So, what happened to the driver who hit him?"

"They never found him, or her."

"He's lucky to be alive." He blew out his breath. "I bet it's weird though, with the three of them together."

"Totally," she agreed, grinning, "but they're being very mature about it."

Malachy laughed at that. "Rather you than me. I can't imagine what my dad would be like if me mam found someone else."

"Do you remember much about yesterday?"

Malachy ducked his head and for a moment; she wished she hadn't asked, but he was just thinking.

"I remember everything up to when, he, y'know. And then, all I remember is the feeling of his fingers, the way they pushed into me and it hurt. The pain was terrible." He shuddered. "Then nothing until the hospital. I thought it was bad enough hearing what he'd done to you. Anyway." He shook himself. "What happened after that? I was dying to ask Seamus, but me mam and dad were here."

Jasmine shifted. "I found Iomlan. Seeing what he was doing, I just got so angry and it was like before. Iomlan just went and before I knew what was happening, he was on the ground. He jumped up and I did it again, and again, over and over. I couldn't stop myself. I just wanted to hurt him so bad." She stopped and rubbed her face. "Anyway, I think he was getting tired. I saw this tree with a broken branch. And——"

"What?" Malachy lent forward.

"I lifted him up, impaled him on it. It was horrible, Mal. I just stood there, watching him as he pulled himself off. And then he just disappeared and I thought, he's given up. I was trying to get you back to the car when John and Seamus came up."

"Seamus was there? How did he get there?"

"I don't know. I hadn't even thought." She stared at him, flabbergasted. "Shit, can you believe that, Mal? I didn't even notice."

He shrugged. "Shock, I guess."

"Yeah, I suppose." She dismissed it, too intent on her story. "But I'm glad he was there. He healed you. I didn't have a clue."

"Seamus healed my ankle?" He looked at his foot. "He did a shite job."

"No, not that, it was the…" She stopped, thinking better of it. "Your ankle wasn't bad. I think he prefers to leave it to nature, if he can."

"Well, I wish he didn't. I'd give anything to stop me mam from fussing."

He gave her a sideways look. "Couldn't help yourself?"

"Yeah, of course. I should've just stood by and let him hurt you."

He didn't answer. Worried she'd been too sarcastic, she sneaked a look at him. He was gazing at his foot with an odd expression on his face, almost as if he were pleased with himself.

"There's something else—"

"Jas, there's something I want to ask you, I've been thinking about it for a while—"

They stopped.

"You first," Malachy offered immediately.

"He told me that me and Iomlan have joined."

His jaw dropped. "Shit, really? Why didn't you say? That's great, it's all over." He caught her look. "Isn't it?"

It came out in a rush, "Seamus doesn't think so. He thinks it too soon, that something's *not right*, whatever that means. That this is what Ellyllon wants, that he's still out there, waiting. Oh, and I don't have the control I should have. I'm not experienced enough. He's told me not to use Iomlan unless he's with me."

"Shit," he repeated softly.

"But it's been almost two days and I haven't seen him, so he must be wrong. And I don't think he realises exactly what I did. I beat Ellyllon all by myself. What could he do now?"

Malachy frowned. "I dunno, Jas. I'd trust Seamus and his feelings any day. It's like when you were in the convent; he knew something was happening to you. He felt it."

"But it's not the way he thinks it is. No, I didn't mean it like that," she backtracked quickly, seeing his expression. More than anything she wanted, needed him to understand. "I mean, it doesn't feel like I can't control Iomlan. It feels like it's a part of me. That we're together. United."

She sighed, frustrated with herself, with her inability to find the words to describe what she meant, what she felt.

"But I don't think he's saying that you're not. He's just—"

"So you agree with him?!"

Iomlan swirled with the anger in the pit of her stomach. For the briefest of moments, she imagined how easy it would be to shut Malachy up. Horrified, she pushed the thought away and took a deep breath.

"Yes, no, I don't know," Malachy was saying. "But I've known him all my life. If he's worried about your control I'd listen to him."

"Well, thanks, Mal, for the vote of confidence."

"Oh Jas, come on, it's not like that."

They stared at one another.

"Look, I'd better go, me dad'll be here soon," Jasmine spoke first. "Don't get up."

"Jas, what I was saying before—"

Getting up, she moved towards the door. "Look after that ankle."

"Jas, wait!"

She was at the door, had pulled it open just enough to slip through. Relenting slightly, she gave him her brightest, most false smile. "It's OK, Mal. Don't look so worried. I won't use Iomlan on my own."

He frowned. "But you need to talk to Seamus and sort it out. And I need to tell you how I—"

"Yeah, you're right. I'll do it. Text you tomorrow."

*

The rain had stopped. She walked home, pushing her bike. She couldn't believe that Malachy had agreed with Seamus. Treating her like a child too. Was that it? He was only a year older than her, but did he really just see her as a kid? And all this time she'd been thinking, hoping… She sighed, the sound loud in the quiet lane, the empty fields. Maybe, they were right and she wasn't ready. What is it that Seamus had said before? With Iomlan, your thoughts can become reality? And she'd had that thought about Malachy. Maybe Malachy was right and she should talk to Seamus. He'd been through the same thing too once. That felt better. She should go straight there, tell him how she felt and he'd see she was able to control Iomlan. Lifting her head, she sped up, unconsciously squaring her shoulders.

Her dad's car was parked outside the house. Damn, he was early. But he would wait, and she could just talk to Seamus and forget the lesson. He'd understand when she explained. But would he? Or would he see it as another example of her immaturity, a lack of commitment? And what if her dad left? She was back to school on Monday; they only had two full days left and then he'd be going back home, to London. Unable to decide, she hovered.

"Jasmine?"

It was her dad, coming around the side of the house.

"You're back! Thank God."

"Dad, hi. No, I was just going somewhere. I won't be long."

"Only I'd love to get out of here," he continued, oblivious. "I knocked but I don't think anyone heard. I think they're still in bed." He dragged his hand through his hair, "Sorry, it just feels a little surreal, thinking of them, together, y'know, and me sat downstairs."

"Oh." She didn't want to think about it. And then she remembered Seamus hadn't said a time; she could always go later. "OK, I'll just put me bike away."

She slipped off the saddle and began wheeling her bike towards the gate.

"Sorry, did you say you were going to see someone?"

"No, it's OK. I'll go later. They won't mind."

*

In the end, she directed him to the town of Boyle and they had a drink in a little café there, right on the river. Made of thick, grey stone, the café used to be the bridge house, with three tiny rooms looking out over the river, filled with mismatching brightly coloured chairs and tables jostling for space and a sandwich counter. A small vase of flowers adorned each table, and in each room a turf fire burned brightly in one corner. Jasmine chose the quieter room, and a table close to the river. With the lowness of the building, if she'd opened the window and had stretched her hand as far as it would go, she'd've been able to touch the water or caress the waterweeds moving softly with the current, just below the surface.

Her dad had got the drinks, coffee for him and a Coke for her and now he joined her, sitting opposite. For a moment neither of them spoke, both too busy looking down into the water.

"Jas, we've talked about so much in the last couple of days. I can't remember when I've talked so much. Or enjoyed it so much. But we haven't talked about what happened before I went to Canada."

He paused, took a sip of his coffee.

"I talked to my counsellor a lot about this, and it helped me to see things a little clearer." He sighed, and the hand that lowered his cup trembled slightly. "Looking back I can't believe I put my feelings, my stupid hurt pride before the chance to see my daughter grow up. But I did it and I can't change it, but without trying to justify it, to make excuses for myself, I need to explain. I've been given a second chance and I'm not going to muck it up now."

"Dad—" she began, but he held up his hand to stop her.

"Please Jas, just let me say this. I want to do it before I lose my nerve. When me and your mum separated, and this is such a cliché, it was only then that I realised what I'd lost. But I told myself that if I worked hard, proved to her that I'd changed, then there was a chance that she'd take me back. Oh, I knew it wouldn't be easy, but I knew that I still loved her and I believed that she still loved me. But then she started seeing John. That was a shock, I must admit. Your mum and my best friend." He shook his head. "But still I thought, and I'm not proud of this, let her get it out of her system and when she's ready she'll come back to me. But she didn't. And now there's no chance. The worst thing is that even after everything, I still love her, and I've only myself to blame for losing her."

"Oh, dad!"

Reaching out, she touched his arm. Unbidden, Iomlan moved inside her. Soft, gentle, it followed her instinct to comfort. She made as if to push it away, but something stopped her. Warm, it rose up inside her then slipped down her arm into her hand. Played across her fingers and onto the skin of her dad's arm. He smiled suddenly, his eyes becoming huge, vulnerable.

"But your mum's happy, I can see that, and that's all that matters."

What was she doing?! Exactly what Seamus predicted. Appalled, Jasmine pulled Iomlan back and let her hand drop.

"Of course, at the time I genuinely thought it would wear itself out," her dad continued, staring at his hands. "I knew, of course, that John was in love with your mum, had been for years. But I didn't think it was serious for her. I thought she was just paying me back for all those years. How egotistical is that?"

"John was in love with mum?" She remembered what he'd said the night of the takeaway.

It was so obvious. "*She was always very special to me*". How had she not seen it?

"Of course, he never said anything, did anything, to me or your mum. John would never do that," he replied quickly. "It started when I met your mum, just after Uni. I could tell by the way he looked at her, the way he was with her. I guess he thought he was hiding it, but you can't hide love, not really. And when they got together, I thought of how stupid I'd been, how I'd given him the chance he's been waiting for, longing for."

Jasmine looked down, embarrassed. The way John had said it, now she knew what he was really saying, was so different. It was as if he'd been trying to explain a generous, hopeful love, full of longing and sacrifice for the two people he loved, not the selfish, manipulative love her dad was describing.

"I know it wasn't really like that." Her dad laughed, seemed to know what she was thinking. "But it was the way I was thinking. I just want you to know how messed up I was, in my head."

He paused, flicked her a look.

"It was always there, you see, how John felt, in the back of my mind. And he and your mum were always close, always got on really well. I used to wonder if it hadn't been for me if they'd've got together sooner. Or if something had happened… maybe… when I was out—"

"You think something happened?!"

"No, of course not." His face reddened. "But when you're jealous you imagine all sorts of things. And when they got together the thought was there and this time it wouldn't go away and then when they announced their wedding, well, I saw red, I guess."

"I don't think mum would've done that."

Her mum knew all too well the pain of an affair; there was no way she'd do that.

"No, of course not. Honestly, Jas, I do know that," her dad reassured her, seriously.

There was another silence. Jasmine looked at the river again, wondered how deep it was and what secrets lay beneath.

"So, you and John getting on OK?" her dad said eventually, his voice bright, casual, changing the subject.

"Yeah, we are now. It was bad in the beginning; I just wanted you and mum to get back together. But it's OK now. I know him a lot better, and I, er, like him."

He nodded. "I can see how much he cares for you."

It was her turn to blush. "But he's not my dad; I've only got one of those."

He smiled at that, glanced at his watch then drained the last of his coffee.

"Are you ready to go?"

She lifted her can and gave it a shake. There wasn't much left.

"Yep."

*

Jasmine's mum was rummaging through the kitchen cupboards.

"Just writing a list." She waved a piece of paper at them as they came through the door. "I don't think John did any shopping while I was away. There's a lot to get."

"Kate, do you mind if I go and lie down for a bit on the sofa?" her dad asked suddenly.

He looked suddenly ill, pale, the colour drained from his face.

"Of course not. Do you want a blanket?" she asked, concerned.

He shook his head. "No, thanks. I just need fifteen, twenty minutes and then I'll be fine."

He touched Jasmine's arm as he passed. She watched him disappear into the lounge, closing the door behind him.

"I wondered where the two of you had got to. Where did you go?"

"Just to a café."

"You could've had a drink here."

"I think Dad wanted to talk."

Her mum turned. "Is everything OK?"

"Yeah, he just wanted to explain a few things. He'd been to some counsellor, in Canada."

"That's good, as long as you're OK."

"Yeah, I'm fine."

"If you're sure." Her mum closed the cupboard door. "I was going to go now, but if you prefer me to stay?"

"No, I'm fine."

Gathering up the bags she'd left on the floor, she slung her handbag over one shoulder and opened the kitchen door. "I won't be long."

Needing the loo, Jasmine tiptoed past the sitting room door and, kicking off her trainers, went quietly upstairs. She opened the door. John was there, stood in front of the bathroom mirror with a towel wrapped around his waist and his back to her. One hand was raised, holding his shoulder as he examined it in the mirror. At the sound of her, he stopped and, half turning, looked at her over his shoulder.

"Sorry—" she began.

And then she saw it and her stomach dropped. A wound, about an inch thick, the width of a small branch, lay in the centre of his shoulder. It had almost healed: the swelling, the redness disappearing into the stark whiteness of his skin. She opened her mouth to speak, but nothing came out. John stared at her, his face calm and still, his eyes empty of colour. And then her feet were moving, backing her slowly out of the room, her heart pounding. At the top of the stairs she whirled and, using the bannister, threw her body down the stairs. Her feet tripped and tumbled; she missed a step and would've fallen but for her hand gripping the bannister. She hit the ground and grabbed her trainers, struggling her way into them. Her hands were shaking, she couldn't get her fingers to work, to lift the backs and let her wriggle her heels inside. Half sobbing, she glanced back, expecting to see him on the landing, coming for her, but it was empty. Desperate, she tried again, her fingers tearing at the material. Finally her shoes were on and she was grabbing the door catch, turning it and pulling and flinging the door wide open. The floor creaked over her head and she looked back. He was there, his black eyes fixed on her, his foot poised on the top step. Her stomach churned and Iomlan surged through her, flashing upwards. She saw him fall backwards but didn't wait to see and was turning away again, stumbling out of the door and down onto the path.

Chapter Twenty

Jasmine tore along the lane towards Seamus' house, her feet pounding. *It's John*. The words ran through her head, unstoppable. *It's John, it's John*. She gasped for air, her lungs cramping, but she daren't slow. Risking one glance back, her feet stumbled, but there was no sign of him. But he was coming, she could feel it.

She was almost there. Just ahead, Seamus' house was obscured by trees, a thick hedge. Perfect for an ambush. She ran towards it, her body tensed, anticipating. It towered high above her, the foliage dense. Iomlan churned, pushing at the edges of her control. She flinched, preparing to twist her body out and away. There was no one there. Almost crying with relief, she ran through the gate and up the path. The front door was open and she could see Seamus coming along his hallway, carrying a mug, talking to a figure behind him, and then he saw her and he dashed to the door.

"Seamus!" she tried to call, but her voice was barely more than a croak.

He stepped outside, dropping the mug as he half ran to her. It hit the path, smashed, bits bouncing into the grass, but he ignored it.

"Jasmine, what is it?!"

"It's John," she gasped, her chest heaving.

He grabbed her elbows. "What's John?"

"It's John. He's John."

He cocked his head slightly. "What's that sound? It's like a hum, but it's—"

"I saw the wound!"

Her mouth felt dry, her throat thick. Her chest whistled.

"What wound? What are you talking about?" His shoulders straightened, "Jasmine, I need you to calm down for me. Your Iomlan's all over the place. Now, I want you to breathe for me. Deep breaths, that's it Jasmine, nice and steady."

She breathed, feeling the air and the quiet authority of his voice calming her.

"I went into the bathroom. John was there, looking at his shoulder, and, and then he turned. He has a wound in his shoulder. It's the same, it's from the branch, from where I lifted Ellyllon up. And his eyes, they were the same. Seamus, I think John is Ellyllon."

Seamus stared at her, flabbergasted. Then, slowly, he shook his head, "You're wrong. John isn't Ellyllon. He can't be."

"But it was him, I know it was. It was Ellyllon."

"Jasmine, I'm absolutely certain John isn't Ellyllon."

How could he be so certain, so sure? If he'd seen him, like she had, he'd know.

"It couldn't be, because John's here with me. And has been for a while. Look."

Half turning, he indicated behind him. John was standing in the shadow of the door, listening to them.

"But I don't understand, I thought—"

John stepped forward. "It wasn't me, Jas. Seamus is right. I've been here a while."

"It must have been Ellyllon pretending to be him," Seamus offered, his voice soft, soothing. "Remember, we talked about that, about Ellyllon doing something like this. And I would know this better than anyone. I promise you, Jasmine, John is not Ellyllon."

"I was so sure. I didn't stop to think." Something was bugging her, something wrong, out of place.

"Why would you? You believed your own eyes. Did he do anything? I mean, try to hurt you in any way?"

She thought about it. "No, nothing. He just stared at me."

"Hmm." His eyes glazed. "It's almost as if he wanted you to think he was John. Now, why would he want that?"

She still couldn't put her finger on what was wrong. Her mind felt sluggish, refusing to work.

"Seamus, you have to do something!" John's face twisted. "This has gone on long enough. She's not safe."

Seamus' eyes refocussed. He looked at Jasmine.

"John, you should go," he said loudly. "And Jasmine," he said, pulling gently at her elbow, "let's go inside."

His tone jarred. Jasmine cocked her head, and then it hit her.

"Oh my God, you know, don't you?"

John shook his head. "I've got to go."

"No!" She shook off Seamus' hand. "You know, don't you? About me, Iomlan, Ellyllon. Did Seamus tell you?"

"Yes," Seamus answered, but John too was answering.

"No, I knew already."

"You knew already?! Why didn't you say anything?" She looked at Seamus. "You didn't want me to know? Why?"

Seamus stared back at her, his face blank.

A thought occurred to her and she turned back to John. "Have you been spying on me?"

"It wasn't spying. It wasn't like that. I was just making sure that you were OK."

"John!" Seamus' voice held depths of warning.

Memories flashed through Jasmine's head. Their house in London, catching a glimpse of John watching her out of the corner of his eye, his constant questions, where she was going, what she was doing.

"How *long* have you been watching me?"

"Why don't we go inside, talk there, explain," Seamus tried again, making to take her arm, but she pulled away.

"I don't want to go inside. And I don't want to talk. I want to know what's going on."

Her voice rose. "How long have you been watching me?"

"Since you were a baby."

"Oh, John," Seamus breathed, his eyes wide. "This is the last thing she needs."

"But I'm tired of it, Seamus! I'm tired of all of it!" John lashed out suddenly. "The lying, the pretending, keeping my mouth shut. It's time she knew; she has the right."

"She does. But we agreed, not now. Think, John. What reason could Ellyllon have to make her think you're him? He wants her confused, not knowing who to trust. This does exactly what he wants. It plays straight into his hands. When the time was right, we would've told her."

"Well it's too late now, I can't take it back. But, maybe, if I hadn't listened to you, we would've told her already and he wouldn't be able to use this against us."

Inside, Jasmine was reeling. She could hear them talking, arguing in front of her, but they seemed so far away. She didn't know what she'd been expecting John to say, but it wasn't this.

"A baby," she repeated. "I don't understand. How could you know about me then?"

John moved closer. "Because I felt your potential for Iomlan when

I first saw you. You were six months old."

"But how?" She looked at Seamus.

He rolled his eyes and sighed. "John had Iomlan too. It was how we met. I was his mentor."

"John has Iomlan! But why didn't he say?" Confused, she looked from one to the other. "But if John has Iomlan, wouldn't I feel it? Wouldn't I know?"

John and Seamus exchanged a look.

"I did have, but I don't anymore." John's face twisted with pain. "Something went wrong and… it died."

"It happens sometimes," Seamus interjected. "No-one knows why. But the person always retains something of it. A sense, inexplicable feelings."

"So you felt it in me."

"Yes, I felt it. And I couldn't believe it. People like us aren't common. To find, to know another one… it was like I was being given a second chance. I'd already lost the chance of having the two things that meant the world to me. And I couldn't tell your mum or your dad; they'd never've believed me, would never let me near you again if I'd tried. I did the only thing I could do. I told Seamus. And he came over to London to see you, to check for himself."

"It was the only way to be sure and I was concerned, concerned that for John to feel the potential in you so young it must be very strong in you," Seamus explained, taking up the thread. "Your father and John were taking you out in the pram. I met them seemingly by accident. You were sleeping and it's nothing to reach in and move a blanket, touch a baby's face. And for me it was enough." He glanced at John. "I knew then that John was right. And with such potential Ellyllon would be drawn to you. And as you got older, the risk increased."

"But if there was nothing he could do, what did it matter?"

"With a potential so strong, I feared that he would circle and wait his chance. Your Iomlan could sustain him for longer than most; it would've been worth the wait. And there are many places you could've gone and woken Iomlan by accident. John told me you have a fascination for Neolithic sites." He gave a wry smile. "I think we're drawn to them. It's natural, like a bee to a flower. When it happened, I wanted to be close by, not just to guide you but to protect you."

She looked at John. "That time in Avebury, you were so weird, wanting to know what I'd done. You were so insistent, it scared me."

"Those sites are considered sacred, although not for the reason people think. John offered to be my eyes and ears, to check on you occasionally, and I accepted."

"You were the daughter of my two closest friends. Knowing the dangers, what else could I do?"

Another thought struck her and it was so awful she recoiled from it.

"That's not why you're with my mum? Because of me? What you said about her, loving her, it was all a lie?"

"No, of course not!" He snapped, his voice thick with disgust, "I love your mum. She means everything to me. She always has. That's why I kept going away. I had to come and check on you, but I just couldn't stay and see the way your dad treated her knowing how I could have loved her if only she'd let me."

Jasmine froze. She'd dismissed her dad's suspicions, preferring John's gentle love story, but John had kept the secret of Iomlan all these years, had lied and manipulated to do it. Not just once, but over and over. Even here, what he'd seen, what he must've known she was going through, in the tomb, the bus crash, the plate, he never said anything. Never hinted, not once. His whole life was a lie. If he was capable of that, what else was he capable of?

"So, the way he was in London, about me going out, my friends, that had nothing to do with Iomlan or Ellyllon?"

She was looking at Seamus now, asking him. Couldn't even look at John.

"That was my doing, I was worried about you, your heart and the influence of other people on you. You know the harm we can do with Iomlan even when we try to use it for good. But what do you think would happen if we grow up bad, our hearts corrupted? These children you were with, your *friends*, were selfish, petty, ignorant. I couldn't risk it, so, I asked John to intervene. When that didn't work we decided that the only thing was to bring you here. Joining with Iomlan is an honour; I had to be sure you would grow up worthy of it."

"Worthy! Honour!" she sneered, even the sound of the words incensing her. "Those friends of mine you call selfish, they weren't like that at all. But you didn't know, because you didn't know them. But what did that matter when I was so easily led!"

Iomlan swirled, stoking her anger like a blast of air on a catching fire. Next to her, Seamus tensed. She felt his Iomlan and knew instantly what he was doing. He was preparing, getting it ready, just in case she lost control. But there was more. She felt him. She gasped, rocked by the power inside him.

"You felt that, didn't you?" Seamus thrust his face into hers. "Without any effort, any need to focus, you felt what I did. And more than that, you got a glimpse of me, even though I didn't mean for you to. That's a measure of the power you have, of what you can do. Of what you'll be able to do as you learn and realise your power more and more. And yet you refuse to see why we did what we did. Maybe you're right and me and John could've told you, could've tried to explain. But as I said before, would you have believed us? Of course you wouldn't! And what if we'd left you in London? With those so-called friends? What do you think they would've done if they knew what you could do? Have you thought about that?"

"But why didn't you tell me afterwards?" she pleaded, needing desperately for him to understand, to see what he'd done. "Like after the bus crash and the plate. You knew what it was like. I thought I was going mad. I hurt Malachy!"

"I wanted to tell you so many times, but we'd agreed to wait and I was afraid," John interjected miserably. "You were finally beginning to trust me and I was afraid this would just make everything worse."

"So you were too scared to tell me?" she sneered. "And after the bus crash, you driving me to school, what was that about? Making you feel better?"

"No, of course not. I was scared for you and I thought Seamus' plan was too risky—"

He stopped, shutting his mouth with a snap.

"What plan?!"

"Nothing." He shook his head, his face reddening.

"Jasmine—" Seamus began.

"What plan?" she insisted.

He took a step back and for a split second she thought of using Iomlan to prise it out of him, but then Seamus was there, in between them.

"It was my plan; why don't you ask me? Or is it that you can't use Iomlan against me?" His voice was cold, but the auburn flecks in his eyes burned. "Can't use it to torture the truth out of me? You want to know so badly? Well then, I'll tell you. I used you. I used you as bait to try and stop Ellyllon. And I used John's belief in me, his trust, to secure his help, his silence. I was trying to draw Ellyllon out, to make him so desperate to feed that he'd ignore the dangers. And then I'd have him. He can't be killed, but there's other things I can do. I don't expect you to understand, but you were my last chance to stop him feeding on our kind once and for all. I'll never see another like you in my lifetime, a person on the brink of joining with enough power to make him forget his own safety."

He sighed, ran his hand through his hair and looked suddenly old. "That day at the lake I was there, hiding. We can shield ourselves from one another, if you know how. But even then Ellyllon can sense us, not fully, but enough so I couldn't be too close. You two were supposed to stay at the top of the rock, to wait for John there, but you didn't and by the time I realised… So now you see this was nothing to do with John. This was all me. What I didn't know, what I didn't realise, was the thing I was hunting was as clever, if not cleverer, than me."

He lifted his chin. "That's the truth I've told you, Jasmine. I've left nothing out. And tell me, do you feel any better for knowing it?"

"No," she replied quietly.

"And now you really know what having Iomlan means. The choices we sometimes have to make." His eyes softened. "When the time was right I was going to tell you. To explain. But now, you must listen to me and think about Ellyllon. Not for me, for my plan or for John, but for yourself, for your own survival. I'm telling ye, this is what he wants. To separate you from me. I don't know why, but it's the only thing that makes sense. He's trying to manipulate you. Don't let him."

"Him manipulate me?" she repeated, incredulous. "I can't listen to this."

She took a step back.

"Jas," John said, moving around Seamus.

She held up her hand at him. "Leave me alone. I don't want this. I don't want any of it."

"But, Jas, this is it. This is you. You can't deny it."

"What, so I can end like him? Using everyone and everything around me?" She rubbed a hand across her face. "I can't think. There's all this stuff in my head, these voices telling me what to do, I can't think straight! I'm tired. I just want to be like everybody else."

"But you're not, Jas. You're not, and you never will be." John stretched out his hands, his eyes pleading. "Look, come inside. I promise we won't say anymore. We'll leave you to rest. It'll give you time to think, and you'll be safe there." One hand lifted, the fingers curling, ready to cradle her arm. "Come on."

"No! Get off, me!" Pulling away, she began backing down the path. "Don't try and stop me!"

John moved to follow her, but Seamus stepped in front of him, barring his way. "Let her go, John. All she needs is a bit of time to get it straight in her head."

She couldn't believe it. He was talking as if she was the one with the problem, as if he still couldn't see that he'd done anything wrong. The realisation of it was like a cannonball blasting through the centre of her. Turning, she went back through the gate and left without a backward glance.

Chapter Twenty-One

She walked home, oblivious to the road beneath her feet, the glare of the low winter sun as it darted in and out of the trees.

"Jasmine!"

Her dad was stood outside her house, his back to the still open front door.

"Where the hell did you go?" he demanded, coming down the path. "I woke up and I couldn't find you or your mum. And the front door was wide open. I know it's quiet here, but that's just asking for trouble." Then he took her hand. "I need to tell you something. I just got a call from your Granddad. I've got to go back to London. Today."

"Why?"

"It's nothing to worry about, but it's your Nan, she's had a fall. She's hurt her hip. She's in hospital. He says she's got to have an operation. It's nothing serious, but at her age, well, I need to be there just in case. I've got to go. I've got a flight booked, but I won't be long. I'll come back as soon as I can, OK?"

She looked at the ground and nodded, not trusting herself to speak. It was too much; all she wanted to do was to crawl into bed and go to sleep.

"I will be back, I promise—" He stopped, looked closely at her for the first time. "Jas, what's wrong, you look terrible?" Reaching out, he touched her chin lifting her face. "You're crying! What's wrong? What's happened?"

She pulled away, wiping furiously. "Nothing, I'm OK."

"You're obviously not. Tell me."

"It's nothing."

He looked at her for a moment then pulled her to him, holding her tight. When she was little, his arms felt like the safest place in the world, but this time they held no comfort. After a few moments she gently extricated herself.

He frowned, the movement tightening his scar. "Jas, maybe we should go inside. It's cold out here."

"No, I'm OK, you've got to go."

"Well I'm not leaving you alone, not like this. Come inside, come on." As if to parody John, he took her arm and began leading her up the path.

"I'm not going in there!" she cried, pulling back, her arm slipping out of his grip. "Someone might be inside."

"Who'd be inside? Your mum and John are out." He gave a small laugh. "I'm sorry, I wasn't serious about the front door. Look, there's no one inside. And I should know. I went into every room looking for you."

He took her arm again and, holding on tight, propelled her inside.

"Where's your mum? This isn't like you. I think she should know how you are before I go."

"She's shopping," she replied, sniffing, watching the stairs.

"Maybe I should call her?" He took his phone out of his pocket.

She shook her head, pressed her sleeve to her runny nose. "No, she said she won't be long. I'm sorry, I'm being silly. I'm OK really."

"What about John?" He lifted his finger, held it poised over the button. "Maybe I should try him?"

"No, not him!"

His eyebrows lifted. He stared at her at her then wordlessly put his phone away, back in his pocket.

"OK, are you going to tell me what this is all about? Why you don't want me to call John?"

"It's nothing, just a stupid row."

"Jasmine, I don't believe you. You wouldn't react like this over some stupid little row. I can see something's wrong and, to be honest, I don't like the fact that it's about John." He took his phone out again. "I'm going to cancel my flight. I'm not leaving you until this is sorted out."

"You can't! What about Nan?! If anything happened and you weren't there… Please dad, you have to go." She flapped her hands at him. "I'm fine. Really."

"I can go tomorrow. Or—" His eyes lit up. "How about this? Why don't you come with me? I know you've got school, but it'll be just for a few days. It'll give you some time away from John, and then when we know your Nan's OK we can come back and sort it all out. Together." He paused. "What d'you think?"

A wild overreaction, and yet it was tempting. A chance to leave everything behind her, to pretend, even for a few days, that it wasn't happening.

"Oh Dad, I'm sorry. I'm just being silly."

The light in his eyes went out.

"OK, I understand." He nodded, swallowing. "To be honest I was just being selfish. Thinking how much it would help me with you there. Help me deal with stuff, y'know, the things I find difficult. And take me and your Granddad's mind off your Nan. Y'know how he fusses over you." He sighed. "I think I'm more worried about how he'll cope than how your Nan's operation'll be. You know how she does everything for him. But you're right, you need to stay and sort this out. It's the adult thing to do."

Jasmine stared miserably at him. She felt terrible, as if she'd raised his hopes then ruthlessly dashed them. She thought of the journey he'd face, the worry about his mum and dad, her operation and what that might to do him.

"OK, I'll come."

"You will? Great." He grinned, looked at his watch and then, as if he was afraid she was going to change her mind, began to talk very fast. "Right, you've got about ten minutes to grab a small bag. This is the last flight we can get, so just bring the basics. We can buy anything else you need in London. I'll write your mum a note and book you a seat. You go on upstairs and I'll find a pen and some paper."

"There's a pen in the kitchen drawer, I think."

"OK." He disappeared into the kitchen.

She looked at the landing. It was empty. Taking a deep breath, she grabbed hold of the bannister and took her first step. Nothing happened. She took another, then another, watching carefully. She reached the top. Silence. She moved towards her bedroom, passing the open bathroom door. Still, undisturbed, the surface of the sink gleamed, the flannel was neatly folded and the soap sat neatly in its dish. She moved on. Up ahead, all the doors were open, where her dad had gone searching.

"Jas," her dad's voice shouted suddenly. "Don't forget your passport and don't bother with toiletries; you can buy them the other end."

"OK."

Her room was as she'd left it, only she'd forgotten she hadn't made her bed. The duvet was still crumpled, showing where her body had been. Ten minutes, her dad had said. She went over to her wardrobe, and reaching up, pulled down her rucksack.

*

Fifteen minutes later and they were on their way, her dad turning left on the main road, heading towards the village.

"Dad, it's the other way." She pointed. "Knock's that way."

"Oh, we're not going there. The first flight to London out of there isn't until tomorrow. We're going to Sligo, getting a flight to Dublin and transferring from there."

"Oh."

They'd reached the village and as her dad slowed, preparing for the junction, a small red car came flying in the opposite direction.

"Hey, dad, I think that was mum!" Jasmine grabbed his arm and pointed.

"Was it?" He glanced around. "We've missed her. Not to worry, you can call her when we get there. That's if you still want to go?"

Looking out the back window, she watched the car disappear.

"Yeah, of course." She turned back.

Neither of them spoke. Lulled by the movement of the car, Jasmine closed her eyes. Inexplicably, she thought of Malachy, and opening them again, reached into her bag and took out her phone.

"What, what are you doing?"

"Just texting Malachy." She began typing, the buttons clicking. "I forgot to tell him."

"But you're only going for a few days!"

"Yeah, but I said I'd be round tomorrow." Finishing, she pressed send.

Just past the town of Ballymote, Jasmine wiggled uncomfortably.

"Dad, sorry, I need the loo."

"What?" He looked around him, "There's nowhere to stop."

"It's OK, I can go in the hedge."

"Oh, OK. But be quick; we don't want to miss the flight."

He stopped at the nearest gap and she hopped out.

*

Half an hour later, manoeuvring the car into a space in the airport car park, he turned off the engine.

"Can you pass me the paperwork?" He pointed to the glove compartment, "Thanks. I just need to check with the hire company where they want the car. Will you be alright here for a sec?"

She nodded and he got out, shut the door and walked off in the direction of the airport building. She watched him go then settled down to wait, her left hand supporting her cheek. Malachy hadn't bother to reply to her text. And given the note her dad had left, she was surprised her mum hadn't called sending the air blue with the very expletives she complained to Jasmine about. She lowered her hand. Now she was thinking about it, it was odd. Bending over, she unzipped her bag and reached inside. Her phone had slipped down; she found it at the very bottom and pulled it out. It was turned off. Surprised, she turned it back on again, and almost immediately the screen began to flash with missed messages from her mum, John and Malachy. With a loud buzz, it began to ring, the screen illuminating. It was Malachy.

"Jasmine, where are you? I've been trying to phone you. Why did you turn your phone off?"

"I didn't. But there's no big panic. I'm with dad and I'll be back in a couple of days."

He wasn't listening. She could hear him talking, then other voices in the background, sounding muffled as if his hand was over the phone.

"Jas, John told me everything. He's here with Seamus."

"So, you're taking their side now?"

He sighed. "Jas, it's not about sides. John told me Ellyllon was in your house. What makes you think you'll be safe from him in London?"

"I—" She hadn't even considered that.

"Jas, where are you? I checked on my phone; there's no flight from Knock."

"Yeah, we're flying from Sligo to Dublin then to London."

He swore. And then he was repeating exactly what she said and she heard someone, maybe John, exclaim and the line went dead. The door to the driver's seat opened and she jumped.

"It's all sorted. We can leave it here. Ready to go?"

He saw the phone in her hand and studied her for a moment, his eyes anxious.

"Not having seconds thoughts, are we?"

She put her phone back in her bag and shook her head. "Nope, I'm coming."

She followed him into the airport terminal, looking around her curiously. She'd never seen an airport so small before, the corrugated ceiling and iron beams making it look like a converted hangar cut into sections.

"Over here, I think," her dad said, pointing at desk over to their right, where a woman, youngish and fairly attractive, was sat looking bored.

There was no one else there. As they approached, the woman

attempted a smile, but her heart really wasn't in it.

"Good afternoon, is this the check-in for the Dublin flight?" Her dad flashed his best smile.

The effect was instantaneous. The woman's face lit up, her eyes sparkled and totally unaware she was doing it, she lifted her hand and touched her neck, her hair. Jasmine rolled her eyes. It was always the same. If she hadn't grown up with it, she'd never have believed that it could happen outside films.

"It is. Have you got your tickets, sir?"

"No, I booked online. Is that OK?"

Her dad leant over the counter and stared deep into the woman's eyes. Playing with the small pendant around her neck, she laughed girlishly.

"Not a bother, I can retrieve them for you and then check you in. Have you got your passports?"

Her dad handed them over.

"Thank you. Is this your daughter?"

Her dad said something Jasmine didn't catch and the woman laughed again.

"Jas." He cocked his head. "There's a café over there, why don't you grab us a drink and I'll join you in a minute?"

"What do you want?" She sighed, shouldering her bag.

"Just a coffee." Already, he'd turned back.

She went to go.

"Oh, Jas, wait a minute." Stopping her with one hand, he reached into his trouser pocket. "You need money."

"It's OK. I've got enough."

"OK," He let his hand drop.

"Sir, do you have any luggage to check-in?"

"No, wait." He leant in close. "Y'know Jas, I want you to come with me more than anything, but if you've changed your mind, that's OK. We can call your mum."

"No, I want to come with you. It'll be good to get away."

He grinned at her; his face, inches from her own, was a mass of gleaming teeth. "Then you're coming with me of your own free will?"

"Y-e-s." She gave him a doubtful look. "I suppose."

"Good, I just wanted you to be sure." He glanced at the woman watching them, waiting. "I won't be long."

*

Grabbing the nearest table, Jasmine placed her dad's coffee on the table and sat down opposite it. Still chatting, his hips twisted, he played with the woman's pen. Jasmine dropped her bag and, resting her Coke can on the table, opened it with a hiss. She took a swig just as her phone rang. Dropping the can down, she scrambled for it. Pulled it out and checked the screen. John. Frowning, she answered it.

"Jasmine—" he began.

"I don't want to talk to you."

"Please, Jasmine, don't hang up, like you did with Malachy."

"But I didn't—"

"Please, Jas, just hear me out. We're not far from you and won't be long. We just need five minutes with you, just to talk, nothing else, I promise you, please, Jas, please," His voice shook; he took a deep breath, "Will you do that?"

"Just talk?" she asked, softening.

"Yeah, I promise. And if you still want to go after that then we won't stop you."

She thought about it. "It's OK, I am coming back. I told Malachy I'm fine, I'm with Dad. I just needed to get away for a bit."

"I know, but we still need to talk."

"OK, five minutes."

"Thank God." He sighed with relief. "OK. Now, when do you board?"

"I dunno." She squinted, trying to see the departure board. "It's saying fifteen minutes."

"Damn, I'm not sure we'll make it!"

Behind him, someone snapped.

"Bloody hell, Seamus, how can I do that?" John swore loudly, his breath hissing between his teeth. His voice receded as he moved away. "Ok… but isn't it…? OK, OK… I'll try. Look Jas, we're going to have to do this now. And please don't argue with me, just listen. Whatever you do, don't get on that flight. I don't know how else to say this, but that's not your father. It's not Justin."

"Don't be stupid, of course it is." Laughing, she glanced over at her dad. Reaching over the desk, he took hold of the woman's name tag and very gently straightened it. The woman tapped his fingers away, but she was smiling. "Trust me, that is definitely my dad."

"No, Jasmine, it isn't," John said slowly, his voice grim. "It's Ellyllon."

Chapter Twenty-Two

For a moment, she thought she hadn't heard right.

"Do you have the necklace he gave you on?"

"Yeah, course."

"Then you need to take it off. Seamus says you have to take it off and focus. To look past what Ellyllon wants you to see, the illusion of your dad, and see what's real."

"Is that really the best Seamus can do?" she snorted. "God, he's so desperate. And pathetic. Don't you think I know my own dad?"

"Did you know me? Did you know Malachy? Please, Jas, just take off the bloody necklace!"

"I can't believe he told you about Malachy," she bristled. "That's not—"

"Just take off the fucking necklace, will you?!" He roared suddenly, deafening her.

Shocked, she'd never heard him yell like that, not even in their worst arguments, or that day with her dad when they'd actually punched each other. She took it off.

"Is it off?"

"Yes."

"Good." He breathed out. "Look, earlier when you came to find Seamus, he heard something. A noise. Do you remember?"

"No, I don't. And I don't see what that has to do with any—"

He cut across her. "It doesn't matter, but he did. Look, we don't have time for this, so just listen. Seamus believes that noise was coming from the necklace. That it's like, er, a charm, or a talisman, and somehow it stops you from seeing Ellyllon as he really is. And what better person for him to pretend to be than your father? Someone you'd trust more than anyone?"

"But why? Why would he pretend to be my dad? What's the point?"

"Who else could take you away from us, from Seamus? Who else would you *choose* to go with?"

She went cold. *You're coming with me of your own free will?*

"If you think about it, isn't it all a bit of a coincidence?" John's voice continued. "That your dad should come back at exactly the right time? Saying exactly what you, what everyone, wanted to hear?"

She didn't answer and John pressed his advantage. "OK, Jasmine, you think we're wrong, you think that's your dad. Why don't you prove it, prove me wrong? You've taken off the necklace, so why don't you use your Iomlan? If we're wrong, then what's the harm?"

It was true, she realised, and would only take a second to do it, to prove that he and Seamus were wrong. But what if they weren't?

"But you're wrong. We're going because me nan's in hospital. We'll be back in a few days. He explained it all in the letter."

"What letter?"

"The letter me dad left for mum and… Oh, God!"

"There was no letter. Only a note saying you'd gone out. If it hadn't been for your text to Malachy…" His voice hardened. "Do it, Jas. Do it now."

She closed her eyes.

Breathing deeply, Jasmine centred herself, then opened her eyes. Still turned away from, her dad's focus was entirely on the woman in front of him. Knowing exactly what to do, she let Iomlan build and then, frowning in concentration, very slowly allowed it to slip gently from her. For a moment nothing happened, and then he lifted his head and turned to look directly at her. The air around him shimmered, his face blurred and she jumped back, fighting for control. His face twisted, his features merging and remerging and then sharpened into two, her dad's and Ellyllon's, and she was seeing them both together, one face on top of the other, the two of them somehow managing to occupy the same space at the same time. She recoiled, her breath catching.

"Jas, what's happening? Jas, answer me. Can you see him?"

"Yes," she managed to whisper.

Iomlan faded and once again it was her dad's face looking at her and John was talking urgently in her ear.

"We're not far aw… Seamus is driving like a… lunatic. He says to… in the open, near people… don't get on the plane and don't…"

"What? John, what did you say?" Her dad was striding towards her. "John, you're breaking up, I can't hear you!".

He was almost there.

"… if you… don't use Iomlan… him again…"

"What? Why?"

Coming closer, his eyes bored into hers. The phone went dead.

"Who were you talking to, Jasmine?"

He'd reached her.

"Um… just Malachy. I hung up on him."

"They're ready to board; we need to go." Stood over her, he tapped his foot, impatiently.

"But… you haven't drunk your coffee. And I… I haven't finished my Coke."

It was all she could think of. She looked desperately at the departure board, thinking it might help her, but it had changed and was now telling them to board.

"It's probably cold and you can get another." He shrugged, touching her on the shoulder.

She flinched, then tried to hide it by pushing her can away.

He cocked his head. "You're not wearing your necklace."

The hand on her shoulder began to press.

"God, I almost forgot it… it's given me a bit of a rash, must be allergic to it." Flushing, she pushed back the chair, knocking his hand away. "I'm sorry, I've got to go to the loo. I won't be long."

She stood up.

"It's too late for that. We've got to board now. You can go in Dublin." He grabbed her arm, just above the elbow. "Don't forget your necklace."

"Oh, right, sorry." Her heart thumping, she reached down, going as slow as she could, playing for the time.

She lifted it off the table, pretended to fumble and let it drop. Fast as a snake his hand was there, clutching the pendant in a tightly closed fist.

"Oops a daisy." He smiled, leaning across her. "You can put that on later. It's time to go."

Slipping the necklace in his pocket, he tugged at her arm.

"I don't feel well." She tried to pull back, but he tightened his grip and pressed his face towards her ear.

"I don't think there's any more point to my little pretence, do you?" he said softly.

His breath moved across her skin, making it crawl. She looked sideways at him. His smile was smooth, urbane, but his eyes, the blue of her dad's, were vicious. Her mind flew; without Iomlan there was only one thing for her to do. She opened her mouth to shout.

The tannoy sounded suddenly and a woman's voice began to speak, calling out their flight details, telling everyone to board. Jasmine froze. Immediately a queue began to form. Next to her ear, her dad's mouth was talking again.

"I wouldn't do that if I were you. Do you see that little boy over there? No, over there." He tugged viciously on her arm, pulling at her to get her to look, his nails digging so sharply that she had to stop herself crying out in pain.

At the front of the queue, the check-in woman stood talking with a woman and a little boy. He was turning slowly, twisting his mother's hand and arm as he gazed curiously all around him. The check-in woman said something and, smiling broadly, bent down low to talk to him. He stared back at her, his dark eyes solemn as he nestled in close to his mum, pressed his cheek into her leg.

"What's the name of your cousin? Darling Kate told me. Hugo, that's it. A brave little soldier, fighting for his life. Children are so small, so fragile. So easily hurt. Makes you want to protect them." He sighed. "But a blink of an eye is all it takes and then they're gone, taking their parents' hearts with them."

"I know you. You can't do anything to hurt that boy. Seamus said—"

"Seamus said!" Ellyllon sneered, jerking her arm again, "What does he know of what I can do? What do you? Or do you think you can stop me like you did at the lake?" He laughed softly. "Look how well that turned out. And even if you had the wits to stop me hurting him, if you broke the first rule and used Iomlan in front of all these people… Well, as you can see, there's more here to play with. You can't save them all."

He watched her for a few moments, letting his words sink in.

"Seamus, I'm sure, told you about Influence, what it can do. They won't even know who did it. Now. Are you ready to go?"

Walking tight together, they joined the queue. Waited, the minutes ticking. Jasmine looked desperately back, towards the airport entrance, but the door remained firmly closed. The queue took a step forward and then stopped; the check-in woman was chatting, examining boarding passes, and the queue moved on again. It was moving too quickly. Jasmine looked at the airport clock, the armed guard stood casually by and prayed for something to happen. Ellyllon's fingers tightened. It was their turn.

"Hello again." The woman smiled, "Can I see your boarding cards?"

Ellyllon ducked his head and grinned and they handed them over, and if the woman noticed anything she didn't say. She flashed him one last warm, playful smile and let them through. They were the last. Jasmine slowed, trying to delay them, but his hand pulled her on. They reached the door and, ushering her through, Ellyllon pushed her out onto tarmac.

It was beginning to get dark, the shadows creeping as the sun lowered, preparing to set. Disorientated, Jasmine looked about her. A small plane lay near the start of the runway, about a hundred metres ahead of them. Two men, dressed in the long, smart coats of businessmen, were mounting the steps, while the rest of the passengers made their way across the tarmac, following a rough, straggly queue. The little boy, jiggling with excitement at the end of his mother's hand, had reached the tail.

"Where are we going?"

"I told you. Dublin, then London."

"But we've joined; you can't separate us. There's nothing you can do."

He sniggered and pressed his mouth to her ear again, his voice hissing with contempt.

"Separate you? Why should I want to do that? Is that what the old fool told you? Madra Rua, the cunning old fox!"

The mother and little boy had reached the steps. Bending down, she slipped her hands under his arms, but he squirmed away from her with a loud shout. She relented, and letting him go, took his hand instead. Together they climbed the stairs, the mother's head bent as she watched his legs stretch awkwardly over gaps way too big for him. His foot tripped and he would have fallen between the steps, down on the tarmac below, if it hadn't been for his mother's hands taking his weight, steadying him. Watching her, Jasmine thought of Seamus, of John and the way they'd tried to protect her and felt sick.

"I don't understand what you want," she said, hoping to distract him, to keep him busy.

His eyes glittered, the twitch of his lips telling her he knew exactly what she was trying to do.

"Did the great Madra Rua tell you anything important? Anything worthwhile? Why do you think it's called joining? I could've taken Iomlan, could've taken it at any time, but why would I want half? Only one part, when the whole is so much the greater?"

His words ringing in her head, they reached the tail. Bunched at the bottom of the steps, a handful of passengers waited as the mother and son reached the top. They stopped, the little boy taking one last look around. Then he scrambled inside, his mum following. Inside Jasmine, something clicked. A memory flooded through her, Seamus talking earnestly to her, telling her about the joining, and synergy and suddenly she knew exactly what he'd been trying to tell her. It was all so clear, so obvious, if only she'd been listening. She'd been so busy thinking that all the magic, the power lay in Iomlan, that she, her body, was little more than some kind of empty vessel and only important because of what, by a freak of nature, was inside her, but it wasn't like that at all. It was the two of them together, merged, that produced the real power. Seamus' feeling had been right; Ellyllon didn't want to consume her power, he wanted to use it, wanted to use them both. She stopped, the movement propelling Ellyllon in front of her. Swinging back, his lips bared, he pulled at her, twisting her arm, but this time, knowing now what was at stake, she held herself firm.

"No!" Drawing herself up, she looked at him full in the eyes, "There's nothing you can do with my power if I don't let you. I'm not going to let you use me or Iomlan."

Surprised, he took a step back and, for the briefest of moments, his hold on her lessened. It was enough. Quick as a flash, she threw herself backwards, her arm slipping out of his hold and away. She began to back away from him, keeping him in sight, but with a curse, he jumped after her, one hand raised.

"Hey!"

They froze.

"What are you doing?!" The voice shouted again.

It was one of the passengers. Ellyllon span and Jasmine saw a man walking swiftly towards them, the rest of the passengers turning to watch. Ellyllon lowered his hand and, giving her one last smile, disappeared. The man stopped, his eyes widening in shock; behind him someone gasped, and then Jasmine was spinning, turning around and around, searching desperately for Ellyllon and dreading the feel of his hand on her shoulder. But there was no sign of him. Two more passengers were moving towards her now, a second man and a woman, their faces twisted with concern. Without a word, others followed, but more slowly, as if feeling they should do something, but not really sure what. Where was he? Jasmine took a step back, away from the plane and towards the grass verge that lined the runway. The faces moved closer, caught in the fading light; they looked strangely similar, their cheeks and eye sockets dark and hollow. She studied each one desperately, searching for features she recognised, for something she remembered that would tell her that this wasn't Ellyllon.

"It's OK." The woman stepped ahead of the others. "It's OK. We'll get someone for you. We'll find airport security. It's OK, you're safe now. You're safe with us."

Her hand was stretched out towards Jasmine, filling the gap between them, saying trust me, trust me: trust me. She stared at it, torn between wanting to believe and doubting. The fingers were inches away from her; another step and they would reach out and take her hand or grab her wrist. Iomlan stirred, cutting through the fog in her head and she realised what she was doing and her heart thudded.

"Keep away from me!" she shouted.

Iomlan was there, preparing, but she daren't use it. She pushed it away. And then her feet were moving again and she was running, running away from the woman and the other passengers and down the other side of the runway. She glanced back. Pulling away from the others, the woman was following, her step measured, purposeful, and she knew that her instinct was right; she was Ellyllon. Another glance, this one left, to a high wire fence, the sand dunes behind it reaching down to the sea and the twinkle of distant houses. On the right were grass fields and the grey of one, lone stone building. It looked easier. Turning right, she ran across the runway and onto the grass verge and then out, into the grassland.

Chapter Twenty-Three

She ran, her heart pounding, the sound filling her ears and making her head throb. Underfoot, the grass was changing, becoming taller, thicker, the ground beneath it pitted and ridged. Her ankle twisted; for a moment she thought she was going to fall, but somehow her body righted itself. She slowed. Ahead of her, the ground rose into small, uneven lumps before falling away altogether. Behind it, dark blue rippled. The sea! Stopping, she whirled, looked left then right. She was wrong; it wasn't a field, it was sand dunes, with the sea beyond. Without knowing, she'd run into the tip of a peninsula, a dead end with only one way out. She glanced back. Her dad once more, Ellyllon was still coming. Cutting her off. She pushed on.

She hit the first of the sand dunes, her feet sinking and sliding as she clambered up the side. And then she was over the top and back on grass. She ran down the other side and halfway up the next one, slowing as she hit sand again but afraid to stop. She scrambled over the top, pausing just long enough for another, desperate look, her chest heaving. The building she'd seen from the runway loomed ahead of her, slightly to her right and back towards the mainland. It was a church, a ruin, the walls crumbling and half-buried by the sand. Quiet, empty, it lay in shadow, silhouetted against the last of the day's sun. Gravestones, fallen sideways, dotted the sand behind the churchyard wall, like confetti thrown all ways. More sand had collected next to the church wall, pushing the gravestones upwards into a high, grassy mound, topped by an intricate, High Cross. Against the darkening sky, they looked like people huddled together, sheltering while they waited for a storm to pass. A memory clicked. This was Killaspugbrone, the church Malachy had told her about, the village buried by sand. Iomlan stirred inside her. Ellyllon! She looked around. The dunes and grass were empty; there was no sign of him. He could be anywhere, could reappear anywhere, or right next to her, his fingers twitching as he reached out towards her. She shivered, forcing her legs, her aching thighs, on.

Without meaning to, she headed for the church, her instinct towards shelter. Almost to the graveyard, and the ground rose steeply. Grass caught at her legs, thick, hard tufts tripping her feet. She fell, the world tipping, and clutched at the grass, tried desperately to keep herself upright, but the sharp blades sliced and cut.

"Ow!" Somehow still on her feet, she sucked at her fingers, tasting blood.

The flow eased and she continued, clambering, dragging her protesting legs up. She reached the churchyard gate and, grabbing the flaking iron post, pulled herself inside.

Holding a stitch in her right side, she staggered towards the church, following the rough path that led through the sand dunes. Narrow, it twisted, meandered through the lumpy ground. Gasping, her steps followed her breath, in out, in out, the two, like a litany, pounding through her head. The mound was close, the High Cross looming. She glanced back; her dad's head tipped the churchyard wall, and she threw herself forward. Two, three steps, her foot snagged, caught a clump of grass and she fell. Her impetus took her, threw her body forward and she hit the ground, bouncing. Sprawling, she came to rest at the bottom of the mound, the breath knocked from her body, but still she wouldn't stop. Dragging herself up, she sat panting, her legs tucked under her. Another look back. The gateway was empty. He hadn't followed her; maybe, he couldn't follow her and she was safe. Pressing down with her hands, she tried to lever herself up. Nothing happened. She pressed down again, but all the weight seemed to have gone in her arms, her legs.

"Jasmine!"

He was stood, leaning against the High Cross, one leg casually crossed over the other. Her body sagged, she felt the mound against her shoulder and closed her eyes. There was nowhere left to run. There was only one thing left to do; she thought of Seamus, and using Iomlan, let that her thought fly.

"It's funny, to think of all the effort Christians expended to eradicate our beliefs and usurp our heritage," Ellyllon said thoughtfully, sounding like a person on the bus determined to start a conversation with a stranger. "Yet somehow they always seem to come through."

She opened her eyes, looked up to see him pat the High Cross. He saw her watching and grinned, and then he was coming down the mound towards her, stepping lightly, effortlessly across the sand and through the gravestones.

"Maybe it's just that underneath it all, we're all still pagans, heathens feeling the rhythm of the earth beneath us. The desire for life."

He joined her on the path.

"Why do you keep on running? You know it gets you nowhere. Just round and round and back to me."

He sighed and, shaking his head, slowly lowered himself to the ground. Their eyes met. Still her dad's face, but the eyes were Ellyllon's.

"You're waiting for Madra Rua. Holding out for him. I know what you did, I felt it. But you must know by now that he's always just that little bit behind. That little bit late. And he can't kill me, no matter what he thinks, what he believes. Can't keep me from you. I've wasted too much time on you, too much effort, to give up now."

He shifted slightly, as if settling himself. Lifted up his hand and stared at it.

"You see, when I first sensed you, your potential, I made a vow to myself. A decision, if you will. There are things I've been wanting to do for a very long time. I just needed the power of someone." He dropped his hand and looked at her. "Someone like you. Just like you."

He inched closer, his black eyes round and unblinking. "Someone like you comes along so rarely; it can be years before another becomes ready, and even then they'll probably have one tenth of your power. Of course, Seamus could help me, but he won't. He's an unforgiving man. Stubborn. So, you see, Jasmine, I don't have any more choice in this than you do. I need you. Just you."

His face was inches from her, his voice soft, silken. A voice inside her was screaming, telling her to stop, to look away, but she couldn't.

"I can wait. I've waited longer, much, much longer. Wherever you go, I'll be there. The slow drip of the tap in the silence, a fly in your brain, driving you mad with my incessant buzzing. Only sometimes the buzzing will stop and you'll cry with relief, and thankfulness, but then you'll start to wonder, to think to yourself, when will it be back. And you'll never know, all you'll know is that one day, I will be. And when I do, I could be anyone, a friend, family or..." He paused, touched his lips with the tip of his tongue. "Lover. How will you know who it is inside that body, behind that face?"

Iomlan stirred, responding to something she couldn't see, but she ignored it. Ellyllon's eyes seemed to blot out the sky.

"And when you've finished, when you've worn yourself out, running and watching and waiting, I'll be there. Exactly where I am now." His eyes gleamed, the light inside them swirling, pulling her down into their black, bottomless depths. "I don't want that any more than you do. I don't want to hurt you; all I want is one or two little things. Things that are nothing to you, would take nothing from you, but would mean everything to me and leave you free."

She nodded, feeling strangely soothed. It would be so simple, so easy to give him what he wanted and have an end to it. Her head dipped, her body leaning, almost imperceptibly, towards him. She was drifting away, giving herself over to him and she couldn't stop it.

"That's it," Ellyllon whispered. "Open your mind to me, let me in."

"Jasmine! Jasmine!" Seamus was calling her, not outside, but inside her head.

It jolted her wide awake and broke Ellyllon's spell. Iomlan flooded through her.

"No!" she cried, pulling away. "I don't care what you do, I'll never let you use me and Iomlan. I'd let you kill me first."

He leapt up, her dad's face twisted with fury, venom.

"Gwirion!" he spat. "Killing you would be a gift compared to what I can do to you; to the people you love."

Abruptly, he turned away and looked over the sand dunes and back towards the airport. Revitalised by the power flowing through her, Jasmine got to her feet.

"Seamus is coming; you can feel him, can't you? It's over."

"Over?" Her dad's face was gone and it was Ellyllon's that finally swung back towards her. "How can it be that so much power lies inside such as *you*? What did I tell you? Did you think that it was a lie? This will never be over. You'll never be rid of me." He waved his hand towards his face. It shimmered and then Malachy appeared, glaring. "I told you, I could be anyone. You will never be sure, be certain who it is you're with, who it is that's listening to you, who's laughing, kissing, touching you. Nothing will be hidden from me. Nothing. I'll know you better than you know yourself; your dreams, your hopes, your desires."

She stared at the horror that was Malachy's face talking to her like that, his words corrupting her feelings, and then he laughed. His face shimmered again and this time it was John's face that was laughing.

"But I already know those. Know how you'd like it if Malachy ran his hands all over you. But it's me, not him, that knows what your lips taste like. And I can tell you they taste exactly like your mother's."

Jasmine took a step back, her stomach clenching. Iomlan was

straining; it took all her control, but John had said not too. She forced it down.

In front of her, Ellyllon's face was changing again. But more slowly this time, as if he wanted her to see this transformation. The nose, long, with wide nostrils was all too familiar, the lips… she gasped.

"Seamus was right! You were there!"

Her old friend Ade's face smiled.

"Of course I was there. I told you, the time, effort taken with you. Years. Each step brought you closer to me, and away from your idiot stepfather. In his eagerness, his zeal, he did half my work for me, but just when I thought, when I was this close…" He lifted up his hand, almost but not quite pinching his thumb and forefinger together. "He took you away, brought you here. So I began again."

Ade's face's disappeared, and it was Ellyllon's face staring at her, his black eyes gleaming with malice. "Did you ever think to ask, why did I show myself? On the boat, in the field. On the bus, in the convent, when I felt your Iomlan in the palm of my hand. I could've taken it then, ripped it out of you—" Jasmine's hand went instinctively to her stomach and his eyes followed it, glittering. "There was nothing Madra Rua could've done, but I resisted."

He wiped his lips with his tongue, as if savouring a remembered taste. "How do you think I've survived all these centuries, these eons? I know all about people, their pathetic little hearts. It suited me to have you scared. To have you needing them. Believing in them. And then, when the time came, and you saw through them, their lies, your fall would be all the harder. And who would be there to pick you up? Your father."

It took her a moment. "But, but, you took a chance. What if he'd come back?"

He smiled, his eyes burning into hers, the malice in them now so strong that it made her flinch. Her stomach dropped.

"Where is he? What did you do to him?!"

"I told him the truth. Told him he'd lost everything, his wife, his daughter. Had nothing left to live for."

"But that's not true!" she spat. "He wouldn't't've believed it anyway."

"He did take quite a bit of persuasion. But you know yourself, I can be very persuasive."

"You're lying!" She shook her head stubbornly.

"Am I? Really? Your father was a weak, vain man. I did you a favour, as well as myself."

"You're lying!" she repeated, shouting. "He's in Canada."

"Canada?" Ellyllon laughed, thrusting his face towards her, sneering and vicious. "He never even left London. Is still there, if there's anything left of him after the fish have finished."

"Shut up! Shut up!"

Her control slipped and Iomlan flared. It surged through her, her stomach, her throat, burning with the white-hot fire of fury and ice. It burst out of her, towards Ellyllon, the power of it taking her breath away. Catching him full in the stomach, it lifted him off his feet and sent him high into the air before crashing him to the ground, halfway up the mound. Quick as a flash he was back on his feet and grinning at her. "Is that the best you can do? In my time, they'd have peeled the skin from me, layer by layer. You're no warrior; you're a child, a nothing. Too weak, too scared to avenge your own father's murder."

"Too scared?" Gritting her teeth, she let Iomlan fly.

Stronger this time, it hurtled up the mound, skimming the ground and catching Ellyllon low in the stomach and sending him even higher into the winter sky. For a split second, he hung, transfixed, and then, just as he was about to drop, she thrust again. His body snapped back, the violence of it forcing his arms and legs wide, spread-eagled. Iomlan coursed through her, fuelling her anger, as she pushed him over and over, squeezing his body like a lemon, determined to drain every last drop of life out of him, but to her amazement he just turned towards her and smiled. She froze and Iomlan faltered. Something was wrong. He wanted this. She let Iomlan fade, but somehow, Ellyllon stayed where he was, as if he were holding himself up, bracing himself against an invisible wall. Abruptly, his head flexed, and then slowly began to press against the hidden barrier. The sky around him blurred, small creases began to appear, radiating outwards from his head, like a pillow giving way. What had she done? The creases were growing, becoming folds. Desperate to get him down, she refocused, strengthening Iomlan as she sent it out towards him again. She twisted it in midair, trying to prise him off.

"Jasmine, stop!" Seamus appeared out of nowhere, gesturing wildly. "You have to stop."

Her ears were ringing with the power running through her, the sound in her head deafening. She groaned, feeling as if her body was going to be pulled apart. Above her, Ellyllon's body was beginning to shudder.

"I can't, I have to get him off!"

Seamus bounded over to her, shouting so loudly that she could hear him even over the noise in her head.

"No, this is what he wants. You're helping him. Look!"

He pointed. The sky behind Ellyllon was beginning to tighten. She could actually see it stretching out away from him, rippling like satin or air in a heat wave.

"Quickly!" Seamus cried.

She concentrated, tried to pull Iomlan back and away. Nothing happened. She tried again. Felt the strain in her body, her legs, her throat, but Iomlan still continued to pour out of her. She couldn't stop it.

"I can't——" Her legs buckled.

His Iomlan lashed out, moving across her, heavy, smothering. Their powers collided and the whole world seemed to shake and then she felt her Iomlan weaken, stutter and fade. She fell forward, onto all fours, but Malachy was there, reaching out for her, grabbing her arms and pulling her onto her haunches, John close behind. And then she heard Malachy swear and the three of them looked up towards Ellyllon.

"Shit!" Malachy swore again, his eyes stretched wide.

The sky above them had become completely distorted, pulled all out of shape. And now the ground around them, beneath them, was beginning to follow, the sand dunes, gravestones, the church all beginning to stretch, as if reality itself was being pulled, distorted into a giant bubble, with Ellyllon at its epicentre.

"We're too late!" Seamus was shouting next to them.

There was a loud roar, like an airplane flying close overhead, and the bubble burst, the pressure easing so suddenly that Jasmine was sent sprawling forward again, Malachy with her. They untangled themselves.

"Jesus, Seamus, what is that?" John shouted, grabbing his arm and pointing.

Back on her feet Jasmine stared, open-mouthed. A golden light surrounded Ellyllon, silhouetting his body, growing slowly but steadily. He was still smiling, the look on his face happy, blissful almost, and she knew then that this was his last, triumphant manipulation of her. She looked down and saw Malachy still on the ground.

"Oh God, Mal, what have I done?"

He looked up at her helplessly. Ellyllon's body was beginning to curl and buckle, his arms and legs moving towards one another, coming together as he was pulled backwards into the light. Seamus put on hand on her shoulder, talking fast, his eyes huge.

"It's a void. He's like a cork saving us from the worst. But if that gets any bigger it'll suck him in and us along with him. And then everything else. Jasmine, I need you, I can't close it alone. I need you to focus, to work with me, follow me and think only of closing it. And whatever you do, don't stop until I say."

He grabbed her hand, pulling her closer to him, and together they focussed. She closed her eyes, concentrated on closing the void and resisting the urge to fight as Seamus dragged her power to his. Side by side, like two torches trained against the darkness, their powers multiplied, they began to draw the edges together, but the forces behind Ellyllon were immense; it was like trying to close the edges of a tent in a hurricane.

"We're doing it! Keep going," Seamus yelled, his voice straining.

A shriek split the air. She opened her eyes and saw Ellyllon glaring at them, his body squeezing outwards as they closed the hole around him. He tensed, pushed backwards, trying to reverse what they were doing and draw his body further into the void, the movement catching Jasmine and Seamus unawares. Their hold on the void slipped. With a roar, the edges burst, pulling Ellyllon inside and releasing a wind so ferocious that it took Jasmine off her feet, dragged her hand from Seamus' and hurled her after him. She caught herself a few feet from the edge and in the blinding light she just made out Malachy as he tumbled past. Iomlan flashed within her, reacting much quicker than she could, and caught him just before he too disappeared. He hung suspended for a moment, his upper body dark against the light, and then very slowly, inch by inch, she began to pull him towards her. Behind him the void was still growing.

"Jasmine, the void!" Seamus howled.

Battling the wind, she turned to look at him. Incredibly, he was still standing, with John behind him, crouched low and holding on to his legs. She refocused, training Iomlan back onto the void, yet somehow managing to keep something back and pull Malachy closer. It wasn't working. The void was still growing and she could sense Seamus' desperation, feel it rising with her own panic. She refocused again, Iomlan subtly shifting, and now the void was beginning to close, but she couldn't hold Malachy. Her grip weakened. He began to slip away from her, but she stopped him with a jerk and he groaned in pain. His legs had disappeared again; he was up to his waist in the light. She could just make out his face, lined with fear.

"I've got you!" she screamed, but the wind took her voice and whipped it away.

Below them, Seamus was desperately changing his Iomlan, trying to compensate for her and allow her to pull Malachy out. She tried again, tweaking Iomlan with the lightest of touches. She had it! The edges of the void were coming together, the light around Malachy shrinking. She was pulling him clear.

"That's it! It's closing," Seamus encouraged. "Keep going."

But she was tiring. She'd never used Iomlan so furiously for so long, not even beside the lake, and it was draining her. Her chest heaved with the effort, her body trembling. She reached out for Malachy's hand and it was only through pure will, pure stubbornness, that she managed to pull him towards her. Their hands touched and held.

The void was closing more quickly now, the forces that ripped it open gathering momentum as they worked in the opposite direction. Jasmine steeled herself for one final pull, the pull that would get Malachy out just before it closed completely. Obedient to her will, Iomlan surged upwards and she shouted against the effort that was becoming pain. Malachy slid towards her, his feet and ankles the only things left inside, and he was so close to her now that she could see the look on his face and she allowed herself a quick thrill of excitement, of relief. They were almost there. One more tiny effort and Malachy was free, and somehow, they were all getting out of this alive.

"Something's got me!" Malachy yelled suddenly, his face twisting in pain and alarm.

He was pulled backwards so violently that he jerked out of her grasp and back into the void, his body disappearing in front of her.

"Malachy!" she shrieked, stopping him.

His arms, head and shoulders were the only part of him she could see. She reached for him again, shouting at Seamus for help, seeing the light tighten around Malachy and knowing they had only seconds before the void closed. Seamus was there suddenly, his hand too reaching out to Malachy, the tips of his fingers millimetres away. Malachy's head and shoulders jerked again, his eyes caught hers briefly, and then he was gone, the void closing abruptly behind him. The wind died instantly and Jasmine plummeted to the ground. She fell hard, her body bouncing over the uneven sand until it came to a stop between two dunes. She lay still, the breath knocked from her body, unable to do anything but look up at the rapidly darkening winter's sky. The cry of an oystercatcher sounded, all alone and eerie in the sudden quiet.

Chapter Twenty- Four

Jasmine woke as the movement beneath her stopped. She opened her eyes. She was in Seamus' car, lying across the back seat. Outside the window, the sky was black, the thick cloud parting just enough to let the moon through. It illuminated the edges of the cloud and the front of her house, turning them both silver. John and Seamus were in the front of the car, talking, their heads bent towards each another and their voices low. Grabbing hold of the seat, Jasmine pulled herself up. Immediately they stopped and turned around to look at her just as the front door flew open and light from the hallway flooding the path. Leaping out, her mum dashed towards them, calling Jasmine's name. She wrenched the back door open and, ignoring John's reassurances, grabbed Jasmine's arm and pulled her out of the car. Jasmine swayed, just managing to stay on her feet as her mum threw her arms around her, squeezing her tight.

"Jas, are you alright? What happened?" she asked, her eyes wide.

"Kate, I think we should go inside."

It was John's voice, close by them. Their voices washed over her. Resting her chin on her mother's shoulders, she closed her eyes.

*

Stirring, Jasmine opened her eyes. She was in bed. Someone had left her bedside lamp on, the soft warm light keeping the darkness at bay and giving the room a cosy glow that clashed surreally with the hollowness she felt inside. Time felt wrong, disjointed, as if there were gaps, things she was missing. She remembered falling to the ground, John and Seamus rushing over to her and Seamus putting a hand on her forehead. Remembered arriving home, her mum walking her inside and the three of them talking around her, but she hadn't really listened, and after a while her mum had steered her up the stairs, into her bedroom and Seamus was there again, with his hand. But none of it had seemed real, seemed almost to be happening to someone else. Only Malachy was real, the shout he'd made, the look on his face the split second before he disappeared. She shuddered and dipped her face below the covers, as if to hide it from the world. It was all her fault. If only she'd done as Seamus had said, and hadn't listened to Ellyllon, his deliberate, manipulative barbs. The knock, when it came, was so quiet that for a moment she wasn't sure if she'd really heard it, but then the door opened and someone slipped into the room, closing the door carefully behind them. She closed her eyes.

"Jasmine."

It was John, his voice soft, only just above a whisper.

She didn't answer. With a sigh, he joined her on the bed, the mattress dipping.

"We need to talk. I need to tell you what we've done and, er, said about your dad, and about Malachy."

Reluctantly, she lifted her head. The lamplight behind him framed his face, darkening its contours, the lines and furrows.

"Are you OK?" He frowned.

She was thinking about it, thinking of how exactly to answer when he sighed again.

"It's not nice, but we had to do something. This is the last thing you probably want to hear, but it's important. I know it's early days, but there will be so many questions. Malachy's parents will want to know, but at some point, the Guards might want to interview us all."

"The Guards?"

He nodded, seemingly encouraged by her question, or relieved maybe at hearing her answer.

"Yeah. Obviously, Malachy's parents will report him missing, and that would mean a lot of questions, searches even. But if the Guards think he's just left, gone away, then maybe they won't ask the same questions or be as thorough." He paused, rubbing at his forehead irritably. "Seamus has arranged it. He's left a note for Malachy's parents, in his handwriting. It'll look as if he's gone to England to "find himself". It's no secret that Malachy and his dad have argued a lot over the last few years. A father and son arguing, well, that's no big surprise, but the note made it sound like something more."

"But you can't do that!" she exclaimed, her voice thick with horror. "They'll think he's still alive. They'll be left wondering, waiting for him to call them, to come home. They'll never know what he did, what he was trying to do. You can't do that to them."

He looked at her grimly. "What else could we do? Leave him just disappeared, gone? Have the police searching the local area, the fields for him? At least, this way it will all – calm down, eventually."

"But what if they blame themselves? Or his dad, because of the arguments?" The idea appalled her, the thought that someone else would take the guilt that was meant for her. She pulled herself up, the bed rocking. "You can't let them. It was me, all my fault."

"Jas, we can't tell them the truth. They'd never believe it."

"They would if I showed them."

"You know you can't tell them," John said sadly. "You know no one can know about Iomlan."

"That's why you're doing it, isn't it? To protect Iomlan, to protect me." She fell back, exhausted suddenly. "I wish I'd never heard of Iomlan. Without it, without me, Malachy would still be here."

"Oh, Jas, you can't think like that." John touched her gently on the arm, but she shook it off. "You can't blame yourself for Malachy. It was Ellyllon's fault. He manipulated you. He manipulated us all. Your mum, me, playing on our sympathy, our feelings. I sensed something about the necklace and I told myself that I was just being jealous. Ellyllon knew that, knew that's how I'd feel, and used it against me. He even did it to Seamus." He shook his head in wonder. "He wasn't just manipulative, he was clever, so clever."

"But it was me that opened the void."

"But you didn't know what you were doing, what it meant. Only Ellyllon did." His voice rose. "Can you imagine how Seamus is feeling? How much he's blaming himself?"

"But it was my fault! Seamus tried to tell me, to warn me, but I didn't listen. If I'd done that Malachy would still be alive. I killed—"

"Don't you dare start that shite, Jasmine, not with me!" John snapped. "I know what guilt does to you. How it eats you up inside. You can't go back, can't change things." He took a deep breath, steadying himself. "No matter how much you want to. You can only keep going. And learn from it, for Malachy's sake."

He leant forward and, to her surprise, gave the top of her head a quick kiss. He smiled, his blue eyes shining and she felt something inside her break. She looked away, swallowing hard, and he quickly wiped at his face.

"There's another thing I needed to tell you. Seamus is outside. He wants a word, will you see him?"

She couldn't answer; she nodded. He stood up, the bed bouncing beneath her. Without another word he left, leaving the door slightly ajar. She heard him on the stairs, his footsteps slow and heavy.

Wiping her eyes, she waited, trying in vain to prepare herself for what might come next. She heard a creak and Seamus appeared, pushing the door gently open. He looked terrible, his eyes were red with fatigue, the skin of his face grey and drawn, the lines around his eyes and mouth etched deep, as if the Croi had taken his chisel to them.

"Seamus!" she exclaimed, shocked by the sight of him.

"I know. You're not looking so good yourself," he joked with a weak attempt at a smile.

Closing the door, he moved to the edge of the bed and sat down. They sat in silence for a few minutes.

"I'm sorry about Malachy."

She nodded. Swallowed again.

"But I have to talk to you. I know you've a lot to take in, but we really don't have much time." He paused, giving her a thoughtful, assessing look. "We have to go after Ellyllon."

"What?!"

"I've been doing a bit of thinking, thinking maybe I should've done a while ago. We both know he wanted the void opened, that he deliberately used you to do it. And at first, I couldn't think why, but know I think I know, and if I'm right, we have to stop him."

"But I thought—"

"He was dead? Why would he want that?" He shook his head. "No, one thing we know about Ellyllon, he's a master of manipulation, and a strategist. I think he had a second plan, a plan B, if you will. He used you to send him somewhere he couldn't go. And we can follow him using the tombs at Carrowkeel. We need to leave first thing." He stood up. "John'll take us tomorrow."

"Oh my God, you're serious, aren't you?"

"Of course. We have to stop him and I can't do it alone."

"But I can't come. What about Malachy?"

"Staying here not's going to help him."

"What?" Her voice rose. "I can't believe you said that. Malachy's dead and you don't even care. All you care about is Ellyllon, about stopping him. Whatever it takes. Look what happened—" Her voice broke, the tears coming again, but now she was talking, she couldn't stop. "I can't do it. What if I do something worse the next time? I won't do it. I hope I never see him again." The tears were pouring down her face with the violence of her grief, falling off her chin and trickling down her neck. "Ellyllon murdered my dad, and now Malachy… and, I've, I've lost them both. And you just want me to leave?"

She hid her face in her hands, unable to bear how she was feeling, what she'd done. Seamus watched her cry.

"Jasmine, I am very sorry for yer loss," he said eventually, his quiet voice cold. "But when it comes to Malachy, those tears of yours, are they for him or yourself? Your own guilt?"

Dropping her hands, she gasped. Her cheeks reddened; it looked as if he's slapped her.

"You're not the only person to have suffered, to have known grief, loss, and pain," he continued, his eyes hard. "There's plenty, and some not so very far from this room, that have known more hurt than you can possibly imagine. But they carry on, not because of any virtue, but because that's all any of us can do other than lay down and never get up again. Why should you be any different?"

His eyes bored into hers, flecks of green and brown mercilessly reptilian. There was no comfort there, and after what she'd done, she didn't deserve any. She looked down. Iomlan twisted inside her, turning with the knife in the pit of her stomach. Another moment passed and then Seamus sighed, sat down on her bed again.

"Do you know that when I met you, I thought what a thoughtful, intelligent girl you were. Older than your years. Someone our ancestors would be happy for me to leave our legacy to. But you seem determined to prove me wrong. I told you there are consequences to what we do, I told you to take care, to think before you act, but you, who've been joined all of two minutes, knew better. So let me tell you again. What happened to Malachy is a consequence of what I did, what you did, whether we meant it or not, and the harm Ellyllon inflicts now is also a consequence of what we did or didn't do. So what are we going to do about it? Cry and wail how sorry we are and leave him free to do as he pleases? Or do we try and stop him?"

She could feel his eyes on the top of her head, willing her to look at him, and thought inexplicably of Ellyllon. *Open your mind. Let me in.* She looked sideways at the carving the Croi had given her, sat in its usual placed beside her bed. Even then, Seamus had been trying to protect her. John too. All those years, being driven away by her mum and dad, seeing them together, but always having to drag himself back, to honour his vow and make sure she was OK. And Malachy, risking his life for her, without a second thought. She sighed, feeling a weariness that went beyond simple tiredness and into her very bones. She was so tired of fighting; John, Seamus, her mum, Malachy, Niamh, the very world. What was it John had said? *Learn by your mistakes, for Malachy*. Or as her beautiful, glorious dad had told her when she'd gotten into a fight at school: *you got to learn to pick your battles, Jas, and fight for just the important stuff*.

She lifted her chin. "We try to stop him."

Seamus smiled, the smile spreading across his face and reaching all the way to his eyes, their flecks of red warming her with their soft auburn glow. "I knew it! I knew there was strength in you. But then again why should I be surprised when—" He stopped, closed his mouth with a snap. "What I said was harsh enough, but I can't be soft with you. With Iomlan, with the power you have, you'll need to be tough, and hard with yourself too. As hard as I am on yer. But you're not alone. I'm here and, whatever we do, we have to be together. We're going up against Ellyllon, and sure, he's going to use every nasty little trick he has against us. If we're not together, if we're not honest with each other, he'll see it and he'll use it. So no more secrets. From either of us, you, but me as well." He dipped his head. "I've learnt that meself. I was wrong to keep things from you. I should've trusted ya."

"No more secrets."

"And while we're talking, there's one thing I need to tell you. I wasn't sure before, didn't want to be getting your hopes up, but we'll start as we mean to go on. It's about Malachy."

"Malachy?" Her heart skipped a beat.

"Yes." Frowning, he looked away, as if he still wasn't sure. "I may be wrong, and we both know how wrong I've been, but seeing you how you are, I can't—"

"Seamus!"

"Sorry." He flushed, reminding her suddenly of John. "I've been thinking if Ellyllon could survive the void, then why not Malachy?"

It took her a moment. "I don't understand."

"Ellyllon is human enough to need oxygen, and if he can breathe then so can Malachy. That's why I wrote that note to his parents. With any luck, we won't just be stopping Ellyllon, we'll be finding Malachy and bringing him home."

Jasmine's head whirled. He was alive; Malachy was alive! She pulled her legs up and hugged her knees. If Malachy was alive, then anything was possible.

"Do you know where he is?" she asked, her voice trembling.

Seamus shook his head. "No, but I think the reason Ellyllon wanted the void open was so that he could go back to the time of the druids. If I'm right, then that's where Malachy will be."

"Time? You mean time travel?"

He laughed softly at the look on her face. "After everything you've seen and done, is that really so impossible? The old places, tombs, stone circles, activate Iomlan because of the power they contain. It's an old power and it's very strong. It magnifies Iomlan, enables us to do things that would normally be impossible."

"How? Where does it come from?"

"No one knows. To our kind, it has just always been there, but I've always wondered if it comes from the planet, the Earth itself. The power is part of what they are, imbued in the stone. But I've never used it to travel into the past; it's not something I ever wanted to try. Some things are best left alone, but it's not like we have a choice." He stood up. "Now, I need to go, to prepare. But there's just one more thing. I know I said no more secrets, but I meant between us. You mustn't tell John about Malachy. He'll have to face his parents every day, as well as your mam. I don't want him having to carry any more than he has to."

She thought of all the years he'd lived with his secret, never able to tell anyone, to explain. To her, or her mum. Her mum!

"Seamus, how long will we be? What about mum? If John can't tell her, what will she think? I'll just disappear, like Malachy. She'll think something's happened to me."

"It's alright. John'll tell her something to stop her worrying. She'll know you're OK, and hopefully we'll be back before long."

"But maybe now is the time to tell her, to explain?"

"And you think that'll stop her worrying?"

She thought about it, imagined her mum thinking all kinds of things. They were going to go back in time; all kinds of things could actually happen. Her stomach fluttered with excitement. They were going back in time. Seamus was right; there was nothing else to do.

"OK."

"I must go. Let you sleep."

"I don't think I'll be able to get any now."

"Oh, I think you can," he retorted, leaning over and touching her lightly on the forehead.

She fell instantly asleep, missing the look he gave her as he pulled her duvet up and tucked it around her shoulders before slipping silently from the room.

*

The next morning, leaving her mum fast asleep in bed, John drove them to Carrowkeel. The Bricklieve Mountains shone in the morning light, the grey granite tinged almost purple against a bright blue sky. The early morning air was crisp as they climbed up the path, the wind keen. At the final ridge Seamus walked slightly ahead, as if to give Jasmine and John a last chance to talk.

"You will look after her, won't you?" Jasmine asked after a few minutes.

"Of course I will. I hate lying to her, I always have, but if she knew the truth, well, let's just say it's better this way. At least she'll think you're safe. And if she thinks you're with Malachy, then she'll think you're happy." His blue eyes looked out over the hillside. "But when you get back I'll tell her everything, explain everything. Not just now I mean, but when you were a baby, what me and Seamus did. You were right. You have to stop the secrets sometime and I want her to know. And I'll accept whatever she decides."

Jasmine frowned. "We'll both tell her. This isn't just down to you. This was never just down to you."

He didn't answer, so she tried again. "Y'know mum, she'll be furious with us for a few days, but she'll come round. She always does." She nudged him playfully with her elbow. "I did."

He smiled at that. "Yeah, you're right. So, does this mean that I'm forgiven? By you?"

"I'm working on it!" she joked, then immediately sobered. "I think I understand it all better now. Why you did all those things. I know now you were only trying to protect me. When I think what Ellyllon was trying to do—" She shivered in a sudden gust of wind. "I think maybe if I'd been you, I'd done the same."

Surprised, John stopped and turned to face her. Out of the corner of her eye she saw that Seamus had reached the top of the path and was waiting for them to catch up. To his right the tombs loomed high above his head.

"It's time to go." Seamus' voice carried down to them.

"Coming," Jasmine called up to him, but stayed where she was, gazing at John. "I wish I'd known all this sooner. I wish I'd known what you were doing. I wouldn't have been half so horrible."

"Only half?" He grinned then threw his arms around her, hugging her so tight she could barely breathe. "Just come home safe. And remember that I love you. I always have, more than you can ever imagine."

"I love you too." She admitted it finally, hugging him back.

They broke apart and walked the last few paces to Seamus in silence, not looking at one other.

"Are you ready?" Seamus asked.

They nodded. Jasmine took a step, John moving with her, but Seamus held out his hand to stop him.

"No, John, you'd better not go any further. You still have traces of Iomlan and I don't know how it could affect you."

John opened his mouth, as if to protest, then closed it again. The two men embraced.

"Take care of her, Seamus," John murmured softly. "Bring her back to us."

"I will."

They broke apart. Jasmine and John hugged for a second time and then she and Seamus began to make their way up the hill. She looked back at John and he waved, but the second time she looked back, he was gone, out of sight with the curve of the land. They continued in silence, hearing nothing beyond the sound of each other's breath.

They reached the entrance.

"Right, Jasmine, if you're ready, I'll go first and you follow. Once inside I need you to take my hand and keep a tight hold; we don't want to separate in there."

He slipped down and into the tomb. After a last, lingering look around her, Jasmine did the same.

Left at the bottom of the ridge, John paced up and down. Although it seemed like forever, he knew it was only minutes since they disappeared. The cloud was moving in, coming from the North; it smothered the view and he could only just about make out the faint outline of Benbulbin in the distance. He wondered what it would look like to Jasmine and Seamus when they emerged out the other end, how everything would look. The ground beneath him shuddered and his stomach lurched. Feeling sick, he spotted a large boulder and went over to it. His stomach continued to churn and he placed his hand over it, willing it to stop. It was too familiar, a tiny part, a ghost of what had once been there. The beautiful, exhilarating flow that had made him feel more alive, more real, than anything. The churning stopped. They'd gone. Not quite anything, he thought to himself, remembering Kate, how she'd looked when he'd left he, all soft skin and hair, curled around inside the duvet. It was time to get back to her, to explain, and tell one final lie that he suspected would be one lie too many. He stood up and took one long last look at the ridge before starting down the track. He moved quickly, a lone figure in the brown and grey of gorse and granite.

Turn the page and discover *The Emerald Tree*,
Book II of Nina Oram's Carrowkeel trilogy!

The Emerald Tree

For Malachy, the light was blinding; even with his eyelids tightly closed it seemed to find its way into his eyes, into his head. Ellyllon had released his ankle and was moving beside him, his elbows and body bumping into him. Fearful of being left alone, Malachy grabbed at him, holding on to anything solid, only to be shaken off before grabbing again. There was a deafening roar and Ellyllon was violently pulled away, Malachy going with him. Despite the forces around them Ellyllon shook himself once, twice, heaving Malachy from him and sending them both tumbling away in opposite directions. Malachy felt the faint breath of cool air and then he was out of the light and falling through darkness. Wind whipped at him, stinging his face and hands. He opened his eyes just long enough to see the white of sand before he hit the ground and everything went dark.

Malachy woke, feeling something cold and wet and sniffing loudly poking him in the chest, neck and face.

"Here; out of it. That's it. Let's have a look."

The voice moved closer as it spoke and he felt hands turning him over onto his back. He coughed, his throat raw, his body shivering with cold. He opened his eyes; a man, his face lined and weathered, knelt over him, his hat and clothes soaked by the light rain misting around them.

"Where did ye come from? Were ye out in that?"

The man instinctively looked up, as if surveying some kind of devastation, then returned his attention to Malachy.

"Have ye a name?"

Malachy coughed again. "Malachy. Costello." He managed his voice a deep rasp.

"Malachy Costello, is it?" The man squinted at him. "There be no Costellos round here. You're a long way from home, ladeen."

The man looked up again, thinking, then back at him, deciding.

"You'd best come home with me. Can ye walk? It's not far."

He placed his arms around Malachy, helping to lever him up first into a sitting position then slowly onto his feet. Malachy's head span and his body swayed. He could feel the man's grip on him tighten.

"I've got you. Now, we'll be taking it nice and slow. That's it. My name's Thady, Thady Padian."

They began to walk, Thady taking almost all of Malachy's weight, and all the time talking to him, encouraging, reassuring him. The ground beneath them was soft and their feet sunk into it, making the way hard going. Malachy's chest heaved and he coughed again. Looking down, he saw only sand, but he was too tired to question what that meant. At a hedge Thady stopped, letting them both catch their breath, and for the first time Malachy looked up. Ahead of them lay the usual green and brown of grass, hedge and track. A small cart sat the other side of the hedge, tied to a ragged looking pony. Malachy glanced back, the way they'd come: behind them a huge bank of sand disappeared into the distance. Over to the right, something grey; it looked like part of a wall, or a tower, rose out of it.

"There's nothing we can do for the poor souls." Thady shook his shoulders softly, but his face, looking in to Malachy's, was heartbroken. "Come ladeen, we need to get you home. Into the warm."

They stared at one another for a moment and then Thady led him through a gap in the hedge and out onto a track. Propping Malachy up at the end of the cart, Thady held him upright with his body, then, with a gentle push, used gravity to press him back into the bottom of the cart. He grabbed his legs, heaved them up and pushed him further onto the cart. Malachy put out his arms, trying to help, but they flailed helplessly. He didn't seem to have the strength.

"There," Thady said after few moments, breathing heavily.

Malachy's eyes were closed. With a shake of his head, Thady shrugged out of his coat and laid it over him. Shivering against the rain, he patted Malachy's ankle and moved around the cart to the seat. The cart dipped as he clambered heavily into it and, taking the reins, gave a loud whistle. His collie appeared, running furiously across the uneven ground, his tail flying. He bounded through the gap in the hedge and with one long, powerful jump, landed in the cart.

"Settle down," Thady admonished him and immediately he sat.

Brown eyes regarded Malachy curiously. He shifted forward and gently placed his nose next to Malachy's outstretched hand. Thady turned around, clicked his tongue and the pony moved off. The three of them were heading for home, taking Malachy with them.